Lost In Reincarnation

By

Samantha Jo Purdy

First published in Great Britain in 2021

This edition published in 2021 by Amazon Kdp

Copyright © Samantha Jo Purdy 2021

The right of Samantha Jo Purdy to be identified as the Author of the work has been asserted by her in accordance with the copyright, Designs and Patents Act 1988.

All rights reserved. No part of this publication may be reproduced, stored in a retrieval system, or transmitted, in any form or by any means without the prior written permission of the Author, nor be otherwise circulated in any form of binding or cover other than that in which it is published and without a similar condition imposed on the subsequent purchaser.

Trade paperback ISBN   979 8 541 47335 3

Business email:

Samantha.jo.purdy@gmail.com

Acknowledgments

Thank you to all the people who didn't make life nice or pleasant for me.

My message,

To those who have struggled or are still struggling.

To those who have felt failure.

To those who have lost someone.

You all inspire, even when at your lowest, you still glow.

Beautiful things can be born from the bad.

Magic exists everywhere.

Table of Contents

Table of Contents..iv

Chapter 1 The Obscure 2

Chapter 2 A Day in the Life of Amira 11

Chapter 3 Tefut and Akil 27

Chapter 4 Echoes of the Past 37

Chapter 5 Digging for Knowledge 45

Chapter 6 The Plot 51

Chapter 7 Calm Before the Storm 57

Chapter 8 Kidnapped 65

Chapter 9 Facts Speak Truth...................................73

Chapter 10 Dress for the Occasion 77

Chapter 11 Good Old Fashioned Detective Work 89

Chapter 12 Like the First Time...............................95

Chapter 13 The Discovery 103

Chapter 14 Tale of King Toke & Queen Runa. 109

Chapter 15 Akil & Tefnuts True Intentions..........121

Chapter 16 Hope 133

Chapter 17 The Reak Queen Runa 143

Chapter 18 The Proof...153

Chapter 19 Ignorance is Bliss 163

Chapter 20 King Toke 169

Chapter 21 The Edge of Knowing 177
Chapter 22 The Third Wheel Plan 181
Chapter 23 Grandma Lena's Story 189
Chapter 24 Double Edge Knife 195
Chapter 25 The Invitation 201
Chapter 26 Home and Inspiration 209
Chapter 27 Coming of Age 219
Chapter 28 A Gift from the Royal Twin Flames . 229
Chapter 29 The Twin Flame Ceremony 239
Chapter 30 Life Goes On 251
Chapter 31 Why I Left Your Mother 263
Chapter 32 Life after Death 277
Chapter 33 Practice Makes Perfect 289
Chapter 34 The Day of the Big Presentation 297
Chapter 35 And The Prize Goes To… 309
Chapter 36 The End of College 319
Chapter 37 Birthday Brunch 337
Chapter 38 Getting A Sign 343
Chapter 39 Ladder of Success 351
Chapter 40 The Journey 361

Chapter 1

The Obscure

  In a realm that lies not too far from the earth there is a dark, vast space filled with millions of star-like figures glistening all around. At first glance it looks very much like the night sky, but upon closer inspection, the millions of little stars are in fact, millions of little orbs. In among the orbs it is easy to see that some shine more brightly, and others not so bright at all. All of the orbs are placed around the room on different types of strange furniture. In the center of the room lies another orb that is a bit different from the others. It is one of the dullest ones in sight and it barely lights up enough to be noticed in the dark space. This particular orb seems different from the others, as it is held by a much grander looking ornament, more exquisite than all of the others, carved with such intricate detail and historic symbols.

  Across the endlessness, two doors swung open revealing a wall, showing that this is not just a great space but an extremely large room. From the light of the doorway, two figures slowly enter the room. They appear very crippled with curved backs. They seem very old but walk with ease. It's an old man and an old woman and both wear light colored tribal looking garments. The woman has white hair styled into many tight braids, the old man beside her is bald, and even in very little light, it is easy to see how elderly they are from their deep-set wrinkles and their saggy skin.

A moment later another two figures enter the space. They also appear to be old but with much straighter backs and took stronger strides. They are two gentlemen who are very smartly dressed and they both have grey hair. One has a neatly styled beard, and the other was very clean-shaven. Both had deep wrinkles, but their skin was not nearly as saggy as the couple in front of them who was leading them towards the dull orb on the grandly carved piece of furniture in the middle of the room.

As they walked along they were followed by one more person. He was a strong, tall, broad, silhouette of a young man, and looked like he was at his peak of potential, youth, and sexual maturity. His back was straight, his hair thick, and the sides of his head were shaved. As soon as he entered the room the two doors slowly closed behind him. The young man follows the other four older people into the middle of the room where the dull orb sits.

The young man eventually reaches the orb and begins closely observing it, gazing at its dimness with curiosity and gently touching its smooth, curved edges.

The two old, smartly dressed gentlemen walk around to stand behind the young man. The one with the beard says, "Time is running out, my king." He sounds very well-spoken and very British.

The others nod in agreement.

The other smartly dressed gentleman offers his advice "There is not much time before the worst could happen. We should take new action" His R's were rounded as he spoke, revealing his American accent.

The young man continued to look longingly at the orb and reached out again to touch it gently. He looks to the old man and woman, who are still standing across from him on the other side of the orb, who haven't spoken a word yet.

"I've employed so many to try and find her, and nothing. I don't understand… I need you both. You're my last hope. I need you two to find her. Will you do that for me, Tefnut and Akil?" said young King Toke. His voice was a mixture of deep commanding and desperation, he had an unusual accent whose origin could not be guessed.

The old bald man, Akil, steps forward and replies "It's been centuries, we're out of practice, and we may have lost our touch." He looked back at the old woman, Tefnut, smiling and putting his hand on hers.

Tefnut brushes a tight white braid behind her ear and says, "But of course we will try. We wouldn't lose our king for anything, would we dearest?" Both Tefnut and Akil have whispers of Egyptian tones in their accents.

Akil smiles in response, "No of course, not for anything."

King Toke was still looking upon the orb, unable to look away from it.

"Good. Then it is agreed, there is less than a month left before … Go now and locate her, when you find her or learn anything new, tell me immediately." orders King Toke.

Tefnut and Akil bow their heads making their backs click slightly from the action. They straighten up, as much as their bodies will allow them to, and leave the room arm in arm as they walked out of the double doors, leaving the King alone with the other two gentlemen.

The two gentlemen, Thomas and Johnny, stand either side of the King, and both watch Tefnut and Akil leave through the double doors. They breathe a sigh of relief and turn to look at the young King, whose eyes were sad, glistening, and still gazing at the low glow of the orb.

Thomas and Johnny wait for the doors close before they speak.

"There's something off about those two, I can feel it, but I can't put my finger on it." said Johnny

King Toke smiles "You never did like them, did you, Johnny?"

"Can't say I do either, your majesty." said Thomas as he scratches his beard.

King Toke continues to talk as he goes back to looking at the glowing orb.

"But I trust them with this. They have the most experience after all and aside from me and … her. They are one of the oldest in this realm, remember?"

"I'm sure they will find them, but perhaps we should help as well? Under such circumstances?" says

4

Thomas, who has a smile on his face resembling something like a rebellious but sweet child.

The King looks at Thomas with a sly smile and gives in. "Perhaps you're right. I do need all the help I can get at this point. But don't tell the other two. You know how they can get. They'll take offence and I'll never hear the end of it."

Thomas and Johnny smile and bow to the King as they link arms affectionately and reply "Sounds good to us, your majesty."

They all exchange a smile, and both Johnny and Thomas give the King a confident wink before they both turn on their heels and leave. King Toke remains in the room alone. It is the only way he can feel remotely close to his beloved, and it has been so long, longer than ever before. His thoughts are filled with hopeless feelings, and a single tear falls down his cheek as he continues to look upon the dim-lit orb. He takes both hands and holds the orb, then presses his forehead against it.

"Please come back to me."

***

(Meanwhile on earth)

In a sweet small town, in a nice big house, lives a rather ordinary girl called Amira. Just like every other Monday, for the last two years, she is getting ready for college. Her room is slightly messy and she's focused on getting dressed, not being late, and maybe looking pretty. Amira quickly brushes through her long dark blond hair, grabs a pair of light colored blue jeans from the back of her desk chair to put on along with a plain, black, long-sleeved top. She tries holding her hair up with her hands, but after looking at herself in the mirror for a few seconds, decides it's not a good look and lets it down again. Amira fishes out her favorite pair of knee-high boots from her wardrobe and puts them on. She stands in front of her full-length mirror and judges her overall look. Amira always wanted to wear prettier clothes, but she always felt stupid whenever she tried. She thought it would make her life a bit easier if she had been better blessed with her looks. She cups her breasts, turns to the side, sighs and releases them, and then she rests her hands on her waist. She turns her back to the mirror and looks down at her butt. Unimpressed, she gives up and admits defeat yet again. She sits down at her dressing table/desk and looks closely at her face. . She used to feel so pretty when she was little, and she certainly never used to feel self-conscious, but she will be tuning 18 soon, and all the other girls are always wearing makeup and wearing stylish things. Not that Amira ever felt comfortable putting makeup on or dressing to impress. There was something about it she didn't like the thought of. She let out a sigh and opened her top drawer where there were masses of unopened makeup products. Every piece of makeup you can think of was in her top desk drawer. At the very top was a new pack of makeup that her mum had bought her called 'The beauty face kit'. She looked at the foundation and the contour sticks inside the pack but suddenly decided to chuck it back into the drawer and slam it shut. She didn't want to have to bother with all that faffing around to be pretty. 'Why can't people be allowed to be pretty without this stuff' thought Amira to herself. Instead, she picks up her trusty and very used eyeliner pencil, draws on her bottom lash line, and smudges it a little. She looks at herself in the mirror. 'A bit more' she thinks to herself. She shuffles a little closer to the mirror and draws a thin line on her top lash with a little flick at the end with the eyeliner and then finishes by applying some mascara. She looks at herself in the mirror and tries smiling.

 She sighs. "Standard"

 Amira grabs her black bag containing the things she needed for college and her black coat. She leaves her bedroom, closing the door behind her, running down the stairs into the kitchen, and throwing her coat and bag on the island in the middle. Amira begins to rummage through the cupboards and grabs a pack of sliced bread and pops a few slices in the toaster. She opens the fridge and finds a box of eggs with only two left in it, which was lucky, one each. She takes the eggs out, chucking the box aside, cracks the two eggs into a pan, and switches on the stove, and watches as they begin to fry. The toast pops up, perfect and evenly brown. Amira loved the smell of toast in the morning. She took two plates from the rack and placed them on the island next to her bag, collecting both slices of toast and placing one on each plate, her fingertips burned slightly. She quickly butters them, grabs the eggs out of the frying pan with a spatula and slides a cooked egg on top of each piece of toast.

Happy with the presentation, she walked around the corner and shout up the stairs, "MUM BREAKFAST IS READY!"

Amira sits down at the other side of the kitchen island and begins eating her egg on toast with a knife and fork. There was no point waiting until her mum got there; she could be ages. By the time she had finished her breakfast and had put her plate in the dishwasher her mum finally arrived in the kitchen. Sharron was a mature woman who had her hair tightly pinned back into a French twist, she wore high heels, a tight fitted grey dress, with a matching blazer and a deep shade of lipstick. Her mum always got a lot of attention, but she always thought that was because of all her makeup and she looked after herself by hiring a personal trainer 4 times a week. Sharron was actually in pretty good shape for someone who was in her late 40's. She never left the house without her makeup done, and never, ever, missed a session with her personal trainer.

Her mum sat down and began to cut up her egg on toast into very small pieces to avoid ruining her lipstick as she began eating.

Sharron looked her daughter up and down, noticing that she hasn't touched any of the makeup she has given her, yet again. She thought her daughter was beautiful, of course, but she did wish Amira would be more outgoing and experimental.

"Amira? Don't you like the new makeup pack that I gave to you?" asked Sharron.

Amira rolled her eyes while tidying up the mess in the kitchen.

She turned around with an apologetic look on her face "its great mum, I just don't feel comfortable with putting it on, I guess."

Her mum smiled. "But you'd look so much prettier with it on. Trust me! I wouldn't be where I am today if it wasn't for make-up! Do you know how many daughters would love it if their mum gave them new makeup?"

Amira blinked a few times to process everything she just heard her mum say. Sharron was a successful social media influencer and had been for the last ten years after her modeling career ended.

"Anyway, I am going your way this morning. Do you want a lift to college?" asked Sharron.

Amira looked at the kitchen clock and admitted to herself that she could use a lift to college. She was running too late to just walk there.

"Yes, please," she said eagerly.

Amira's mum finished her last piece of toast and said, "Right then, let's get going" and handed her plate to Amira, who took it and shoved it in the dishwasher and subtly kicked the door closed in a well-rehearsed manner. She lunged for her bag and coat as she quickly made her way to the door.

Chapter 2

A day in the Life of Amira

(One week later)

Amira was sat waiting in the car, clutching her bag. She was waiting for her mum as she usually did whenever a lift was offered, a typical Monday for Amira. She had her black coat on, and the label was itching the back of her neck. She had been meaning to cut it off for some time but had always ended up forgetting about it. Her mum finally left the house and walked towards the car while taping and clicking on her phone. Amira watched her mum slowly make her way to the car and thought that she would nearly be there by now if she had walked to college instead. Her mum made one of her usual excuses about getting ready such as 'I was just swapping my shoes for some different ones' or 'I wanted to change my outfit'.

But today, her mum said; "I was just uploading a photo for a new product I'm promoting." As she got into the car and strapped herself in she gave herself a final check in the mirror. She turned on the engine and pressed the button to lower the car roof.

Amira was glad she kept her hair bobble on her wrist from before and quickly put her hair up into a bun just in time for when her mum started the car. The air started to waft about them, making it a little harder to hear.

Her mum with a raised voice, said "By the way do you finish college at four today!?"

Amira replied, "Yeah! Why!?"

Her mum said, "Good because we're going to your grandmas for a visit. I'll meet you there at four and wait for you in the car park."

Amira hadn't seen her grandma in ages and had been meaning to visit, so she was excited to see her. She enjoyed being around her grandma. In many ways, she was just as much of a mother to her as her own mum was, not just that, but they were just like best friends. Amira has always found it so easy to confide and tell anything to her grandma.

"Yeah, ok, I'll be there!" replied Amira.

Her mum pulled over at the side of the college and stopped for Amira to get out of the car. Amira said thanks to her mum and closed the car door. She fumbled for the handles of her bag and pulled it over her shoulder and quickly walked to the entrance. Once she walked through the main doors, she began to slow down her walking pace to cool down a bit before she got to class. She climbed up the stairs towards her usual business classroom where she could see that there was already a queue outside the door. She walked towards the familiar faces of her college group who were chatting and gossiping whilst waiting for the teacher to arrive.

Amira didn't really bond with anyone there, nor did any of them befriend her how some of them did with each other, like magnets. It was of little matter to Amira, she didn't mind being alone. She found that she preferred it most of the time. She sometimes thought maybe it was her own doing that she had no friends. Even though she was nice and pleasant to anyone and everyone she interacted with, maybe she just seemed too closed off and reserved. Amira walked up to the end of the queue and leaned against the wall, and listened into the conversation the two girls in front of her were having.

The pretty blond called Tammy was talking to her best friend, Rose.

"This guy I met last week on a night out, you know, the one that kissed me, he asked to see me again." boasted Tammy.

Tammy had turned 18 last week and celebrated it with a night out; apparently she had been going out long before, even when she wasn't of legal age. The girl Tammy was talking to was called Rose, Rose was casual but beautiful in a less obvious way compared to Tammy, and she had very dark brown hair that was up in a low ponytail which really helped show off her slender face. Amira assumed that Rose went on the same night out as Tammy but by the look on her face Rose didn't enjoy that night out as much as Tammy had. Amira observed that Rose seemed to look down every time Tammy mentioned 'that guy'.

Rose tried to smile and looked up when Tammy had finally finished talking and said, "So when are you seeing him again?"

Tammy replied, "Not sure he just asked me when I was out again."

This reply seemed to give Rose some satisfaction, not that her friend Tammy would ever have noticed, she seemed very self-absorbed and attention-seeking, which Amira thought must have been very tiring.

The business lecturer, Mr. Clark, finally arrived. He opened the classroom door and ushered all the students to go in. Amira always made sure she was at the back of the queue to the classroom. When everyone in the class was in a friendship group, she would feel awkward if someone had asked her to move so they could sit near a friend.

Everyone entered and sat down. Amira found a seat that was next to Tammy and Rose. Everyone plonked their bags on the floor, turned their computers on, and turned their chairs to face Mr. Clark who was at the front of the classroom getting ready for the lesson. Mr. Clark also turned on his computer and the electronic whiteboard. He was Amira's favorite teacher. She wished that the teachers in school would have been more like him as he always looked out for his students, even when they were difficult. He always gave them the benefit of the doubt. As Mr. Clark was talking to the class he uploaded his PowerPoint to the big screen, and it said in big letters, 'THE FUTURE'. Anxiety began to stir up in Amira. She had no idea what she wanted to get out of this business course. All she knew was that she wanted to do something she was good at and meant something, not that she had any idea what that would be of course.

Mr. Clark went around the classroom and asked if anyone knew or had any ideas about what they wanted to do after the course finished, which would be in a few months. A boy called James was the first to share, saying that he wanted to sell luxury cars. Another guy called Mark wanted to be a consultant for other businesses and Tammy wanted to work in cosmetic treatments, which Amira suspected as much. A few others in the classroom said stuff like security. A boy wanted to have his own local delivery business for special occasions, traveling, becoming a partner, and working for a company or wanted to teach. They all sounded great to Amira but hearing all of these did not inspire or give her any ideas of her own about what she wanted to do after this course finished. The thought of not knowing made her anxiety flair up a little, and she could feel it in the pit of her stomach,

Mr. Clark finally got around to Amira and asked her what she was thinking about doing in the future. She looked back at him with lost eyes and was relieved when she could see that he understood and he didn't press her.

"Maybe you will have a better idea about what you want to do in the next two weeks." said Mr. Clark.

He gave a kind smile and returned to the front of the class. Amira let out a little sigh of relief that helped her tummy ease a little.

Mr. Clark then announced to the classroom, "Your assignment for the next two weeks is to make a business plan and present it to our entrepreneurial star guest, Darren Wilson."

Some of the room gasped in excitement, but Tammy blurted out, "Whose Darren Wilson?"

Amira only knew about Darren Wilson as her mum had mentioned him often. Her mum was a big fan of Darren Wilsons' TV show that was well known for investing in small businesses and giving guidance to people who had good ideas on how to make them better and come to life, it was a big hit, but he hadn't made any new shows for the last year or so.

James, a very eager boy who always did his level best to stay at the top of the class was the first to give a frustrated and yet excited reply to Tammy's question.

"He's only a freaking legend! He's like the Steve cowl of the business industry!" said James.

Mr. Clark laughed and said, "That's actually a pretty good way of putting it."

James, in sudden realization and panic, said "Two weeks, sir? That's not nearly enough time!"

Mr. Clark pulled a sympathetic face "Yes, I know it's a bit of a tight deadline, but Darren Wilson didn't give us much time with his schedule and all. He said he's very busy, so we are really quite lucky to be getting him at all."

This response satisfied the majority of students in the room. Amira however, was trying not to have a panic attack. How was she supposed to develop a PowerPoint presentation about a business plan when she had no idea what that business plan would even be about? She crossed her arms to hug herself and tried not to think about it too much.

Mr. Clark went back to his computer and got everyone to settle down after the exciting news and said,

"Darren Wilson has sent a video that will hopefully answer all your questions." He then pressed the play button.

The video was a little dramatic. Those who did not know of Darren Wilson before today found it amusing, but those who knew Darren Wilson were inspired by it and eager to start. It was quite cheesy to watch but it was a well-made video with a few special effects on it.

Darren Wilson's last words on the video were: "If you can manage to impress me, you'll be going places; there might even be a prize for whoever has the best business plan!"

Mr. Clark allowed the class the whole day to research for business ideas for the assignment instead of lessons. Amira was upset that she didn't have an idea already like everybody else in her class did, and she dreaded the very thought of presenting a business idea, never mind thinking of one. 'So how much worse is it going be if I have nothing to present at all?' Amira thought to herself; the thought made her stomach churn.

She turned to her computer and logged on. She was sitting next to Rose, who was already logged on, with PowerPoint at the ready and typing things into Google. Next to Rose was Tammy, who appeared to be looking at other cosmetic businesses to get ideas from. Amira looked again at Rose, Amira thought that she seemed nothing like Tammy at all, almost the complete opposite to each other, but they were apparently best friends, which was almost impossible to believe for Amira. Rose seemed like a really nice person; she was pretty ambitious and outgoing, which Amira admired about her. In fact, she didn't see why they couldn't be good friends. She watched as Rose typed and scrolled and thought maybe she could help me out a bit.

Amira was curious and decided to ask, "Rose, what's your business idea?"

Rose looked at Amira with surprise, she was always so quiet and shy, but she was pleased by the question and was happy to answer. She could see Amira was having trouble thinking of something.

"Well, I want to supply people with the tools to understand themselves and be at their happiest state. Loads of things get in the way of that, I think, like plastic surgery. I think that's a big one. People just need to see themselves without the filters they have collected throughout their life mentally and physically."

Amira was surprised and asked, "Oh, so you'd be offering a service. And what do you mean exactly? Like what?"

Rose replied, "Like people do what they think others want them to do and ignore or suppress what they actually want. Like people that wear loads of make-up to look different, or who have surgery, it must have an impact on who they truly are on the inside."

Amira thought it made perfect sense. It made her think about herself and maybe why she felt so weird about all the unopened makeup in her top drawer.

"I think that's a great idea." said Amira.

They both exchanged a friendly look.

Tammy mumbled, "It's the stupidest idea I've ever heard."

Rose and Amira rolled their eyes and stared back at their computer screens and pretended that Tammy didn't say anything. Rose wasn't the sort of person to be put off easily. She was always very sure of herself.

Amira thought about Rose's idea and was a little jealous she didn't think of it first. That sort of thing was right up her street, and she wanted something that would pay well and give her a fantastic lifestyle, but to also deliver a very meaningful and useful service, one that wasn't a rip-off, one that was real.

***

A whole 2 hours had passed and Amira was no closer to finding an idea for her business plan. Instead she had been watching business success stories on YouTube, hoping that something would inspire her, but nothing. She sighed, plucked her bag off the floor, and followed the others into the cafeteria for a lunch break. She was standing in the queue for food behind Tammy and Rose. She felt like a ham sandwich if there was nothing good on the hot counter. The queue moved a little and, behold, there was a pasta bake, chicken, garlic and tomato with cheese.

'Screw the sandwich.' Amira thought, 'I'm having that'.

When Amira had collected and paid for her pasta bake and a bottle of coke zero, she turned to look where to sit. To her surprise, Rose called over to her, "Sit with us." Amira, of course, went over and sat down. It made a nice change from sitting on her own. Rose had gone with the all-day brunch option, and Tammy had a cereal bar with a banana beside it. Tammy was occupied with something on her phone as Rose was tucking into a very full looking sausage. Amira pierced her fork into her pasta bake, and got good catch with lots of melted cheese and placed it into her mouth; it tasted very strongly of tomato and had plenty of garlic in, just the way she liked it. The warmth, the flavors, and the texture of the pasta bake and cheese helped her relax instantly. Rose looked up at Amira as she cut up one of her hash browns and dipped it into an egg yolk.

"What's your business idea going to be?" asked Rose.

Amira shrugged her shoulders, swallowed her food and said, "I have no idea. I think I want it to involve people getting a service that I supply, but I don't know what it is yet."

Rose made her mouth into a line as she thought, "You mean like customer service? Or personal shopping?"

Amira did like shopping. She tilted her head to one side and said, "If I can't think of anything else by next week, I'm definitely going to go with that! Thanks!"

They giggled and continued eating. Tammy put down her phone and opened her breakfast bar, and took a bite out of it, looked at Rose and then Amira, looking her up and down and at the food she was eating.

When Tammy swallowed her small bite of the cereal bar, she said, "Was that your mum that dropped you off today?"

Amira was taken back for a second and replied, "Yeah."

Tammy said, "She's got a nice car, and she's so pretty. What does she do?"

Amira wasn't surprised by that question. Of course, it would be about the flash car.

"She sells and promotes beauty treatments and makeup lines. She works with a few different ones." Tammy's eyes lit up with excitement.

"Oh, she's an influencer! That's so cool. Does she get lots of free samples?" asked Tammy, wagging her eyebrows.

Amira wasn't sure she liked where this was going.

"She gets some samples, yeah; she uses them every day and does giveaways on her Instagram page." Amira hoped this would stop Tammy from asking her for free stuff.

Tammy was a little less excited. She knew she had better not ask for any free makeup but handed her phone to Amira.

"Add her for me on Instagram." demanded Tammy.

Amira took the phone and quickly typed in her mum's Instagram name and handed it back to Tammy. Rose was mopping up the last of her beans with her last slice of toast. Tammy looked at her phone using her finger to scroll. Amira was just happy she could continue eating her meal while Tammy seemed busy looking through all of her mums Instagram posts.

When Tammy had finished her cereal bar and banana, she looked back at Amira and put her phone back down, and said, "I would never have thought she was your mum in a million years; she's practically Instagram famous! You know she's got like over 600,000 followers!"

Amira smiled and hid that she was a little offended 'Does she mean to say that I'm not pretty?' she thought to herself.

"What does your mum do?" asked Amira, eager to change the subject.

Tammy leaned back in her chair and said, "She's a nurse."

Amira nodded and looked quickly to Rose and asked the same thing before Tammy could get another word in.

Rose said, "Mum and dad run a restaurant together."

This made Amira think that she hadn't seen her own dad for a while, since he moved out a few years ago, as he frequently travelled with work.

"That's so cool. Do you work there too?" asked Amira.

"Yeah, whenever I want, or if they are busy. It's nice to get some easy money!"

Tammy smiled and sat upright and said, "My dad works in nightclubs. He's a promoter, slash, manager. He always brings me presents. What does your dad do, Amira?"

Amira took a sip from her bottle of coke zero and said, "My dad is a health inspector. I don't see much of him because he travels with work."

Tammy says quickly, "Are they divorced?"

Rose flashed Tammy a warning look.

Amira happily replied, "Yeah, they've been broken up for years now. They were never married."

Tammy nodded and said, "Yeah, I know how that is. My parents got divorced a few years ago."

Tammy looked down and seemed deep in thought. Amira was glad that it didn't lead to further interrogations from Tammy, which would have made her anxiety brew.

***

Amira spent the remaining two more hours on YouTube, watching interviews and business success stories for inspiration, but she still had no idea whatsoever what to do. She looked at the clock and it was 15:50. She started to think about going to meet her mum and seeing grandma. She sighed, switched her computer off, and put on her jacket. She grabbed her bag from under the desk and asked Mr. Clark if it was alright to leave a bit early.

"Yes, of course. If you need any help with this presentation, feel free to email me." he told her.

Amira thanked Mr. Clark and turned to leave saying goodbye to Rose and Tammy on her way out. Amira began to walk to the care home that her grandma was in. It was only 15 minutes away. As she walked along she saw a group of girls and boys walking with each other. Some were being very flirty towards one of the girls, she was beautiful, she had long blonde hair, pink lipstick and wore a tight skirt and top, and she had a good figure. Amira looked away and began to think that maybe she should have used that makeup kit her mum had gotten her after all. She used to have a massive crush on one of the boys chatting that blond up, and he never looked at Amira twice. She wrapped her coat around herself and picked up speed getting ahead of the group. Amira arrived outside the care home and saw an extremely old couple sitting on a bench outside. Amira smiled politely and gave a little wave to be courteous. She regretted it immediately as she got no kind of response back from the old couple. 'God, you'd have thought I was a sack of crap or something' she thought to herself.

Amira turned into the drive and was in the car park where she could see her mum's bright red car and her head popping out of the driver's door.

Her mum shouted, "Hurry up, Amira! I've been here for 10 minutes waiting for you!"

Amira looked as her mum got out of the car and stood with an impatient look on her face, so Amira broke into an easy jog until she reached her.

"Sorry, I did actually leave 10 minutes earlier than I was supposed to" Amira said, a little out of breath.

Her mum linked her arm and said, "Well doesn't matter now, does it? Now then, it's your grandma's 100th birthday soon, she might not be around for much longer, so be nice to her."

Amira wanted to snap back at her mum for that but decided it wouldn't be worth it. Amira and her grandmother always had a strong bond. She loved spending time with her especially when she was growing up. Grandma would tell her lots of stories, stories that she can't really remember a lot of these days, but she was the closest thing to a friend Amira had ever had. They walked into the main entrance and signed the guest book at the reception. After that they carried on down the corridor until they reached her grandma's room; the door had the name 'Lena Nilsson' on it with a sticker of a butterfly next to it.

Chapter 3

Tefnut and Akil

Akil and Tefnut walked arm in arm down a wide and very grand hallway in the realm of twin flames. They were both wearing hooded black robes now, and the length was trailing behind them as they walked. Tefnut, although very old, had an unmistakable presence of confidence. Akil had a sense of sophistication and strength despite his withered looks. They had strength to them, the kind that cannot be seen but sensed.

They arrived at the end of the corridor where there was a black door. They opened the door and skulked inside. In this room, it was immediately obvious it was strange. There was no furniture, no windows, and no decorations. But there was a huge map of the world that covered an entire wall, it looked very old and very detailed, but it was up-to-date. Both Tefnut and Akil stopped and stared at the map for a moment. They turned to face each other and spoke in soft tones.

"What is the plan, Akil?" asked Tefnut as she pulled the hood of her cloak over her neatly braided hair.

Akil looked back at her and said, "I'm not sure, Tefnut. Maybe we should track her down. It has been a while, after all. If we want the plan to work we should know exactly where she is at all times. After seeing the king just now he may resort to other options besides us."

"He still seems to trust us, my love; I think all will be well" Tefnut reassured as she touched his arm affectionately.

Akil nodded and stroked his beloved Tefnut's wrinkly, sagged cheek and put up his hood too.

"Let us see if she is still there." said Akil.

Tefnut nodded in agreement, and both turned to face the detailed map that filled the wall. Tefnut whispered a name in a tone too deep and too soft to be heard by normal ears. After a few moments, a little light appeared on the east side of the British island and twinkled there.

Akil huskily said, "She's moved again."

"Well, it has been a few decades my love." replied Tefnut. "It was expected."

Akil sighed "Let us go."

Both Akil and Tefnut focused on the lit up speck in the middle of the map. They both simultaneously placed one hand on the map, leaving their other arm to rest by each other's side. In less than one second their resting arms flung up and clasped together. The tiny light grew larger and larger until it was completely covering them. Then ZAP. They both vanished from the room and the light quickly faded back down to the little speck and went out like a small candle flame being blown out.

Outside the care home, in a small town near the seaside, Akil and Tefnut miraculously appeared. Even those passing by didn't notice them. They were simply shadows at the side of the road with their cloaks and their hood up. With these cloaks they could go anywhere undetected by humans. The only thing that this cloak didn't work on was twin flames from the realm. They took down their hoods, to get a better view of the location, and looked around, still holding hands from when they both arrived. They observed many older people inside the building that they had arrived next to, and a handful were sat outside on benches or in wheelchairs, wrapped up in blankets and wearing hats and gloves to keep them warm. Akil and Tefnut observed that all the younger people around the building were all wearing the same blue clothes. They carried on through the main entrance of the building walking with some ease despite their crooked backs. They reached a mirror and they stopped and stared at themselves.

"Looks like we will fit right in." said Tefnut with a grim look on her face.

Akil lifted his eyebrows in agreement and said, "You're still beautiful to me." he smiled sweetly at Tefnut. "These places are odd...the homes for the elderly, not sure I would have liked to have ended up in a place like this, even back in our lifetime."

"Nor I, my love, let us put our hoods back up." replied Tefnut.

The coast was clear, so Tefnut and Akil carried on looking in the mirror as they put their hoods up and watched as their bodies began to fade into their surroundings. They looked away from the mirror and carried on up the hallway, looking in all the rooms. When they arrived at room 44, they paused and read the name stuck on the door. Akil tapped his finger quietly on the door in acknowledgement. Tefnut nodded in reply, being careful to stay quiet. Carefully they looked upon the old woman who was sleeping in her chair inside the room. She was just as old as they were, dressed in a long purple skirt and cardigan, and her thick, white hair was beginning to mess. Akil and Tefnut looked at each other, nodded, and turned back to walk down the hallway, and back out of the main entrance so they could find a place to talk in private. They passed by all the nurses who took no notice of them. Akil and Tefnut were cautious about not bumping into any of them, which they found a bit difficult as a few came rushing out of nowhere. When they arrived back outside, they looked around to find a quiet place to sit down and talk. They noticed a red car parked next to the main entrance of the building and a glamorous woman carefully applying makeup.

Akil looked and shook his head. "And they wonder why they can't find love."

Tefnut pointed to a bench near the car park entrance about 50 meters away. They linked arms and slowly wandered over to it and sat down, keeping their hoods up the entire time. When they made sure no one was around, they took their hoods down. It felt good to feel the breeze, it blew Tefnut's braids about her neck, and Akil's head felt its cold embrace.

Tefnut sighed in frustration. "So, what are we to do?"

"Perhaps we should do nothing." replied Akil.

Tefnut glanced at him in surprise as Akil was usually always the one for action "We can't just do nothing, what about a plan B? What if he sends someone else! We cannot risk someone else finding her."

Akil stroked his bald head in thought. "Perhaps we should tell him some of what we found out all those years ago. Only some, just to make it look like we are getting somewhere, and by the time he thinks were are getting somewhere, it will be too late."

Tefnut tilted her head to the side for a moment. "So he will think we are doing our best and that we are doing everything in our power, but because we will stretch it out, by the time he asks someone else to find her, they won't have enough time."

They looked at each other for a moment and gave each other a little smile.

"So we keep the trust?" summed up Tefnut.

"Keeping the trust, yes." confirmed Akil.

Akil took Tefnut's hand and enclosed it within his own "I wish we had a better plan, but this will do nicely enough."

Tefnut looked at him and said, "It might just work, my love." She had never met anyone as smart as her Akil, and she felt so safe around him.

"We had better lay low for the next few days or so and make it look like we're doing the work." said Akil.

Tefnut nodded in agreement. They both looked away from each other to look at the scenery. It had been a while since they last came to earth. Tefnut rested her head against Akil's shoulder when they saw somebody moving towards them, and they looked on. It wouldn't matter if a human saw them now. They were old people at an old people's home. But as this person drew nearer and nearer they got Akil and Tefnut's attention, and they looked on in disbelief and confusion. They looked upon a young girl. She had long dark blonde hair, knee-high black boots, jeans and a black coat. Her face was deep in thought, but she looked directly at Akil and Tefnut. Their bodies stiffened, both of their gazes were locked upon her. The girl smiled at them then someone shouted, and the girl looked away and ran off towards the red car that was parked in the car park next to the care home. Akil and Tefnut carried on watching her with great intensity as she ran away.

Akil and Tefnut were still tense and alert. They looked at each other suddenly and in confusion.

Tefnut said, "The guest book! We must check it for that girl's name."

Akil seemed one step ahead of her as they both put their hoods up and got up immediately, the sounds of cracking and clicking riddled through their joints making both of them groan in pain. They walked as quickly as they were physically able to towards the reception desk where the guest book was. As they entered, they could see the girl and the woman just turn the corner at the very end of the hallway. They both hunched over the guest book and read:

'16:15 - Sharron Nilsson & Amira Hardy'

Akil said, "Look! That must be the girl's name, Amira! This Sharron must be her daughter because their last names are the same. But Amira does not share that family name. Why?"

Tefnut shook his head and pointed to Sharron's name "Well, if this woman had a child, it is likely that the child took on her father's last name. It seems she did not marry, or else she would also have Hardy as her last name."

"Come, let's inspect some more." said Akil quietly.

They both turned on their heels and began back up the long corridor again. They turned the corner and found room number 44 again. They approached it cautiously and slowly. They looked into the room and saw the young blond girl sitting next to the elderly lady in the chair, who was now wide awake and smiling. They were chatting and laughing. The glamorous woman was sitting on the bed when her phone began to ring.

The glamorous woman stood up, looking at her phone and said, "Sorry mum, I've got to take this, its work. Amira, look after your grandma."

Akil and Tefnut recoiled from the room and turned away from the door looking outside of a nearby window as the glamorous woman hurried past them, not even noticing them, as she answered her phone.

Tefnut said with quiet excitement, "Quick let us go back outside!"

They turned and walked as quickly as they could back out of the main entrance and sat on the same bench as before but kept their hoods up this time.

Akil said, "This changes everything, Tefnut! This is exactly what we needed! It couldn't be more perfect."

Tefnut smiled back in agreement. "She looks just like her, right down to the last detail! A doppelganger!"

Akil said, "Yes! So here's the new plan. We will wait until they leave, and then we will begin our work. We will take her back to our realm and tell the King that we have found her!"

Tefnut smiled, and then her face turned serious in thought.

"Won't he know it is not her when he sees her? And the girl may not be easily fooled."

Akil says, still smiling, "The girl won't be a problem. You know how gullible they are when they are young, she will easily be persuaded. After all, the king is a handsome man."

Tefnut replies, "That's true! She will definitely be attracted to him… but what about the king! He won't be easily convinced!"

Akil coughed in slight laughter. "Did you not see the king just now? He is a mess. He hasn't seen her in nearly 100 years, he is desperate, and his heart is clouded by sadness and desperation. If we tell him she died 18 years ago and was put back into the life cycle and reincarnated here, he would surely believe it."

Tefnut smiled as she thought about it "It's perfect."

They held each other and embraced, sharing a passionate kiss in celebration.

***

"So then Johnny, where do we start?" said Thomas as he played with the tip of his beard.

The two old men looked at each other, then back at the large old-looking map covering the wall.

"Well, let's see where her name shows up." said Johnny in his American accent.

Thomas focused on the map and whispered a name that was too quiet and deep to hear.

They both looked at the map and watched as a small light appeared on it.

Thomas stroked his white, neatly trimmed beard and said, "That's in Hungary, wouldn't you say, Johnny?"

Johnny, still looking at the map said, "Yes I believe so."

Johnny and Thomas looked at each other with a little concern, Thomas still having one hand on his beard.

Johnny scrunched his face up and said, "...You don't think…"

Thomas looked at the map and back at Johnny and said, "No! If she did, then why is her orb still the same? It's still glowing. And the tracking speck on the map is lit and not black. It seems strange though. The little speck seems a different color than usual."

Johnny dropped his hand and said, "Thomas, I've seen dead glow worms brighter than that orb was just now. And I suppose there is something different about the speck. Almost like it's trying to tell us something."

Thomas rolled his eyes. "If she truly died her orb would have gone, and another would have taken its place, along with the knowledge of new name and a restored light."

Johnny waved his hand in agreement and thought for a moment, then said, "The things that happened thereafter", he said as he gestured to the speck on the map. "It's going to be really hard to trace."

Thomas nodded, looking at Johnny, and said, "We'd better get started then. There's not much time left."

Johnny stroked a loose strand of his hair back into place with a slick hand movement.

"Looks like juice won't cut it this time. Good old fashioned detective work is needed." said Jonny.

Thomas smiled at Johnny, remembering their life on earth together and how they met in the First World War. They walked right up to the map on the wall and stood side by side. They both placed the hand furthest from each other on the map, leaving their other arm to hang next to each other. As the light began to grow and grow, becoming so bright, they clasped their hands together and ZAP. The light consumed them both, and then they disappeared. The light became duller and duller on the map until it went out like a small flame.

Chapter 4

Echoes of the Past

Amira had barely been with grandma for 5 minutes before her mum had a work call and left to take it. Not that she minded, of course, she did enjoy visiting her grandma and now she had her all to herself. Her grandma was asleep when they had first arrived but seemed lively enough now. Amira's grandma's name was Lena Nilsson. She was dressed in a baggy purple dress with a black cardigan and an old-fashioned pair of slippers. Lena was happy to see Amira. She reminded her of how she used to be when she was her age. She had the same eyes. In a lot of ways it was almost like looking in a mirror, although, from the photos scattered on top of the cabinet of grandma when she was younger, in her late 20's, showed little similarity in looks overall between her and Amira.

Grandma asked Amira, "How is college going, dear?"

"It's ok, we have to come up with a business idea and present it in two weeks' time to the whole class, and a guest visitor called Darren Wilson is going to come to watch and give some prize away." confessed Amira.

Grandma Lena looked down and repeatedly pressed her fingers together in thought, "That name sounds familiar. Doesn't your mum know him?"

Amira smiled "She wished. She's been to a bunch of his talks. You know those ones that you said cost a lot? He has his show on the TV, grandma" explained Amira.

Grandma smiled in realization and said, "Yes, that's right! Oh, she will be terribly excited when she finds out." She shot a playful warning look at her granddaughter.

"Please don't tell her. I won't have a moment's peace if she finds out!" Amira whispered urgently.

Grandma smiled sweetly to Amira. "She won't hear it from me." and gave Amira a subtle wink and a pat on her hand to reassure her.

Grandma sat back in her chair. "So what IS your business idea?"

Amira sighed and glanced out of the window. "I have no idea. I liked an idea one of the girls in my class had, though."

"What was that then?" Grandma asked.

"It was a sort of help center for people who have a bad relationship with themselves, for example, people who have had plastic or cosmetic surgery and don't see themselves clearly anymore, anything to do with the relationship one has with one's self basically."

Grandma nodded. "That's not a bad idea. You know... I had plastic surgery when I was in my twenties... I have regretted it for a very long time."

Amira looked at her grandma in shock. "I didn't know it was even a thing back in those days."

Grandma shook her head and, with a more serious tone, said, "It definitely wasn't as common as it is today, but it wasn't entirely unheard of. It was certainly doable, only to those who would dare or who could afford it."

Amira, still stunned, asked, "Why did you do it? Why get plastic surgery?"

Grandma sighed and thought a moment "Well, I used to look very different. I used to look more like you. But after the holocaust, it was a precaution to have it done..."

Grandma stopped talking, and her eyes started to fill with tears.

Amira felt bad and put her hand on top of grandma's hand.

"I'd rather not talk about it. They were horrible, truly horrible times." said Grandma Lena.

Amira nodded and said, "That's why you never mention the holocaust? Cause it upsets you?"

Her grandma nodded. Amira thought that her grandma got married when she was 25, so she decided to ask one more question and then drop it.

"Did you meet granddad after the holocaust?"

Grandma put her other hand on top of Amira's. "No, I met him in the camp I was put in."

Amira didn't like the thought of her grandma in a holocaust camp. She remembered the images she saw at school when they were learning about it. She stopped herself from thinking about it, as her eyes stung.

Grandma asked Amira, "No boys you fancy at college then?" hoping to change the subject quickly.

Amira gave a little laugh. It was never like grandma to stay sad, "No, not really. They don't seem to notice me anyway. They like girls like Tammy."

Her grandma rolled her eyes and said, "Let me guess, her face is full of makeup?"

Amira was slightly taken aback by her bluntness "Well, yes she does wear a lot, actually."

Grandma smiled and said, "If there's one thing I have learnt in this life, it is that being pretty matters less and less as you get older, and just being yourself is the real attraction. All these girls today trying to make themselves look prettier is a cover-up from the truth that they don't appreciate who they truly are."

Amira thought it was an odd thing to say for someone who has had plastic surgery, but then again, maybe that was why she would know better than anybody else.

Amira asked, "Do you regret getting plastic surgery?"

Grandma picked up a handheld mirror, which was face down on her desk beside her, and looked into it for a couple of seconds, staring at her own face.

"At first, it was a huge relief to get it done. I felt safe. But as the years went on, every time I started to feel like myself again, I'd catch a glimpse of myself in a window or a mirror, and a stranger would be looking back at me. I didn't regret it then because it kept me safe. But when I was in the clear, I couldn't undo what had been done... and well now, I guess I do regret it."

Grandma glanced quickly at Amira and pointed her finger at her, and said, "Do not tell your mother about this young lady."

Amira gave a sideways glance at her grandma and said, "Why? Doesn't she know?"

Grandma slowly shook her head.

Amira's mouth was wide open. "Grandma! All this time, and she has no idea?!"

Grandma said, "Nope."

Amira closed her mouth and gave a cheeky smile. "Then she won't hear it from me."

Amira winked and grandma smiled. She slapped the top of Amira's hand in a charismatic manner. "So what about your business idea?"

Amira smiled and said, "I don't know, I'll have to have a good think about it."

Just then Sharron walked back into the room and said "So what have I missed?"

She plonked herself on the bed, crossed her legs, and waited for an answer.

Grandma spoke "I was telling her about the holocaust."

Sharron looked on in disbelief at her mother and said, "You have never spoken about it before."

Grandma replied casually, "Well, you never asked."

Amira smiled and decided to go along with it.

Amira asked, "SO are you Jewish? If you were in the holocaust, doesn't that mean you are a Jew?"

Grandma Lena said, "Yes, my whole family was Jewish."

Sharron looked in confusion. "So why aren't we all Jewish? I've often wondered after I overheard you talking to dad about the holocaust one night when I was little."

Grandma Lena explained, "Well, after the holocaust, I had no more family, and your dad and I ran into some trouble, so we changed our names and went into hiding. Erik was never Jewish, and for me, well, being Jewish seemed too dangerous. I was scared, and I just wanted a fresh start."

Amira asked, "Did you change your name because it was a Jewish name?"

Grandma replied, "Yes, that was part of the reason. That was the reason for changing my last name, at least."

Sharron asked, "So what was your name before it was Nilsson?"

Grandma replied, "My family name was Fekete."

There was a pause in the room as the new information was being absorbed. Grandma Lena looked impatiently at her daughter and granddaughter before she said, "Well?"

Amira and her mum glanced at each other for answers.

Sharron asked, "Well, what, mum?"

Lena sighed in suspense "Well, what do you think my first name used to be?"

Amira looked at her mum for answers, but she shrugged her shoulders and shook her head.

Amira looked back at her grandma and said, "We have no idea, grandma."

Grandma smiled sweetly at Amira and said, "My family name was Fekete. But my first name was Amira."

Chapter 5

Digging for knowledge

ZAP. Johnny and Thomas emerged out from nowhere in a small town in Hungary. They stayed enclosed in their hooded black cloaks, still holding hands and remaining unnoticed by those who passed by. They walked along and swapped holding hands for interlinking arms instead. They had not been given a task as important as this before, they were both determined to go above and beyond, and they were both very excited for a new challenge. They both loved a good brain teaser. It reminded them of their first life together when they met, back when they were spies. They carried on walking until they came to the town's public library.

Johnny asked, "Shall we?"

Thomas replied "After you."

They took their hoods down and carried on inside. They found a librarian sorting out books at her desk and asked her in Hungarian about finding a relative in the holocaust. Both Thomas and Johnny were fluent in Hungarian, among many other languages.

The librarian replied in Hungarian, "We have some local archives that you are welcome to use, and the computers are just in the room next door if you need them."

They thanked her and walked towards the archives room, stopped and turned to each other.

Johnny said "Computers or archives?"

"I'll take the archives, thank you very much." Thomas quickly replied.

"You'll have to get used to computers some time Thomas."

Thomas sighed and crossed his arms "Fine, I'll go on the computers."

Satisfied, Johnny clapped his hands together "Good, we will look for each other if we find something, alright?"

"Right." said Thomas, in a defeated tone looking away hoping for Johnny to change his mind. When he looked back to Johnny he was already mincing away down the hall. For an older man he had a lot of energy. Thomas admired Johnny from where he sat. He sighed, turned and walked towards the computer room, sat down and began to type things in Google search. He took out a notebook from inside his cloak to take notes on.

Two hours went by and it was time for the library to close. Both Thomas and Johnny, although in separate rooms, heard the librarian calling for people to leave. They both put their hoods up in response and remained perfectly still. Johnny kept some of the papers he was looking at and hid them in his cloak. He had a quick tidy up so that the librarian wouldn't linger around, and he slinked into a corner and waited. Thomas glanced at his computer screen that was still on and switched off the monitor quickly before the librarian saw it. Thomas hoped that she wouldn't notice the hard drive was still on, he was in the middle of something, and he didn't want to lose it all. The librarian was completely unable to see the hooded figures that blended into the shadows. She could have sworn she didn't see those two older gentlemen leave, 'They must have left ages ago' she thought. Convinced that the library was completely empty and tidy, she collected her bag and her jacket from her desk and exited the building, locking it up after herself and left to make her way home. A few moments went by and Thomas and Johnny began searching again, when they were sure the coast was clear.

It was 10 pm when Johnny decided to throw in the towel and put all the bits of paper and folders back into their proper place in the local archives. When he'd finished, he stretched, but as he did the countless cracks throughout his body made him wince. He kept forgetting how old his body had gotten.

"Can't wait until this is over." he thought to himself, still wincing from the back pain.

He wandered down into the next few rooms until he found Thomas, who was still in the library and huddled up in front of the computer typing like crazy.

"For someone that didn't like computers, you seem to be having a good time." said Johnny in a playful teasing tone.

He went over and sat in a chair next to Thomas, whose face was frowning in concentration. Thomas noticed Johnny as he sat down, his expression softened.

"So, what did you find?" asked Thomas.

"I found her old family home address, her school and a couple of local newspaper clippings about her parents when she was a child. And she was on the list of people who were taken to a transit camp in a place called Ricse along with her mother and father." informed Johnny.

Thomas, still looking at the computer, said "That's good."

Johnny watched for a moment as Thomas was continuously scrolling on his computer, waiting for him to speak, but he didn't.

Johnny asked, "So, what did you find? What are you doing?"

Thomas stopped scrolling and said, "Well, I've been talking in this chat room for the last few hours, it's been up fourteen years or so, and I have gone through and read all of it."

Thomas sat looking proud of himself, but Johnny's face looked confused. For the 7 hours that they had been here, that was what Thomas had done with his time.

Thomas said quickly, "Oh, it's a chat room for holocaust survivors! They are in search of family and friends and people they met on the inside and so on."

Johnny's face lit up, and he leaned forward. "Marvelous! What did you find out?"

Thomas smiled and clapped his hands on his thighs, ready to tell him what he'd found.

"Well, I read the entire chat room. I have seen everything everyone said. There are some truly horrible stories in there. Some said they managed to escape with the help of a fellow prisoner and a guard. Anyway, after I read it all, I typed in her name and asked if anyone had met her, knew of her, or knew anything about what happened to her?"

This had Johnny's full attention. "Well? Did anyone reply?"

"Why yes, they did as a matter of fact. A few have! Most said that it was her and a guard who helped them to escape."

Johnny tilted his head and said, "Why would a guard help them escape?"

"Ah, they reckon he was in love with her. One woman said that she was a good friend of hers and that this girl was particularly badly treat by the other guards in the camp there. She was a favorite of the men, if you know what I mean."

Johnny looked sad. "How horrible, could explain why she is so difficult to find and why her orb is so very dull."

Thomas looked in agreement. "Yes indeed."

Johnny asked, "Is there anything else?"

Thomas said, "The best part is this one woman on the chat, the one that said they were friends, well, she says that our lady told her that she was going to escape next and change her name, and that she was to look her up when it was safe and visit her."

Johnny stood up quickly, too quickly his body cracked loudly, and he regretted it instantly, but he was so excited to finally be getting somewhere.

Johnny asked quickly. "So you know the new name?"

Thomas beamed up at him. "Yes!"

He was beaming back at Thomas with joy and said, "Then we have a new lead!"

Johnny held Thomas's face in his and he bent down to give him a great big kiss.

Chapter 6

The Plot

Akil and Tefnut waited outside of the care home car park for over 2 hours. They lingered next to the glamorous women's red car, with their hoods up. Eventually, Sharron and Amira came out. Akil and Tefnut prepared themselves, both stood close to the back doors with a hand on the handle, ready to time their stealthy moves to perfection. Neither Amira nor Sharron noticed the two hooded figures standing on either side of their red car. Amira was the first to arrive at her side of the car and as she opened the front passenger door, so did Akil who was directly behind her. They both sat down in the car and closed the door in perfect synchronization. The same happened when Sharron reached for the car door, in less than 2 seconds, Tefnut opened the door, sat down and closed the door in perfect synchronization. Neither Amira nor Sharron noticed anything at all. They didn't even look back. Akil and Tefnut were mere shadows in the background. The red car pulled up to a large detached house with a decent sized driveway. Tefnut and Akil put a hand on the door handle ready to leave when Amira and Sharron did, again timing it perfectly to not be noticed. Tefnut and Akil followed both Amira and Sharron inside the house, remaining unseen. They stopped and looked around and observed Amira entering the house then closing the door and locking it behind her. Akil and Tefnut slowly walked to the corner in the living room where they stood observed and listened.

***

Sharron was the first to open the house door and slumped on the sofa. Amira followed her mum in and locked the door behind her. She found her mum and slumped down on the sofa beside her. They sat in silence for a moment.

Sharron broke the silence and said, "You think you know somebody."

Amira nodded slightly. "I know, all this time, and we never even knew."

"So you didn't name me after grandma?" asked Amira.

"No, I had no idea her name was Amira, I just remember somebody suggesting it, and I thought it was the prettiest name I'd ever heard." replied Sharron as she stroked her daughter's hair.

Amira was going to mention the plastic surgery but then stopped herself. She promised her grandma she wouldn't.

Sharron looked to her daughter and said, "What do you want for dinner then, I'm starving?"

Amira perked up and gave her mum a look that she was very much familiar with.

Sharron looked knowingly and said, "You want dominos don't you?"

Amira smiled broadly, which made her mum laugh, and then she put her arm around her not so little girl. She would soon be 18 and it made Sharron feel rather old.

"Ok, you order, and I'll pay." said Sharron as she handed her debit card to Amira.

"Deal!" said Amira happily as she grabbed the card, took her phone and began to look at the pizza meal deals on the menu.

About 2 hours later Amira and her mum were curled up on either side of the sofa watching TV with full bellies. Sharron wore some simple leggings and a grey off the shoulder top. Amira had changed into her oversized Coca-Cola T-shirt and a pair of shorts. They had a large empty pizza box in front of them with a few crusts left inside.

Amira's mind began to drift in thought about grandma Lena and to the plastic surgery and her friend Rose's business idea. It all seemed to resonate something with her, but she couldn't figure out what exactly.

She looked to her mum, who still had her makeup on even though it was nearly 11 pm and she wasn't going out again for the rest of the night. Amira knew that her mum cared a lot about looks, particularly false beauty it seemed, even though Amira thought her mum was very beautiful without all the makeup she wore. Amira thought of the influencers on social media that had resorted to cosmetic surgery, they were closer to Amira's age than they were to her mum's. Amira thought that there was a lot of pressure to look good even if you weren't an influencer. She couldn't imagine what the pressure must feel like if your job depended on looking good all the time.

"Mum, have you ever had any cosmetic surgery?" Amira casually asked.

Sharron was taken back slightly but replied, "No."

"Would you?"

"I've thought about having it done since I was about your age, actually."

"Why haven't you ever had any done then?"

"Your grandma wouldn't let me. She always talked me out of it. She said it would ruin who I really was." replied Sharron.

Amira struggled for a moment not to tell her grandma Lena's secret, she had to bite her tongue. After all, who could know better than someone who has had it done?

"Why would you get cosmetic surgery anyway?" continued Amira.

Her mum let out a little sigh and said, "When I was little, younger than you are now, I was bullied at school a lot, it felt like I was bullied by everyone there...the teachers certainly didn't help. When I hit 17 or 18 years old, I changed, my body got some shape, I lost my puppy fat, my face got thinner and I didn't have any spots anymore. I was suddenly so beautiful. When I saw people from school again, around where I lived, they barely recognized me and treat me so differently. And all the boys that made fun of me were asking me out and buying me drinks."

Amira felt bad. She never knew that her mum was bullied; she assumed she had always been popular and good looking.

Sharron continued, "Being seen as beautiful made me feel powerful, and I was so happy with how I looked, until I started to work in clubs and pubs. I noticed the other women that worked there were getting more attention than me. So I started to wear more makeup. After wearing more makeup, I really wanted a nose job, for my breasts to be bigger, and I wanted my lips to be fuller. I felt like I needed more to have the same effect on others like it did with those kids at school who were mean to me, or like those beautiful women I worked with at the clubs."

Amira felt that she understood where her mum was coming from. But there was something that her grandma had said to her earlier that made her want to ask her mum something else.

"If you had gotten all of that done, and you were older, do you think you could look in the mirror and recognize yourself? Or would you see a stranger?" said Amira.

Her mum sat there in thought and wrapped her arms around her legs. Amira had hoped she didn't upset her by asking all these questions.

"Maybe." said Sharron.

Amira felt better as soon as her mum replied, and they both sat quietly for the remaining of the show. Amira, however, was half watching it and half not, she was deep in thought. When it got to about midnight, Amira said good night to her mum.

Sharron said, "Oh, don't forget I'll be away this weekend for business."

Amira nodded. "I'll try to remember."

Amira kissed her mum on the cheek and went upstairs. She brushed her teeth, went into her dark room and crawled into bed. She was comfy straight away.

"What a long day." She thought to herself and went to sleep.

***

Tefnut and Akil watched Amira and Sharron eat a large pizza together while they talked and watched TV. It felt like a long time to Tefnut and Akil, so they decided to sit on the spare sofa on the other side of the room, while still listening and observing and while remaining invisible to Amira and Sharron. Akil and Tefnut perked up and leaned forward when Amira got up and they heard Sharron say that she would be away for the weekend. Tefnut and Akil looked at each other and smiled, knowing that that was the perfect opportunity.

Chapter 7

Calm before the Storm

Thomas and Johnny spent a few more days researching on the computers, emailing and looking on social media for clues, each doing as they pleased to help with the search.

Thomas sighed and said to Johnny, "Why don't we just go back home and use the map?"

Johnny sat back in his chair to look at Thomas and said, "Because we want to save our juice for something important, we might need it. I'm not running out of it again like we did last century."

Thomas went back to his computer and they both resumed scrolling.

After a while, Thomas stroked his smooth wrinkly chin and said, "I think I've found out all that I can from all this."

Johnny Sighed and said, "So have I. What have you found out?"

Thomas replied, "Her name pops up in Switzerland, in Bristol, and it stops at East Yorkshire."

Johnny said, "I found the same, also the husband's name, he was a mechanic, and I found an old advertisement for the company that still exists today. I have emailed the company asking for his address."

Thomas smiled smugly "Well, I have their old address in Switzerland. And I found this Woman on Facebook and Instagram with the same last name; her first name is Sharron. A post said that she used to be based in Bristol, but she has moved due to her mother's health."

Johnny's ears picked up. "Show me."

Johnny got up slowly and walked over to lean over Thomas and look at his computer screen. He saw a photo of a very glamorous looking woman on a beach and cliff tops in the background.

Johnny looked carefully at the photo and said, "Does that look familiar to you?"

Thomas made his lips into a straight line and replied, "In a way it does remind me of that holiday we took, but it could be anywhere along the east coast, and we don't have time to faff around, we need their precise location."

In the background of the photo with the cliff tops, there was a ship that appeared to be for tourists and had a bunch of people on it that Johnny noticed and had pointed it out to Thomas. He enlarged the picture so they could see the boat more clearly. There were a bunch of people on it, and there was a name on the boat that was slightly blurry from enlarging the photo.

58

Thomas said, "That could be a local business. I'll try and Google the name. Can you make it out?"

Johnny moved away slightly from the computer to get a better view "York...shire...Belle."

Thomas typed it into Google along with East riding Yorkshire, and there it was.

Johnny read off the top result that popped up on the search "Based in Bridlington, trips can go up to Bempton and Filey… That doesn't help us narrow it down enough."

Thomas went on Google maps and clicked on an area that looked like it had cliff tops similar to those in the photo. It looked just like the one in the photo and the beach as well.

Johnny stroked his beard and said, "Bridlington it is then."

Thomas looked at Johnny and said, "How will we find her when we get there?"

While still stroking his beard, Johnny said, "I think I have a good idea where to look."

They cleared the history from their computers, switched them off and held hands. A light consumed them and they vanished.

***

Three days had passed for Amira, and she was no closer to knowing what she wanted to do for her business plan. Other people in her class were already halfway through their PowerPoint's, while Amira had done nothing at all. There was only one week left after the weekend to finish it, Amira felt so stressed. She had been spending her time learning about what goes into a business and the extras that people don't think of, so it hadn't been a complete waste of time at least. Amira went home and slumped on the sofa. Sharron could see something was bothering her.

"What's the matter?" asked Sharron

Amira didn't want to tell her about the business plan because then she would have to tell her about the famous Darren Wilson coming by.

"Just college work is a bit stressful right now. I'm glad it's the weekend." Amira said passively.

The answer seemed to satisfy her mum enough to not question Amira more about it.

"Ok, well, I'm going to go and pack for the weekend." announced Sharron.

"Oh yeah, you're going away for work. Where are you going?" asked Amira.

"Manchester this time. You'll have the whole house to yourself! Don't do anything I wouldn't do." said Sharron. She stroked her daughter's hair and went upstairs to pack her bags.

Amira sat defeated for a while and watched TV to give her brain a break from over thinking. When she felt mentally rested enough she had a strong urge to do something related to her college work. She ran upstairs, grabbed her laptop, and returned to the sofa, happy to discover it was still warm from where she was sitting before. She opened her laptop and switched it on, she was about to turn the TV off, but then she thought it would be nicer to work with some background noise. As she waited for her laptop to turn on, she heard her mum fumbling around upstairs packing. When the laptop had fully loaded she began outlining her PowerPoint. She put titles on all the slides, picked out the color schemes, and made it look as professional as she could. She spent 30 minutes making a simple template ready for when she would get an idea. She felt so much better now that she had actually done some work on her PowerPoint. Maybe now that she had officially started it would get the ball rolling so she could think of an idea for it. She felt a bit more satisfied and had some peace of mind; she decided to have an early night. It was nearly 10 pm and Amira was more than ready for her bed, she felt so stressed about the presentation and she had felt that way all day. She couldn't wait to go to sleep. Just as Amira stood up from the sofa her mum came down the stairs, grabbed a glass from the kitchen cupboard and poured herself some red wine.

"Finished packing?" asked Amira.

Her mum headed over to the sofa and sat in the spot where Amira had been sitting.

"Oh, that's nice and warm. Yes, I am all packed and ready for the weekend." said Sharron as she got cozy and took a sip of wine

"What time will you leave tomorrow?" asked Amira.

"Well, before you will be awake I think, early morning." said Sharron.

"In that case mum, I shall say bye, bye now" Amira bent over and kissed her mum on the cheek.

"Now? You off to bed?" exclaimed Sharron.

"Yeah, I'm exhausted. Night mum, love you."

"Love you too. Sleep tight."

"I will. Have a fun weekend." said Amira as she began to climb up the stairs.

"I will do my best" said Sharron as she raised her glass and took a long sip of her tangy red wine.

Tefnut and Akil had stayed in the house for the last few days now waiting for an opportune moment. They watched as Amira went upstairs and they decided to stay and see what the mother, Sharron, would do. About thirty minutes after Amira went upstairs, Sharron switched the TV off, put her empty wine glass in the dishwasher, wrote a note and placed it on the kitchen table. Sharron left the kitchen, Akil and Tefnut lingered close enough so that they could read it, even though they were incredibly old their eyes worked perfectly well. The note said:

'I'll be back on Sunday night. Here's some money if you want takeout or need anything. Lots of love. Mum x'

Akil and Tefnut backed away slightly as Sharron came around the table with her handbag; she took out two twenties and one ten and put the £50 next to her handwritten note. She quickly tidied up the living room and kitchen. She placed the empty pizza box in the bin and the cups in the sink. She looked around the room before she turned the lights off and started up the stairs. Tefnut and

Akil stood perfectly still at the bottom of the stairs. Sharron turned the lights off and went into her room. Akil and Tefnut followed her in and saw her alarm on her phone set for 6am. Tefnut and Akil then moved out of Sharron's room and onto the landing. They looked to the third door along the landing with the name 'Amira' on it with a picture of a cat next to it. They slowly opened the bedroom door, and in the darkness, they saw a lump breathing very softly under the bed covers. Amira was fast asleep. They closed the door again, went back downstairs and sat down on the sofa.

Tefnut whispered very quietly, "Are we waiting until the mother leaves?"

Akil replied in the same manner, "I'm concerned the mother will take too long to get ready and will leave when the daughter is awake."

Tefnut whispered back, "So what if she does? She will be alone in this house all weekend."

Akil nodded. "Ok then. We will wait a while after the mother leaves. Then we will take her."

Chapter 8

Kidnapped

Amira was beginning to come around from a deep sleep. She had a strange sensation in a dream she had that she was moving or swaying; it made her dizzy. She turned on her side and stuck her feet over so she could slide out of her bed. With her eyes still closed, she reached for her water bottle. Her throat and mouth were so dry. She had always kept her drink on her bedside table, but she couldn't find it. She lowered her hand down slightly to find the table; she couldn't find that either. She forced herself to open her eyes as far as they would, she was still tired, and the light hurt her eyes. 'I thought I had closed the curtains,' she thought to herself as she continued to force her eyelids open. Where was her table? Why was the floor black? Where was her desk? Where did her window and curtains go? She had a rush of panic that sank in her stomach and made her heart thump heavy and fast as she felt the adrenaline fill her body. 'This isn't my room' she thought. She looked around at the room; she was on a large bed surrounded by tribal objects, hieroglyphics, and a stylish flat-screen TV that looked very much out of place in a room that looked like a weird museum that was also a bedroom. There were no windows in the room at all, and the floor was clear and black. Amira sat at the edge of the bed and slowly lowered her bare feet on the floor, expecting it to be cold, but it was lukewarm. She stood up and felt the duvet fall off her. She glanced at it; it was actually her duvet, from her home, her room. She looked around again and clutched the duvet back around her. 'I've been kidnapped,' she thought. Just at that moment, as she was about to go into panic mode, she heard the door handle turn. She was scared and a paralyzing panic spread throughout her entire body. She continued watching the door opened, and continued to hold her breath in suspense. Amira observed as an extremely old lady, and a man walked into the room smiling. They both wore black cloaks, and they were both hunched over but didn't hobble when they walked. The man wasn't extremely tall but taller than Amira, he had no facial hair or head hair, only some very silver eyebrows. They both appeared tanned with olive skin. The woman was about the same height as Amira, or she would be if she could stand up straight, her white hair was in hundreds of little braids that came just below her shoulders. Amira was confused but allowed herself to breathe again, she felt a little better seeing that it was a couple of old people who look like they couldn't hurt anyone, even if they wanted to, but she still felt unable to move and she was still afraid. The old man and woman smiled warmly as they approached her with open arms.

The old bald man opened his arms and said, "Welcome back, your majesty."

The old woman said, "It is so nice to have you back again, after all these years."

Amira stared back in confusion and was unable to get her words out.

Amira relaxed a little with the thought that they look liked they could die any day now by how old they looked. "What do you mean, your majesty? How did I get here? Who are you?"

The old couple looked at each other, smiled, and nodded. There was something smug about how they looked at each other. Amira didn't know how to interpret it or what to expect.

The old man cupped the old woman's hand as he said, "I am so sorry, your majesty, where are my manners? Your memories have not returned yet. I am Akil, and this is my beautiful twin flame, Tefnut."

The old woman flashed a sincere smile at Amira, but Amira was so confused, and her mind flooded with questions.

Amira said, "What do you mean my memories have not returned? I know who I am, and I know I wasn't here last night! Who brought me here? What do they want with me?"

Her eyes began to fill with tears in frustration.

Tefnut stepped forward and said, "Do not cry, your majesty. We're not here to hurt you. We are here to help you!"

Amira began to cry anyway, she didn't want to, but she couldn't stop herself.

"How did I get here?" said Amira.

Akil said calmly, "We were looking for you for a long time, your majesty, but we did not bring you here. You appeared to us on the outskirts of our realm. We recognized you instantly when we came across you. Your form is still so young and we expected to find you much older."

Tefnut carried on after Akil and said, "That could be why your memories have not returned. Your natural path has been interrupted, you see."

This didn't make any sense to Amira. She wanted to go home. She dropped her hands to her hips to look for her phone, but she realized she was still in her oversized baggy Coca-Cola T-shirt and shorts, she suddenly felt very exposed.

Tefnut took Amira's hands into hers. They were surprisingly soft. Amira looked down and saw that she was wearing black silk gloves. She noticed that Akil was wearing them too.

Tefnut looked directly at Amira and said, "Don't worry, we will explain it all, come with us, and we will show you something that will help explain why you're here, then we will get you some clothes."

Amira began to stop crying. The thought of getting into some clothes cheered her up a little. But she had so many questions, she was in a strange place with these two strange old people. Her anxiety began to build. Akil picked up Amira's blanket, which she had dropped when she looked for her phone, and wrapped it around her. Amira smiled a little to say thank you. Tefnut stayed by Amira's side as Akil walked across the room and opened the door, and gestured towards Amira and Tefnut to go through.

Tefnut began to walk, and Amira reluctantly followed her out the door. Tefnut kept her hand on Amira's arm as she carried on into the hallway.

The hallway was wide and vast; it reminded Amira of an extremely grand hotel. Paintings lined the hallway, each one with a beautiful young couple in it. The floor was the same in the hallway as it was in the room, black and lukewarm. It felt nice on Amira's feet. They walked for some time. The hallway looked very much the same until they reached a door at the end of it. Akil walked ahead of them to open the door and again gestured for Amira and Tefnut to go through.

Amira's mouth fell open as she entered a grand, black ballroom that seemed to have no end. As she looked across the room she saw vast amounts of stars and a little elegant stairway that led to a very royal looking archway. Her eyes looked to the rest of the ballroom and noticed all the furniture was black, the chairs had silver rims, black tables filled with sparkles, huge black sofas and black chandelier lights that went all along the invisible walls. The whole place was empty apart from Akil, Tefnut and Amira walking along to the other side of the room. As they reached the other side of the vast space, Amira noticed a massive Throne. It had black cushions and gold rims that were elegantly shaped. It looked wide enough for two people to sit on comfortably or maybe it was made for a very large person. Amira felt very much underdressed in her baggy T-shirt, shorts and a duvet wrapped around her.

Akil walked up to the throne and went straight behind it, where there was a door. Akil opened it for Amira, she went through it and was followed in by Tefnut and then by Akil, who then closed the door behind him. Amira looked around this circular room that was filled with white marble walls and floors with red carpets. All along the walls were countless paintings with what appeared to be the same couple over and over again, each time wearing different and more modern clothes the closer it got to the other side. She walked up closer to one of the portraits that appeared to be set in Victorian times. She looked at the man who was very handsome. He had blond hair and wore a smart suit, holding a top hat in one hand. The woman had a very elegant dress that showed off her shoulders. She had pure blond hair that had elegant curls which hung over one shoulder, and the rest was swept up into elegantly styled twists. Amira looked closer at the woman's face. It was familiar, extremely familiar.

"It can't be … but that's...it looks just like..." Said Amira as she breathed heavily and turned to look at Akil and Tefnut in panic.

Akil said calmly, "It's you, your highness."

Amira stepped back, her eyes gazing over all the portraits, they were all of her and this man with blond hair, and these paintings must go back centuries and centuries, thousands of years. The wall was full of portraits of her and him. She felt something touch her knees and felt to find she had backed up into a chair. She sat in silence as she carried on looking at all the portraits that filled the walls of the circular room. Amira was lost for words.

Akil and Tefnut walked closer to Amira.

"See, you belong here, your majesty." Akil said warmly.

Amira's heart sank.

Chapter 9

Facts Speak Truths

ZAP. A light appeared and quickly faded away. From it emerged Thomas and Johnny. After a lot of research and clever ideas, they arrived in this very nice house in a seaside town. They stood still and listened for a moment and knew that there was no one else in the house but them, so they released each other's hand to begin to look around.

Johnny clapped his old hands together and said, "Right then, let's get going! Can't believe how good I am at this!"

Thomas put his hands on his hips and said with some attitude in his voice, "Excuse me. It was my idea to look her up in the phone book."

Johnny stopped what he was doing and looked back "And it was my idea to use the police thingy at the station to trace their number to find this address. Thank you. Now! Let's look for clues."

They looked around the room. Thomas looked at the curtains that were still drawn and decided to open them to get more light into the room and to get a better look.

"That's better." said Thomas.

Johnny found some letters on the floor in front of the door and some more on the kitchen side and began flicking through them all.

"They're all addressed to a Sharron Nilsson."

Thomas came over to have a look. "Do you think she changed her name again?"

Johnny said, "Why would she do that? change her name a second time, so late in life."

"It's just a thought." replied Thomas.

Thomas looked around the living room and observed the coats and shoes that were two different sizes.

It seems like more than one person lives here. I'll go and look upstairs and have a rummage." announced Thomas.

"Right, I'll stay down here."

Thomas went upstairs and began to search in all the rooms. The first room was a bathroom. There were two sets of hair products, towels and toothbrushes, which confirmed Thomas's suspicion that two people were living here. The second room was a very simple room. Indeed, it had no personal touches and was very plain, he assumed it was the spare room. In the second room was a very neatly made bed, modern with luxury grey bedding, there was a pretty dressing table filled with makeup, on it were nail varnish remover pads and anti-wrinkle cream. All along an entire wall was mirrored sliding doors 'I think this is a wardrobe,' thought Thomas. He slid open the two doors in the middle.

"Lord have mercy," he muttered.

There were a lot of shoes and business outfits and going out dresses that were so beautifully organized. Up on the shelves were neatly folded casual clothes, it was very well organized in colors and occasions.

"So beautiful." said Thomas in approval.

He closed the wardrobe, sliding the doors back together again, left the room and went to the last room along the landing. This room was slightly messy, with a desk and a laptop, the bed wasn't very well made, in fact, it was missing its duvet cover, and the curtains were not even open. Johnny just managed to tug one of the curtains to the side, trying not to knock the desk over as he did so. He looked at the room again with better lighting.

"That's better." he said.

He looked to the wall near the bed and saw lots of little pictures all of different shapes and sizes that were stuck to it. He stood and took the time to look at each photo on the wall to examine them all closely. He stopped when he saw a photo that caught his attention. Thomas leant over and took the picture off the wall to get a better look at it. His eyes widened in anticipation and excitement.

"It's her... But it doesn't make any sense." said Thomas to himself.

He looked at the rest of the pictures on the wall to help make sense of his discovery before jumping to any conclusions. Most of them had the same people in it. A young girl, a woman, and a very old woman, they were sitting down in most of them.

He looked at the back of the photo he had in his hand and found a date on it.

"This photo was taken only last month."

He put the photo in a pocket on the inside of his robe and continued looking around the slightly untidy room. He opened the bottom desk draw and found a passport.

"Yes!"

He fumbled, with his old fingers, to open it to the photo page. It was the young girl in the photos, she was almost 18 years old, and her name was Amira Hardy.

He sat on the bed puzzled, looking at the passport and thinking. He could hear Johnny moving around downstairs and talking to himself too. Thomas got up and decided to have a look in the other room again. He opened a few draws before he found what he was looking for, another passport, this one had the woman in it whose name was Sharon Nilsson. He decided he had found enough and went back downstairs to go and tell Johnny what he had found. Something didn't add up to him about this photo. He needed Johnny to get closer to solving the puzzle.

Chapter 10

Dress for the Occasion

Amira still didn't understand. Why was she in all these paintings dating back centuries and centuries ago? Who did these old people think she was supposed to be? What do they want from her? The question that worried Amira the most was: Was it true?

Just as Amira was about to ask one of her questions, Tefnut grabbed Amira's arm and stood up, pulling her up with her.

"Shall we get you into some more suitable clothes, your highness?" said Tefnut.

Amira looked down and saw that she was still in her baggy Coca-Cola T-shirt and shorts with her duvet wrapped around her. She felt extremely vulnerable and slightly exposed, 'clothes would be good', she admitted to herself. Amira smiled politely in agreement at Tefnut and gave her a shy nod in confirmation.

They went back the way they came and arrived back into the ballroom, there were a few others in there now and they were all in pairs. Amira tried to look closer at them all; they all appeared to be very old as well, just like Tefnut and Akil. Except they weren't all in black hooded cloaks like the ones Tefnut and Akil were wearing. They all had their own style, some in very odd clothing and some in very old-fashioned clothing. Others wore an odd combination, a mixture of both of these.

Tefnut and Akil led Amira up to a door along the side of the ballroom and opened it for her. Amira paused for a minute, looking to Akil for confirmation that she was to enter, Akil gestured the way through the door politely and Amira went inside. Tefnut followed behind.

Akil stayed at the doorway and said, "I shall leave you two ladies to it. While you're getting ready, I shall go and tell the King that his Queen has arrived."

Akil smiled politely at Amira, then looked to Tefnut and winked at her before closing the door and went on his way.

Tefnut looked away from the door, still smiling from Akil winking at her. She saw Amira in a state of awe at her surroundings.

Tefnut said, "Do you like our wardrobe?"

Amira looked in disbelief "This is your wardrobe?"

Tefnut replied, "Well, it's the realms wardrobe really; anyone here can use it."

The room was filled with endless shelves and rails and had multiple floors, each filled with clothes, shoes and accessories. It seemed that the higher up the floors were, the older the clothes appeared to be. There was everything from casual wear, to going out, to formal events wear and uniforms. There were a few dresses that particularly caught Amiras eye that she thought were beyond stunning. At the very end of this vast room, there was a platform with some mirrors going around it with a very chic changing room positioned a few meters next to it. Against the wall there appeared to be a large beauty station fully equipped with hair utensils and makeup. Tefnut sat Amira down at one of the chairs at the dressing table.

Tefnut squeezed Amira's shoulders in excitement. "Let's get you ready to meet the King! This is my favorite part!"

Amira couldn't help but smile at Tefnut's excitement. "What part is that?"

"The dressing up, of course! The getting ready part." Tefnut replied, still excited.

She pulled Amira's hair back and began to style it using some of the equipment on the dressing table. Amira thought this was a good time to ask some questions.

"Where are we exactly?"

Tefnut was concentrating on Amira's hair but replied, "Memory still has not returned yet?" She glanced at Amira, and Amira bit her tongue and shook her head.

Tefnut smiled kindly and continued to style Amira's hair. "This is the realm of the twin flames."

"So we are not on earth?" said Amira.

"We are merely next-door neighbors to earth. We can come and go as we please." explained Tefnut.

"So, what are you? Are you human? Are you ghosts?"

Tefnut let out a little laugh as she brushed Amira's hair. "We are all of human origin, we all came from earth, but we are beyond that now."

"Then how did you all get here?" said Amira.

"When we find our twin flame on earth and die, we come here." said Tefnut.

Amira scrunched up her face in confusion. "You mean like a soul mate?"

Tefnut looked towards the mirror on the dressing table to look at Amira. "That's a common misconception." She began to brush Amira's hair again, shaping it effortlessly. "Anyone can find a soul mate, a soul mate is common. A lover, a friend, family, they can all be a soul mate, and a person can have many soul mates throughout their life." continued Tefnut in a passive tone.

"Then what's the difference between a soul mate and a twin flame?" pressed Amira.

"A twin flame is unique, very rare. Its pure romance combined with challenging and encouraging each other to be the best version of themselves. They are each complete souls that fits together as a perfect, much larger jigsaw. They are the ones that can experience love at first sight and feel the most pain if they are separated from one another. It goes beyond the physical; they connect in every way possible, physically, mentally, emotionally and spiritually."

Amira had never heard of a twin flame before, she wondered why everyone in the twin flame realm was old, especially if a twin flame was pure romance. She shuddered at the thought she had about it.

Tefnut had finished Amira's hair, and Amira looked up from her lap and into the mirror to see. It was beautiful. She had given her volume, big gorgeous curls that hung softly down her back, with an elegant tangle of precise weaving and braids that were so different from anything Amira had ever seen before.

"Oh my god." gasped Amira as she gazed into the mirror.

Tefnut smiled. "Do you like it?"

"It's gorgeous. How did you manage it?"

"Oh, centuries of practice." said Tefnut as she laughed.

Amira assumed it was a joke, although she couldn't help but think it was true; just by looking at Tefnut you knew it could be true. But Tefnut's laugh convinced her that it was probably ridiculous that she was centuries old. After all, she did say she was human, didn't she?

Tefnut clapped her hands and said, "All we need now is the outfit!"

Amira looked at all the clothes and then back at herself in the mirror to admire her hair. She glanced down at the rest of the things on the dressing table.

"Aren't you putting any makeup on me?"

"No, your majesty never wears makeup up here in her realm. We all wear very little makeup, if any at all, while we are here. You'll remember it all eventually."

"Then why do you have it if no one ever wears it?"

Sometimes it is used for when we go to earth. It helps us blend in better, like for a party or something formal. These days it seems very odd to go to an event or party without makeup, at least in the last few decades, and we like to keep up to date around here."

Amira raised an eyebrow in confusion. 'Will take more than makeup to help you all blend in anywhere' she thought to herself.

"Why do you go back to earth anyway?" asked Amira.

"I'm sure you'll remember all of that when you get your memory back, your majesty." said Tefnut.

That was starting to annoy Amira. How could she be a part of this world when she had spent all of her life with her mum? How could she be this completely different person, in a whole other realm?

Tefnut obviously had no intentions of answering any more questions, and she turned Amira's shoulders to face all the clothes in the room.

"Pick whatever you like to wear. We don't care whether it's formal or relaxed here. We wear whatever we desire. Some walk around in ball gowns all the time! I couldn't do that myself, the less the better if you ask me."

Amira pretended not to hear that. Amira stopped thinking about that and was instead consumed with the thought of what she would wear. She left her duvet on the dressing table chair and began to walk down the middle of the room. It seemed that the men's clothes were on one half of the room and women's on the other. She looked up to the other levels, and it had the same organization on each floor. It looked like the sort of clothes they wore in the '50s and '60s on the next few floors up going by the frilly skirts. She brought her focus back to the clothes beside her. She seemed to be looking at the more dressy choices in the wardrobe, she hardly dressed up after all, and Tefnut did say she could wear absolutely anything she desired, as everyone does, some even in ball gowns. Amira hesitated for a moment and thought it was a ridiculous thought, she'd feel much comfier in some jeans and a jumper.

"I think just some jeans and a top will do for me, Tefnut." said Amira.

"You want to meet the King for the first time in some jeans?" said Tefnut, "Don't you want to be in something beautiful when you see him again? You usually wear a dress" Tefnut gestured to the dress Amira was standing closest to. Amira didn't want the King to see her in some jeans, she remembered the portraits of him and her in the spiral room and blushed at how handsome he had looked.

'Maybe Tefnut is right' thought Amira.

Amira brushed her hands against the dresses as she walked by and felt the silks, satins, and jewels brush against her hand; they really were very beautiful. She stopped when she came across a pretty lilac color; she felt the fabric that looked like it had a rough sort of netting around it but it felt soft to touch. She took the lilac dress off the rail and held it out to look at. It's over laying netting like fabric floated to a standstill. It was sleeveless and had so much detail on the bodice; it was laced with very small lilac sequins that glistened in a rich light blue color when it hit the light. She tugged it by the sides and was delighted that it was a stretchy material. 'It's comfier than it looks' she thought. She held it further away from her to get a better look at the bottom. It came all the way down to the floor but had an uneven hem that looked like it would show her feet from the front 'And I won't trip over'. Amira smiled at it, she thought it was the most beautiful dress she had ever seen, 'it's perfect'.

Tefnut came and stood by Amira's side, "Shall we try it on?"

Amira's eyes lit up in agreement, and they walked over to the dressing room.

"You go on in there and try it on. I will go and get changed as well. When you are dressed, I will dispose of this baggy garment, and we will see how you look in the mirrors in your purple dress. Ok? Now go ahead and get changed." said Tefnut as she tugged on the edge of Amira's Coca-Cola shirt with uncertainty.

Tefnut shooed Amira into the dressing room and closed the curtains behind her. Amira was a little sad; she loved her Coco-cola T-shirt, it was the comfiest thing she had. She looked at the lilac dress that was cradled in her hands as she stood in the slightly dim changing room and thought, 'It could be worse, I suppose'.

She took off her baggy top and shorts, threw them on the chair beside her and took the purple dress off the hanger. She couldn't find a zip, so she lifted up the skirt to go underneath and popped her arms, shoulders and head through the top of it. She swizzled the dress around a bit to set it in the correct position making sure the longest part of the dress was behind her. It felt very comfortable, and she liked the way the bodice held on to her body and she was confident it wouldn't slip down. It felt perfect, she suddenly felt royal, and 'Maybe it wouldn't be a bad place to live after all' as soon as she thought this she remembered her mum and grandma Lena and felt a little sad and embarrassed that she had almost forgotten about them.

Tefnut's voice said, "Are you finished dressing yet, your highness?"

Amira pulled herself together quickly and opened the curtain before Tefnut could. Amira was in shock to see that Tefnut was not in the black hooded cloak anymore. But Amira wished she would have kept it on. Tefnut was dressed in a tube top and a long skirt with slits that showed both of her legs. Amira was in utter shock at the sight of such an old woman dressing this way. She remembered what Tefnut had said that everyone wore whatever they pleased here and that she said 'the less, the better'. Amira couldn't help but feel that despite the queasy feeling in her stomach, and her eyes hurting from looking at her, that this outfit did suit her in some weird way. With her braided hair and her skin tone, she looked very tribal. She looked at her boob tube top, and wandered how it worked, and stayed up when she seemed to sag so low.

Tefnut extended her arms and walked to Amira. "You look beautiful, your highness."

Tefnut took Amira's hand and realized that she was still wearing black silk gloves. Tefnut led Amira onto the platform at the end of the room with the mirrors behind her.

Tefnut released her and said, "Turn around and see."

Amira turned slowly, she was lost for words. The dress looked like it was made for her, the perfect length and fit, emphasizing her shape. Her hair style suited the dress perfectly. She looked at the rest of herself and twirled. The dress swished up and glistened lilac and blue, the material felt so free and light. She walked about in it and noticed it was very easy to walk in despite its length, probably because it was shorter at the front showing her feet. She looked at her feet and noticed that they were still bare.

Tefnut noticed this as well and said, "Ah, we can sort that out, right this way."

Amira followed Tefnut, she tried not to judge her in this very revealing outfit. So many different styles in every color and style you can think of, all arranged in order of their color. Tefnut had lead Amira to a large part of the wall that was filled with shoes. Her attention went straight to a purple section near the top of the wall, as she did this she noticed that Tefnut was already halfway up a ladder that was against the wall next to the shoes.

"Can you see a pair you would like? Are you a size 6?" asked Tefnut

"Yes, I am! What about that one with a low heel?" replied Amira, as she pointed in their general direction. It gave her anxiety to hold half-naked Tefnut up a ladder and hoped she would get down from the ladder soon in case she fell off it and broke her hip.

Tefnut continued to climb the ladder until she reached the same height as the purple shoes, she dragged her and the ladder to the side moving it along with her arms, and it slid along the wall of the shoes just like the ladders did in libraries. Tefnut grabbed a pair of lilac strappy shoes that had a slight sparkle with a little thick heel. Amira loved them.

"Perfect!" Amira said to Tefnut.

Tefnut climbed back down, and Amira was surprised by how easy Tefnut made climbing the ladder look, especially for how old she seemed 'Someone that old should not be able to move around so well' Amira thought. Tefnut reached the bottom of the ladder and gestured to one of the seats in the middle of the room. Amira sat down, and Tefnut slid the shoes onto Amira's feet. They were comfy and had padded soles. Amira and Tefnut both stood up and walked back to the mirrors for a final look. Amira was delighted by how comfy and easy the shoes were to walk in. She stepped up onto the platform again and looked at herself in all the mirrors, and truly admired herself. She had never looked so perfect or beautiful in all her life as she did at the moment.

"Where was this when I had prom?" She said as she continued to admire herself, her eyes beginning to water slightly.

Tefnut put her gloved hand on Amira's shoulder. "I think you're ready to meet the King now."

Amira's mind came crashing back to her current situation, and her heart sank as she remembered why they had brought her here 'What are they expecting from me?' she thought to herself.

Chapter 11

Good Old Fashioned Detective Work

Thomas went back downstairs into the kitchen where Johnny was reading a large book on the sofa. Johnny looked up at Thomas as he took a seat next to him.

"Did you find anything?" asked Johnny.

"Yes. There are two people living here going by the bedrooms, and these are the two" said Tomas as he handed over the two passports.

Johnny put the book down on the table and took both the passports from him. He opened the first one, "Sharron Nilsson. That's the woman on Instagram we found and the owner of this house." Thomas nodded in reply.

Johnny then opened the second passport "Amira Hardy... her daughter? Why does she have a different last name if it's her daughter?"

Thomas pointed at the picture on Amira's passport. "Doesn't she look familiar to you?"

Johnny focused his attention on the photo. "It can't be... That's...But how?"

Thomas sat back in the chair, somewhat more relaxed, knowing it wasn't just him having difficulty understanding. They both sat in confusion for a few minutes in thought and in silence. Thomas sat back and stroked his beard, and Johnny was lent forward with his elbows on his knees with a passport in either hand.

Johnny was the first to share his theory "Maybe she died and was reincarnated."

Thomas scoffed, "To the very same family? It's simply not possible. That's just too unlikely."

Johnny crossed his arms. "Well then, what's your theory?"

Thomas sat in thought for a moment, then said, "If she is part of this family; she would be our age by now, but that's the thing. The only old woman that is in this family is in this photo I found in one of the bedrooms and she appears to be this girl's grandma and this woman's mother and yet looks nothing like our queen."

Johnny said, "Show me."

Thomas handed over the photo from inside his cloak and gave it to Johnny. After he observed it for a few moments, Johnny picked the book back off the table and started to look through it again. He stopped at a page and pointed to a photo of an 8th birthday party. The photo showed a young Amira sat in front of a big cake and with the mother Sharron and an older lady next to it. Johnny held the photo that Thomas had found next to it for comparison and was satisfied that they were the same three people.

Johnny pointed to the three women in turn as he said "Grandmother, daughter and granddaughter. It has to be!"

Thomas creased his brow. "I think either our queen was reincarnated into this exact same family. Or it might be the grandmother if she is still alive."

Johnny looked in disbelief. "But Tommy, it looks nothing like her."

Thomas snapped back, "Don't people change their looks?"

Johnny was slightly taken back but replied with confidence, "Well, that is almost as unlikely as your first theory, alterations that could be made to such an extent is common enough now! But it wasn't over 70 years ago."

Thomas sat looking at the photo, shook his head and said, "I cannot go on until I find out if this grandmother is still alive, and if so, where she is now. We need to find something that proves what her name is and if it matches the one we got from the group chat. We don't start over until we can completely rule her out."

Johnny nodded in agreement and said, "So how do you propose we find her?"

Thomas looked around the room. "There has to be something here in this house that tells us where she could be."

They continued to look around the house and when Johnny ran his hand over the kitchen top he noticed a small pile of unopened letters that they had sorted through earlier. He picked them up and went through them one by one again. There was one from British gas, one that said private and confidential, one in a small brown envelope and another one from a bank. Johnny stared at it for a moment, went to open it but then stopped himself.

"Thomas, there's a letter from the bank for Miss Sharron Nilsson, a bank statement, I think."

Thomas stopped looking through a set of draws in the living room and wandered over to where Johnny was, who handed him the letter.

"There's only one way to find out." said Thomas as he opened it.

"But what if she notices that it has been opened?"

Thomas scuffed as he said, "She'll probably think she opened it herself, and besides, I love opening other people's post!"

Thomas ripped the bank letter open before Johnny could further exercise his morals. Thomas took the letter out and opened it up. "It is a bank statement."

Johnny came round and stood by him to get a good view of the letter, and they looked through the bank statement together. They went down the list slowly until they got to the last page.

"This one paid monthly. It's quite a bit, could be rent." Johnny said.

Johnny followed his finger to the description that the money was paid to and read out what it said "White House Lodge. What's that?"

"Can we Google it?" asked Thomas.

"Oh, mister, I don't like computers. You've changed your tone. Besides, there is no computer here!" said Johnny.

Thomas thought for a second and remembered, "There's a laptop in one of the bedrooms upstairs!"

They turned on their heels and power walked up the stairs. Thomas led the way into Amira's room, went straight for the laptop, opened it, and switched it on.

"This is a cozy little room. Where's the duvet for the bed?" asked Johnny.

Thomas straightened up and turned to look. "Yes, I thought the same thing when I came in, doesn't seem to be any sign of it anywhere."

The laptop made a startup noise. Thomas sat down at the desk as Johnny observed the pretty purple pattern on the bed's pillow.

"Looks so incomplete when the beds not made." remarked Johnny.

He turned his attention to the laptop and looked on as the screen saver popped up. Johnny and Thomas clenched their fists in celebration.

"Yes, no login." praised Thomas.

Thomas loaded up the Google page and typed in 'White house lodge' into the search bar, and hit the enter key. A few options came up, so Johnny scrolled until he came to a care home in the very town they were in.

"Jackpot! a home for the elderly. That makes sense. Oooh, it warms the heart that Sharron is paying for her mum to stay there." said Thomas.

Johnny was too consumed in the task to notice Thomas at this time. "Yeah, but where is it from here? Is it far?"

Thomas typed in the address of the care home and the address of the house they were into Google maps. It came back with the route and journey time estimation.

"Oyo, that's not too far! What time is it?" said Thomas.

Johnny looked to the bottom of the laptop screen "its 13:37." he said.

"And it takes about 20 minutes to walk there. We should be there by 2 O'clock if we leave now!" said Thomas in an urgent tone.

"Let's go!" replied Johnny in eagerness.

Thomas shut down the laptop, and they both stood up straight, quickly, and both of their body's cracked multiple times. As they did so, they both groaned in pain.

Chapter 12

Like the First Time

Amira looked at herself in the mirrors. Tefnut had left Amira a few minutes ago to go and check to see if everything was ready for the ceremonial reunion with her and the King. She locked eyes with herself in the mirror. 'What am I going to do?' she thought to herself. She looked at her shoes and thought her feet had never looked so pretty. She felt the soft netting overlay of her dress. 'I do look pretty' she thought to herself, something she didn't think about herself very often. She thought of all of those portraits in the room behind the throne, she couldn't deny that it looked just like her, but it couldn't be her. 'How could it possibly be?'

She then remembered what the man in all the portraits had looked like. If those were a real likeness to him, then he would be a very strong built man and a very handsome one at that. Amira couldn't help but be curious. Maybe something would happen when she sees him; maybe that was why no boys were interested in her back home, because she was meant for this King? But that sounded ridiculous to Amira. She couldn't seem to make sense of anything here. She felt very lost.

The door swung open. Amira turned around quickly at the sound and saw that it was Tefnut, and Akil was with her. She gave a little sigh of relief that it was them and not the King. Tefnut closed the door behind her and walked towards Amira who then slid off from the platform and stood up. Tefnut and Akil stopped in front of Amira ready to tell her what would happen next. Akil had gotten changed out of his robe too and into an outfit that complimented Tefnut's outfit, not quite matching but equally revealing. He wore a sort of skirt that stopped at his knees, twisted up and tied through the middle, making them sort of long shorts. Amira wasn't as shocked as she was when she first saw Tefnut's outfit; however, since then she felt nothing would ever shock her so easily again.

"You are a vision, your majesty!" Akil remarked happily.

Amira smiled as politely as she could and said, "Thank you."

Akil put his arm around Tefnut and said, "You always do such a superb job of helping her get ready, my love." And he kissed her on her saggy cheek.

Amira noticed that he was still wearing the black silk gloves, just like Tefnut was. Even after their outfit change, the gloves didn't really match the rest of the outfit.

Tefnut said, "Everyone is ready and waiting for you, your highness."

Amira's heart sank in dread. "What do you mean? Why is everyone waiting for me?"

Akil said, "Why for their King and Queen to be reunited, of course!"

Amira said in a panic "I thought it would be just us, I didn't think there would be a crowd watching! How many are out there?"

Tefnut said, "But its tradition! Don't you remember? All the twin flames are there."

"How many?" Amira said sheepishly.

Akil said, "There's a few thousand. The entire Kingdom is here to watch! Your highness should be thankful! There were more than 20,000 a few centuries ago, remember? Now that was a crowd!" He said as he gave a hearty laugh.

Amira didn't find it funny in the slightest. She was starting to panic 'What do I say? What do I do?' she thought to herself. Before she could over think, and have one of her anxiety attacks, Tefnut and Akil moved to either side and linked an arm each and began to walk her down to the door.

"What's the King's name?" Amira asked as she watched the door getting closer.

Akil said, "Why it's Toke, don't you remember?" That was a very strange name Amira thought, and she was getting extremely frustrated how people kept expecting her to remember something she felt was not hers to remember.

"What does everyone here think my name is?" asked Amira urgently.

Akil said, "Why, your true name is Runa, your majesty."

Just as Akil told Amira the name of who they thought she was, Akil had opened the door, where a vast audience was awaiting. As they stepped out into the ballroom Amira's feet seemed to freeze. The ballroom was full of old people, all stood in pairs, all wearing odd clothes, although each couple seemed to be dressed and coordinated to their twin flame. The huge ballroom was full apart from a path with a sparkling white carpet laid down the middle of it.

Akil and Tefnut both announced to the ballroom, "Our Queen Runa has returned! Now she will be presented to and reunited with her King, our King!"

Everyone in the room clapped five times in perfect synchronization and stopped. Amira still stood frozen in place. She looked to Tefnut for help.

"Just follow the carpet. The King is at the end of it." said Tefnut discreetly as she gave Amira a slight push forward.

Amira couldn't help but keep walking. She didn't want to make an idiot of herself. She kept her eyes down looking at the pretty white carpet. As she looked up she saw all the old people looking at her, some were smiling, and some had an expression she didn't like the look of, she felt so out of place. As she got closer to the turning point she noticed that everyone in the ballroom wore black gloves, just like the ones she had noticed Tefnut and Akil wearing. She reached the corner and turned to face the end of the pretty white path where the throne was, where there was a man standing proudly beside his throne. She carried on walking up the carpet, waiting for his face to become clearer. He looked big, much bigger than Amira was, bigger than she expected. She gulped but continued walking. She looked at all of the old people around her, some seemed very formally dressed, and others were more casual, they were all holding on to each other, some holding hands or simply had their arms around each other. Finally, she reached the end of the path, and the King was but a few meters in front of her. You could hear a pin drop. She looked up to see his face and he was already starring directly at her. His eyes were bright blue, and his expression was serious. Amira couldn't tear her gaze away, she blushed. He began to walk towards her, she felt her heart pounding in her chest. He was directly in front of her now and she felt scared, but stood very still, not taking her eyes off from his. A few moments passed and then suddenly the king grabbed Amira under her arms and lifted her up in the air spinning her and laughing as he did so. Amira screamed in shock and surprise and kicked her legs. The old crowd clapped and cheered. He finally put her down and held her tightly to his chest, she was in shock and was breathing heavily but he felt warm, and for a moment, Amira felt comforted and she closed her eyes to enjoy the hug. It was like it was exactly what she needed.

The King said, "Let's go to our room." His voice was strong and deep and was soothing for Amira to listen to. He had a very slight accent that she couldn't put her finger on.

Amira's eyes opened wide. She was worried to be on her own with him, this stranger, no matter how handsome or royal he was.

He directed her to the door behind the throne, she went in, and he closed it behind her. As he did, Amira turned around, and she watched the crowd disappear as the gap in the door closed.

He pulled her in for another embrace.

"You look as beautiful as ever, my Runa." said Toke softly.

King Toke drew back to look at her face, but she was looking to the floor. She felt awkward and scared. Toke put his hand gently to her chin and tilted her head up to look into his eyes.

"What is it, Runa?"

Her eyes began to water and she couldn't help but cry, "I don't know you, and they tell me that my name is Runa, and I'm not! I'm Amira."

He looked helpless but pulled her to him once more, stroking her hair.

"It's ok, come on, we'll go and talk. Ok?" said King Toke as he reassured his long lost beloved.

Amira stopped crying. She was so glad that someone had finally listened to her. He pulled away and smiled at Amira, and Amira smiled back, she was happy that he was kind to her and didn't get angry. He held her hand and led her to the spiral stare case in the middle of the room. As they walked up she looked at all the portraits of him and her along the walls until they reached the top. Another door opened up to a beautiful spacious room with a large bed in the middle, two desks on either side of the room, a big thick comfy sofa, and a huge TV mounted on the wall. He sat Amira down on the sofa, handed her a cup of water, and sat beside her.

"I know that you don't remember. Akil and Tefnut explained everything to me." said Toke.

Amira was relieved that they had been listening to her. "I thought they were ignoring me."

"You have been like this a few times before you know, and me too. But don't worry; it always comes back to us." he reassured her

Amira was so confused, but the king seemed genuinely nice. She felt she could trust him.

"I don't understand how I can be Runa when I've spent my life living as Amira?" she said as she dried her tears.

"We met many, many, many centuries ago. After we lived our last life on earth together, we came here."

He looked into Amira's eyes and saw how lost and scared she was. King Toke smiled kindly at Amira, still holding her hand.

"I promise I will do anything I can for you, and I will do my best to help you to remember. I'll explain how you came to be in Amira's life." said Toke as he stroked Amira's hand and looked into her eyes.

'Maybe it is possible, I could be Runa?' she thought to herself as she watched King Toke stroke her hand with his thumb, sending warmth throughout her body.

Chapter 13

The Discovery

Johnny and Thomas had walked for 15 minutes arm in arm with their cloaks on and with their hoods fully donned. They had finally reached the entrance of the care home they had looked up, back at the house, and had stopped a few moments to take in their surroundings. They didn't speak, but both pressed on until they got to the entrance and took down their hoods so that they could be seen. They went to the reception desk to ask for some assistance, but there was no one there. They both looked on the desk and saw a bell with a sign next to it saying 'Ring for assistance'. Thomas looked at Johnny who without hesitation rang the bell with his free hand, and they waited.

"Why don't we just have a look in all the rooms?" said Thomas

"That could take us ages." replied Johnny.

"No. This is taking ages." snapped back Thomas in an impatient tone.

Just as Thomas had said this, a middle-aged woman in a blue uniform walked past. She looked busy, as if she was rushing off somewhere but, stopped to look at the two old but healthy-looking men who were looking at her as if they expected something and were waiting for assistance.

Uncertain, the woman asked, "Can I help you?" she said in a thick Yorkshire accent.

Johnny smiled smugly at Thomas and said, "Yes, we're here to visit Mrs. Lena Nilsson."

The woman's face glowed "Well, isn't she popular today!"

"What do you mean?" asked Thomas

"Well, an older lady is visiting her as well, right now. Said she knew her from the holocaust! I caught some of their conversations, oh it was awful, and so sad what she went through."

Johnny and Thomas glanced at each other. They knew a gossip when they saw one, which was exactly what they needed.

"So awful. Yes she helped a friend of ours back then; you know, helped her escape." said Thomas, remembering the conversation he had had with someone in the online chat group.

"You mean with what was happening with her, she was helping people escape? My goodness! I don't like to eavesdrop but how can a woman ignore such a thing? To be used, hurt and mistreated by the guards in such ways, there are scars on her body I always wondered about, but now I know how. Poor lady, she's so sweet too. You know she got me a card for my birthday signed by everyone?"

"You mean she was… abused, sexually?" Johnny said.

"Oh yes, and it must have happened to her a lot when she was there. That's why she changed her name you know. Apparently, the guards were looking for her, even when the Holocaust ended."

Thomas and Johnny gave each other the nod that they had heard enough.

"Can you show us where she is?" Thomas asked.

"Course I can, my lovelies! I'll sign you in if you like, what're your names?"

"Danny Smith." said Johnny.

"Shaun Lockwood." said Thomas.

The woman finished signing them in and introduced herself. "I'm Cheryl, by the way. Right, follow me."

They followed Cheryl up to the end of the corridor and around the corner until they got to room number 44.

"Here she is, love." said Cheryl as she left them to it.

Thomas and Johnny looked at the name on the room door 'Lena Nilsson' they were happy it was her. As they approached the door an old lady hobbled out with a walking stick, she had tears in her eyes, she waved into the room.

"It was so good to see you after all these years. Don't be a stranger, write to me. Bye," said the little old woman. She walked past Thomas and Johnny and said: "Afternoon, don't mind my crying, I have just seen a very old friend, I haven't seen her for over 70 years." She gave a small joyful laugh as she continued on her way.

Johnny and Thomas then looked into the room, but there was no one in there. They looked around. The coast was clear. They put their hoods up and went into the room. It wasn't a huge room, but big enough for a single bed, a couple of chairs and a dressing table with a TV on top of it. They looked out of the window and there was a nice view of the sea. Seemed odd to them both that that old woman had said farewell to an empty room, but they saw it as a good opportunity to snoop. Johnny noticed the photos on the desk top and began to look through them all. There was a wedding photo, when Lena was much younger. He took a closer look like as he was trying to see some hidden meaning in the photograph. Thomas rummaged around in some of the draws but didn't find anything, so he went over to look at the photos with Johnny. Just then, they heard a noise somewhere in the room, and they looked up and noticed there was another door. Then there was a sound of a toilet flushing. They rushed to stand near the doorway before the bathroom door opened. An old lady with grey hair tied up into a bun slowly hobbled over to her chair, sat down and picked up a book. Johnny and Thomas observed her for a few moments and then slowly left the room. They went around the corner and straight down the corridor back to reception. Johnny ran his hand over the sign-in book and the names 'Danny Smith and Shaun Lockwood' disappeared from it. They went outside and leaned against the wall in the shade and took their hoods off to talk.

"She is the same build and height as Queen Runa. And has this newly changed name." said Thomas.

"What was that about her getting a visitor and talking about the holocaust?" Asked Johnny

"Ah well, a few people in the chat group said they were going to visit her and that one of them had kept in contact over the years, so maybe she knew where to find her. One woman did say she was keen to visit soon. Although I didn't think it would be this soon!" said Thomas.

"I did want to talk to her, but I don't think we need to now. We have all the confirmation we need that this is the woman in these photos back from the house, and she is alive. Plus, all that business about the holocaust, I'd rather not put her through that again. She looked very tired just now." said Johnny.

Thomas thought for a moment. "So you think that she is Queen Runa?"

"Although it looks nothing like her, yes, it must be. The 'Amira Fekete' we have been looking for is not dead but spiritually and soulfully damaged, she changed her name, and that is the very same woman in there." argued Johnny.

"Why would she not look like herself?" pressed Thomas.

"Surgery, I suspect." answered Johnny

"Must be! How will it be believed? No use tracking the new name, it won't work unless it is the name given at birth, and we have no proof of what she looked like before the surgery."

"Then we should go back and tell King Toke, and he can come here and see her for himself, and they will both realize that they have found each other. It's the quickest way to go about it."

Johnny nodded in agreement. "Good. Then let's go."

They held hands, the light consumed them both, and they vanished.

Chapter 14

The Tale of King Toke and Queen Runa

Amira was still sat with her hand in-between King Toke's. She did feel safe with him; he seemed kind, and very respectful towards her, not to mention he was uncommonly attractive.

Amira asked, "How did you and Runa meet?"

A flash of hurt crossed his face and then he said, "Before I answer this, would you like me to call you by your last earth name? Do you prefer to be called Amira?"

Amira felt sad for him, but she thought it was best. "I'd like to be called Amira."

He nodded and freed her hand. He stood up and began to pace around the room.

"We were Vikings, we were in separate clans, but we came together to raid larger settlements. When I first saw you, saw Runa by the sea one day, I knew she was the one. I felt my body pull towards her, like a magnet. My body was alight and complete knowing that she was mine and I was hers. She was the most beautiful thing I had ever seen ... she still is, you still are."

Amira blushed. She had never been told she was beautiful before. The idea that this man was a real live Viking also intrigued Amira, for how could that be possible.

"Vikings? But that was like thousands of years ago. I don't understand. How are you still here now?" asked Amira, hungry for more answers.

Toke was still pacing as he answered, "When we find our twin flame and eventually die, we meet again here in this world where we become infinite beings whose purpose it is to unite other twin flames back down on earth."

Amira thought about that for a moment 'infinite beings? They don't look so infinite around here. Everyone, except for King Toke, was ancient and looked like they were at death's door.

"So you don't age here? What about everyone else here? They are all so old!" said Amira.

Toke laughed.

"Royalty does not age here. The subjects of this realm do. There is a 100-year cycle." said Toke.

"A hundred-year cycle? What does that mean?" asked Amira as she sat on the edge of the sofa and pulled up the top of her pretty purple dress to keep herself descent.

"When the King and Queen are brought together to initiate the ceremony, it involves the replenishment of the subject's power, and with it, their youth." said the King, admiring the beauty of his Runa. It had occurred to Toke that he hadn't seen her this young since he had first met her. His heart grew heavy with the fond memories.

Amira could feel his eyes on her, and she blushed and asked, "Why is Runa not here to rule with you? Why leave?"

The king's attention was brought back to the question, "It's the curse of whoever rules here. Every 100 years there is a ceremony. My Queen and I come together in the great ballroom. We both initiate and lead the ceremony, after which one of the royals is immediately reincarnated back to earth while the other stays and waits for them until they are of age and can be reunited. After this, everyone in the realm becomes replenished."

"Why does that happen? Why does one of you have to go back to earth? How do you decide who goes?"

Toke replied with some sadness in his voice, "We never decide. It's completely random. I went back 13 times in a row once. Remember…" He stopped himself, knowing that she wouldn't remember anything, but recovered quickly. "It has to happen, the whole process must happen, or the balance will be thrown. Wars start, natural disasters and plagues happen, just to restore the balance. The royal being reincarnated helps to prevent the very worst from happening, like extinction. Plus it gives us rulers the advantage of growing with the times as they modernize." said the King in a serious manner. It was easy to see that ruling suited him very well.

Amira sat in shock for a moment, this was bigger than she had ever thought, and she never thought that love would play such a huge role in supporting the human race and world peace.

"Wait, so all those things happen because of a shortage of twin flames?" asked Amira, shaking her head in disbelief.

The King nodded in confirmation and took a seat on the table across from Amira. He sat wide-legged and rested his elbows on his knees.

"Are you all supposed to be guardian angels or fairy godmothers or something?" asked Amira.

The King smiled at that one. "You've never called me a fairy godmother before. No, we are twin flames, nothing like guardian angels. Our job is only to reunite other twin flames on earth. It's quite difficult; there are so many obstacles that get in the way."

"Like what?" asked Amira. She couldn't help notice how very masculine Toke was as he sat across from her, which only made Amira feel all the more feminine. She couldn't work out why that seemed so attractive to her.

Toke continued more than happy to help answer any questions and in the hope it might trigger his sweet Runa to remember.

"The main one is people not being in the right state of mind, mental and social barriers, with these in place people wouldn't know who their true flame was, even if they walked right into each other." said Toke.

"Then how do you know if they are in the right state of mind or not?"

"People on earth have no idea of course, but up here, we have centuries of insight and we have tools."

"What tools?"

The

King stood up and held his hand out to Amira. She sat up and shyly took his hand as she then stood up. She had to tilt her head back to look the King in the eyes, he was very tall, and she only came up to his shoulders.

"I'll show you one of them if you like." said the King in his soft, deep tone.

Amira felt her face grow warm from being so close to him and pulled her gaze away from his. He turned and headed back to the spiral stair case, still holding onto Amira's hand, and they made their way down. They didn't go out of the door that led to the ballroom. Toke turned to the opposite side of the round room where there was another door, a double door. He opened them both for Amira and waited for her to go in. Amira was reluctant to head straight in. It was very dark and looked like nothing was inside, but she didn't want to keep the King waiting. She went through reluctantly. It was pitch black. She felt nervous, and she hugged herself, wrapping her own arms around her body. Toke followed her in and closed the door behind him. As soon as the door was closed, the room lit up with little lights that went on forever. It looked like the view was outside of the ballroom, like the night sky, except there were no lights directly above them in here. Some lights shone brightly, some were glowing, but most appeared to be rather dim. Amira stood and took in the sight. She noticed that the closet lights to her were on some sort of furniture, very detailed, almost like a lamp post.

They held the orbs of light at the top. They all varied in size because all of the lights that were dotted about in the room were higher than others and some shorter.

"What are they?" asked Amira.

"Souls that are on earth." replied Toke.

"Are the dull ones, older souls?" asked Amira.

"No, the brightness represents something else. Come and follow me, this way." Spoke the King.

He unraveled her arms from around her and took her hand gently into his once again, and they started to walk amongst the lights in the room, they were endless. It took a few minutes, but there was a table they arrived at and the only table in the room, it seemed. It was very detailed and beautifully made of dark wood that appeared to be very intricately carved. In the middle of the table shot up into a root-like structure that held an orb in place. Toke and Amira stood right up to the orb and Amira noticed it wasn't shining much at all. It was barely glowing.

"This is the royals table of this realm," said Toke. "This is your soul."

Amira glanced at the King and then back at the dull orb.

"But why is it so dull? What does it mean?" asked Amira, who was now alarmed. Did it mean she was dying? Did it mean she would go to hell?

The King noticed Amira's fear and put his arm around her shoulders.

"The light on all of these orbs represents a soul's health, if they are happy and true, and see one's self clearly, believe in their self, the brighter it shines." said King Toke.

Amira let out a sigh of relief, but it saddened her. "Why is mine so dull? I thought I was ok. I feel ok. Sure, I'm kind of uncertain, and I keep to myself but..."

"Well, Tefnut and Akil have a theory about that. They believe that you're younger than you should be because you died before you were ready to and were reincarnated back into the system immediately after. They believe this dullness of your soul still remains from that particular past life as it still suffers from some trauma." said the King as his arms tightened around Amira's shoulders, bringing him in a little closer to him. It saddened him greatly that she had suffered so. He longed to embrace her as his once again.

"If someone is reincarnated, do they always come back looking the same? In each life? I thought people would look different each time they were reincarnated."

"You're not entirely wrong, that is how it works for everyone. But for us it is different, as we are not of earth anymore. Our place is here and the only ones here that get reincarnated every hundred years, is one of us. So when one of us royals is reincarnated, we look exactly the same each time. This form that we have now is the form we had when we first met and came together, and it stays that way until the end of this life."

Amira was satisfied with that answer, maybe she was this Queen Runa, but something still troubled her.

"How do they think I... I mean, Runa died? What do Tefnut and Akil think happened to Runa?" asked Amira.

"They do not know exactly but they traced her as far as the Holocaust in Hungry, but the trace went cold, and your birth name wouldn't work anymore. It's unclear how you died, but what is clear is that you must have experienced some true horrors in that life." He looked thoughtful as he looked at his beautiful Runa, who was once again in his arms. He wanted to comfort her, but he restrained himself, and waited for her to say something in case she still didn't remember yet.

"How can you tell who's orb is who's?" said Amira as she looked around the vast space full of lights.

The King looked a little hurt. He was hoping his Queen would have returned to him after telling her things about her previous life. Nevertheless, he put a kind smile on his face and held on to hope, as she was here right in front of him and would surely remember everything soon.

"We whisper a name, and the orb presents its self to us. We need to use a little juice sometimes, this room is endless, and every year, it grows as the human population grows."

"What's juice?" Amira asked.

"It's what gives us some power, not to do big things but little things to help us do our work. It runs out about every 100 years, which is why the ceremony is so important as it gets topped up."

"So, I could find someone here?"

"You can't at this moment, but I can look for you. What's the name?" Toke was eager to please her.

"I'd like to look up two names, if that's ok?" said Amira. Now that she knew what the light of the orbs represented she couldn't help but check on her mum and dad.

"Sharron Nilsson and Paul Hardy" Announced Amira.

"We must do one at a time, so we will do Sharron first. Who are these people to you?"

"My mum and dad." said Amira.

The King nodded. Although a little sad, he bowed his head and said something very low and extremely quiet, too quiet for Amira to hear. He lifted his head when he had finished and began to look around the room. Far in the distance appeared a vertical light that reached through the roof.

"There, hold on to me and close your eyes."

Amira linked on to his arm and closed her eyes as he told her. She felt a warm wave of air swoosh her hair up, and her purple dress flared up a little too.

"We're here." announced the King

Amira opened her eyes and they seemed to be in a completely different part of the room. The beautiful table with the orb was gone.

"This is Sharron Nilsson's Orb." said Toke.

Amira looked at the orb that was next to her. It was brighter than her own orb was at least. It was what she expected. Despite her mother's confidence, she knew there was a lot of negativity buried within her.

She looked up at the King and asked, "Can we see Paul Hardy's orb now? Please."

The King nodded and bowed his head down and then looked up again in search of the light. It appeared, not so very far away.

"We can walk there. Come." said King Toke as he offered Amira his arm.

Amira took the Kings arm and followed him until they reached the lit up orb. As soon as they arrived, the light faded, and there was the orb. It was very bright, to Amira's surprise.

"It's bright!" exclaimed Amira

"Yes, it's a healthy soul. You seem shocked?" smiled the king.

"I am. My dad left my mum, you see, for one of her best friends after they were together for 15 years." Amira forgot herself for a moment, almost like she was good friends with the King. It made her think of her grandma and how she would talk and tell her anything.

"Ah, it's not uncommon, by the looks of this particular soul, because it is so bright, I'd say that he has already found his twin flame." observed the King.

Amira was shocked and confused. "But how can that happen? He had known of her for years before he left mum."

"Well, twin flames here have a job to push others on earth towards their own. Sometimes this results in finding other people instead. Perhaps in this case, your parents may have both had unhealthy souls, perhaps your dad saw your mum and went with her for superficial reasons such as beauty, but twin flames are deeper than that. It was only a matter of time for your father to find his twin flame. Meeting your mother lead him to his twin flame, one day, his soul was healthy enough to actually notice his twin flame when he saw her." explained King Toke.

"But what about my mum, Sharron? Was she nothing to him?" asked Amira sadly.

"People still connect and love without them being a twin flame. They are referred to as soul mates. Of course, they still mean something. And although your mother's soul was quite dull, when it is bright and healthy, she will find her twin flame too. But these days we only work the bright flames. Dull ones can take up a lot of juice and a lot of hard work. Earth has become a difficult place these days."

"What happens if there are no twin flames?"

"There's no such thing. There are always twin flames." said the King very sternly.

"People can't always be the right age for each other though, can they? What if there are thousands out of sync?" argued Amira.

"Ah yes, in such cases, there is usually a natural disaster, if it is to such an extent. If hundreds around the world are unmatched and are out of sync, smaller things can happen, such as illness, accidents, suicides, murder. All seem horrible and without reason, but they are nature's efforts to restore balance and correctly sync with one another. If we meet a certain target each year for uniting twin flames, it prevents such situations from getting worse."

Amira stood in silence as she looked upon her father's bright orb. She felt overwhelmed and full of hope with all this knowledge. In her wildest dreams she could never have guessed such things could exist, or such horrors could be accounted for, and yet she felt a sort of piece from knowing everything she had learnt so far.

"This explains quite a lot." said Amira, who was almost speechless.

"Would you wish to know more?" asked King Toke softly.

Amira looked up at the King, smiled and said, "Yes".

Chapter 15

Akil and Tefnut's True Intentions Revealed

Thomas and Johnny arrived in the map room, back in the twin flame realm. They were reluctant to be back without having enough evidence or proof, but time was running out. The King must be told what they'd found, and as soon as possible. They walked down the corridor and out into the ballroom where they found some friendly familiar faces. Their favorite couple was there, Antonio and Maria. Antonio and Maria had met in Spain in the early 1600s. Thomas and Johnny enjoyed their company a great deal and had been good friends since the day they first arrived in the realm. Antonio and Maria were both very genuine, kind and most importantly, they were lots of fun. They saw each other from across the ballroom and walked towards each other to meet in the middle. Maria wore a pretty midi-length sun dress, and Antonio wore some tight fitted black bottoms and a baggy half-open white shirt. They were both blessed with dark olive skin with deep wrinkles, and they both had similar hair that was a much darker grey compared to most others that resided in the realm. Most people in the realm were either completely white-haired or had lost their hair altogether. When both couples reached each other, they exchanged greetings with kisses on the cheek and enthusiastic handshakes. Thomas and Johnny noticed that Antonio and Maria were both wearing black gloves, which they found very puzzling.

"Where have you been? We searched for you before the reunion." said Antonio.

"What do you mean?" Thomas said as he gave a sideward glance to Johnny.

"The Queen, of course!" Tefnut and Akil have found our queen Runa! Although she's much younger than we are! It's most unusual, but not impossible, it seems. It is of little matter now that they are finally back together." said Maria happily.

Thomas and Johnny both felt something was wrong, but they couldn't quite put their finger on it. They needed to know more.

"Why do you not look happy? This is fantastic news!" blurted Antonio.

Thomas and Johnny decided to take them into their confidence. After all, if things were as bad as they thought, they will need help.

"Why don't you come to our room and we can tell you where we have been? We've only just got back, and I think that we may need your help. We have much to tell you!" explained Johnny.

"But of course!" said Maria as Antonio nodded heroically.

"We just need to quickly stop at the dressing room first!" said Thomas.

They all made their way to the luxurious and vast dressing room where both Thomas and Johnny picked out their outfits very quickly; they held them up in front of them so they could see themselves in full view of the mirror. They both held up their selected items to see if they matched. They did, and they looked very stylish and smart indeed. They both hurried over towards the shoe wall when something caught Thomas's eye. He stopped dead in his tracks, wandered over to the dressing table, and saw a crumpled purple duvet underneath the table.

He picked it up and held it out. His eyes lit up with knowing, and he shouted immediately to get Johnny's attention.

"Does this look familiar to you?" asked Thomas rhetorically.

Johnny looked amused for a moment, but then his eyes lit up the same way as Thomas's eyes had.

"It matches the pillows in the girl's room we searched, the duvet that was missing." said Johnny.

"If she was the Queen, why would the duvet be here unless ...?" said Thomas.

Johnny finished his sentence, "... She was taken by force."

"My god, they kidnapped her?"

"That's what it looks like. Come on, let's pick out our shoes and talk to Maria and Antonio about it! They could help us."

They looked over to Maria and Antonio who were sitting, waiting patiently at the other side of the room.

Thomas and Johnny hurried over to the wall and with an experienced eye, found and pointed to the shoes that complimented their chosen outfits. Johnny gave his clothes to Thomas to hold while he went up the ladder to collect both of their selected shoes. He climbed up the ladder with great ease and very sure footed, grabbed both pairs of shoes and slid back down the ladder. You wouldn't have thought he was so very old by how he moved until he tried to stand up straight after he had landed, which made his body crack and click. He groaned a little but didn't waste any more time. Thomas and Johnny walked to the exit and beckoned Antonio and Maria to follow. They went back out into the ballroom and started making their way through a light crowd that had begun accumulating. They all made their way up to another door along the ballroom, which went up a long corridor and to their room in the middle of the hallway. Maria and Antonio followed closely behind as they walked through the labyrinth. Johnny and Thomas finally found their room. They opened their door quickly and ushered Maria and Antonio in first. Johnny and Thomas looked both ways to make sure the way was clear before going into their room and locked the door behind them.

"Please sit down, both of you." gestured Thomas to Antonio and Maria. They both took a seat on a smart and stylish lounge sofa that was at the end of a king-sized bed.

"So what is it? Where have you two been?" asked Antonio.

"Well, it is a delicate matter. What we are about to tell you cannot be repeated again outside of this room." said Thomas firmly.

Johnny went behind a trendy room separator that they had in the corner of their bed chamber and began to get changed.

Antonio and Maria looked at each other, gave a firm nod and looked back at Thomas

"We promise." said both Antonio and Maria.

Thomas started as he handed Johnny his items of clothing one by one. "Well, yesterday after Tefnut and Akil left to go and track down Queen Runa. The King asked us to look for her as well."

"Because there was great urgency to find her." said Maria.

Johnny replied as he was getting changed, "Yeah, that's right. He told us not to let Akil and Tefnut know that we were looking for her too."

"But they have found her. So?" said Antonio

"The problem is we don't believe it is our Queen that they have brought here." replied Thomas.

"Why do you say this?" said Antonio as Maria lent forward to listen more carefully. Johnny had finished getting dressed and had now come along to the other side of the room separator. He was dressed in a smart traditional black suit with a stylish blue neck scarf. Thomas went behind the room separator straight after to get changed himself, and he slung his black cloak dramatically to the other side of the room in haste.

"We traced the queen's earth name, and we discovered that she changed it to Lena Nilsson to hide from consequences from the holocaust, she then moved a few times, she got married, had a daughter, who then had a daughter of her own, THAT daughter was also named Amira! AND is identical to look at. But it is not our Queen. This girl here now is her earth-granddaughter. That must be her that is here now! Look, I have a picture!"

Johnny rummaged around for it in his robe pocket that was still draped along the room separator, while Thomas was fumbling around getting his trousers on.

Johnny found the picture and sat beside Antonio and Maria and pointed to the youngest girl in the photo.

"That girl is who is here now! But this girl's grandmother must be our true queen!" said Johnny.

Antonio and Maia looked closely at the photo of the old woman for a while.

"But this looks nothing like our queen." observed Maria.

"Yes, we know, that's why it's so difficult to believe! But we traced the name as far as we could, and through lead after lead, it led us to her who is still alive and of the correct age." argued Johnny.

Thomas was doing up the buttons to his shirt as he added, "We had to come back to tell the King so he can judge for himself and meet her in person. But if this poor young girl is here as you say, and he's with her already, then will he easily be persuaded to consider otherwise?"

"And the ceremony is tomorrow! God knows what will happen if the ceremony is done with the wrong person." Johnny sounded very convincing and worried, and he put his face in his hands.

"We believe you." said Antonio.

Johnny lifted his head up, and Thomas came around the room separator, now fully dressed and wearing a navy blue polar neck jumper, smart trousers, a blazer with a blue cravat around his neck and a matching hanky chief sticking out of his breast pocket.

"You believe us?" said Thomas, he and Johnny looked at Antonio and Maria, smiling and nodding back at them.

"So, what do we do?" said Johnny as he brushed back a stray hair that had fallen out of place.

"Do not tell the King. He will not believe you, not now. I suggest you talk to this poor girl and see if she can tell you anything about her grandmother." said Antonio.

"Right, we will have to get her alone somehow." agreed Thomas.

"But what about Tefnut and Akil?" asked Johnny as he raised an eyebrow.

"Perhaps we should tell them all of this and that they were mistaken, then they will also help us to rectify the situation." said Maria.

Johnny looked at Thomas with uncertainty and then back to Maria, pulling a face.

"That's just the thing, they're not stupid, and I'm inclined to believe maybe they picked this girl on purpose and not as a mistake."

"What makes you say that?" asked Antonio, raising an eyebrow.

"It's just a gut feeling, how they smiled at each other when the King was at the end of his rope wanting to find Runa. I'm not so sure I'd like them to know that we know. What we don't know is why they would go to these lengths." said Thomas.

"Again, we need proof." added Maria.

"Well, I'm so glad you said that." said Thomas smugly as he looked over to Johnny.

"I planted a camera and mic in their room. We would have used our juice, but we can save it for more important things this way. Plus, no one here would think to look for such a device." said Johnny.

"You mean like on those crime shows on the TV?" asked Antonio, who was very impressed.

"Yes, so it's hooked up to our TV. In fact, let's check in on them now. See if they have said anything." said Thomas as he grabbed the remote.

"We wouldn't like to get on your bad side. When did you even put this in their room?" said Maria.

"As soon as they left in search of our Queen. We didn't trust them." said Johnny.

Thomas pressed a few buttons, and there they were, Tefnut and Akil in their natural habitat, their bed chambers. They all sat and watched and listened for a few minutes. They observed and listened, Akil was lying on the bed, and Tefnut looked at herself in the mirror.

"What is it that they are watching on the TV?" asked Antonio.

"I... I think its Love Island." said Thomas.

***

Tefnut was admiring herself in the mirror, straightening out the deep wrinkles on her face using her hands to aggressively pull back the sides of her face round to the back of her neck. Akil was laid on the bed with one hand behind his head, with a remote in his hand.

"You know, I have no idea why I like this show so much." said Akil as he scratched his sagged but hairless chest.

"It reminds me of what being young is like, to be in the prime of one's life again." said Tefnut, thinking back to better days.

Tefnut turned away from the mirror, walked over hunched, and climbed on the bed as best she could to lie on Akil's chest.

"Soon, we will be young all the time, experiencing new things again and not withering away in this place trying to help people like this find their true flame." said Akil as he gestured to the contestants on Love Island.

"Yes, it's mind-numbingly boring, and how exquisite it will be to be young again all the time." said Tefnut as she looked up to Akil and smiled.

"Well, one of us at least." teased Akil.

"But do you think he will keep believing it?" said Tefnut as she stroked his chest.

"I think he will my dear. I think he's completely convinced, and it is in its self very believable! She has the same first name, and she is her doppelganger, identical. No one would ever think to check the grandma who looks nothing like her." Akil started to play with one of Tefnut's braids.

"I suppose that's true. Even if someone did find that out, they would need to prove it to the King now. He won't believe that it is not her, and even if they managed, it will be too late. The ceremony is tomorrow."

"Exactly, see, there is nothing to worry about." They smiled at each other and shared a passionate kiss, and then continued to watch Love Island on their TV.

***

Thomas paused the TV as Johnny, Maria and Antonio all sat in complete shock.

"They must have known for years, decades." said Maria in complete shock.

"I think they've known the whole time. I don't think they've ever lost tabs on Queen Runa." said Johnny.

"So, what do we do?" said Thomas.

Maria was the first one to speak, "I think you should pretend to believe that this girl is the Queen, in front of the King, and definitely in front of Tefnut and Akil. You two need to get proof, real proof. We at least have this proof of what you recorded Tefnut and Akil had said just now. I think that this poor girl knows deep down that she doesn't belong here. I think she will be on our side for sure. You need to get her on her own so that you can talk to her."

"I agree." said Thomas, Antonio and Johnny nodded in agreement.

"But how do we do that? I don't think the King will let her out of his sight. He has been without Runa for almost 100 years and will be without her once again after the ceremony." argued Johnny.

Maria and Antonio looked at each other, Antonio winked, and Maria smiled. They looked back at Thomas and Johnny.

Maria was the first to speak and said, "For now, do not let anyone know you are back, not even the King and especially not Tefnut and Akil."

Antonio added, "We will get the King away from the girl."

"How?" said Thomas and Johnny.

"We will try and convince him that she is not who he thinks she is, and we will say that you two are still on earth following the real queen's trail and have sent word to us about it." said Antonio.

Thomas and Johnny looked to each other, nodded, and both said rather enthusiastically. "Right!"

"Don't forget to wear gloves!" said Maria.

Thomas and Johnny grabbed their gloves from a draw. Thomas went back to the remote re-wound a few minutes and paused it, just in case they needed to prove that Akil and Tefnut had been deceitful. Then both couples all set off to make their plans.

Chapter 16

Hope

Amira was still with the King. They were back in his room after they had finished with visiting room of souls. Amira was looking through things that were supposed to belong to her (Queen Runa). She sat at a desk. On it was a few old coins that reminded her of medieval times, or perhaps the kind that the Vikings used. There were also many papers with the same handwriting but in many different languages. She looked for the King, who was sat at his own desk across the other side of the room, writing rather quickly. She got up and walked towards him passing the large bed and massive TV, which was fixed onto the wall, and a large mirror in the corner next to the bed. She caught a glimpse of herself in the mirror and, for a moment, didn't recognize herself. She had forgotten she was in the beautiful purple dress.

She reached the King's desk and sat down in a very chic but masculine chair placed at the edge of his desk. Amira could see he was busy, so she decided to wait for him to finish writing before saying anything. She looked at his face that was fixed in concentration. Amira couldn't think of anyone she had seen before that was so attractive; not even anyone famous could compete with this god-like figure. She leaned over slightly to see if she could tell what he was writing so urgently. His writing was very neat for being so rushed, so elegant and clear, not of a language she was familiar with, though, 'maybe they have their own language up here,' she thought.

She sat back and began to admire the fabric on her dress and played with the end of a ruffle. Toke did a final swish and a dot with his pen and turned to face Amira.

"Anything come back to you yet?" He asked in a cheery, optimistic voice.

Amira felt a little guilty to keep giving him the bad news. "No, nothing,"

Toke's smile lessened, but it looked like it was an answer he had expected "Then how can I help you?"

Amira answered, "There's a bunch of different papers written in different languages."

"Yes, we speak many languages." said Toke.

"Does everyone here speak lots of languages?" asked Amira

"Yes, it is to be expected up here, you live many lives on earth, and as a soul, you remember them all. Plus, we have to put twin flames together all over the world. Communicating in many languages is a huge asset for us." Toke explained.

"So you all learn as you go? And does a soul remember every other life after dying on earth too?"

132

"Yes, when you get to live as long as we have you end up learning all languages. We still remember languages that have long since died out. Souls are given a clean slate when they are reincarnated to give them a completely fresh outlook and start on life, but when you die, you remember all of them."

"Do you speak Viking?" asked Amira in haste, and in curiosity.

"Yes, although we didn't call it 'the Viking language'. Why do you look disappointed?" said Toke as he studied Amira's face and gave a little laugh.

"No, I just thought you all speaking different languages was something quite magic."

Toke laughed, "We can use juice to understand and speak languages, but it depletes it very quickly. It saves a lot of juice if we just learn the languages, which isn't so hard. Most people have lived many different lives before they come here, by which time they can already speak at least 40."

"But how can that be?" said Amira, confused.

"Well, if a soul does not find their twin flame on earth and then dies, they are reincarnated over and over again until they do, and then they come here. When they come here, they remember all their past lives."

"Wow, so how many lives did you have on earth before you met Runa or … me?"

That gave Toke hope and he gave a sweet little smile. "I had only 77 previous lives before I came here."

said the King, now pleased he might finally be getting through to his beloved.

"So, do you have to reach a certain number before you meet your twin flame?" asked Amira.

"Mostly yes, although some more complicated souls don't. However, there's a hand full that existed long before their twin flames did. They had many, many lives before they met their twin flame, but at least that way, they know a lot of the world by the time they come up here. You might notice some on earth, ones that go their whole lives going from one lover to another, but nothing lasts. They are usually lost souls whose twin flame does not exist yet. Most can sense it deep down if their twin flame is out there or not." said Toke.

Amira was completely absorbed by all of the information Toke was telling her. She thought after finding out more about this place and what they do that she would know if she was the queen or not, but she still didn't feel any closer to knowing the truth or not. Then she got a horrible idea that gave her a little uneasy feeling.

"What if I'm not the Queen?" asked Amira sheepishly.

"But you are, I'm sure you are. We always find each other in the end." said Toke as he reached for her hand.

Amira looked at his hand holding hers for a moment, then looked into his eyes. "But what if I'm not? What would happen?" Amira asked gently.

"If that were truly the case, then we would have to send you back home." said the King dismissively.

"But what about the 100-year ceremony and what If you did it with the wrong person, someone that wasn't your twin flame?" As Amira said this, the King pushed himself back from the desk and sat back in his chair, tapping the desk top with his fingers.

"No one knows. Not for sure." he said seriously.

Amira was at a loss of what to say. She felt that she might have offended the King or perhaps had crossed the line. She looked at all the pages with writing on that were in front of him and saw an opportunity to change the subject.

"What are you writing?" she asked hoping that it might lighten the mood.

"There's a lot of paperwork to do before the 100-year ceremony and it is tomorrow. I don't have much left to write now." replied the King kindly.

"What could there possibly be to write about?" asked Amira.

"Well, what happens after the 100-year ceremony is uncertain, unpredictable. We may die and make way for the next King and Queen, and then they would need to know everything I'm writing about now. This paperwork is also added to our history archives as well." said Toke as he got up from his desk, walked over to the bed and laid down. He faced the huge TV screen on the wall and stared at it in thought.

"You can die up here? But I thought everyone that was here was supposed to be already dead." said Amira.

"When I say die up here, it means to move on and create more twin flames, it's the death of a soul, similar to the death of a star it can make more beautiful things happen, or perhaps transform into something else like the caterpillar and then butterfly." said the King as he closed his eyes.

"So do people just randomly die up here, or does that have something to do with the 100 year ceremony?" asked Amira.

"Yes, it does. At the 100 year ceremony, many souls 'die'. Some may even choose it after being up here for thousands of years. Kings and Queens however, cannot choose. They die when the greater power decides its time." He looked for something under the pillows he was lying on and found a remote.

"But what happens to you when you die?" asked Amira.

"Our souls collide with each other, and many more souls are made, they are put back into the life, love and help cycle. Some even come together to become another being. I believe you would have referred to them as guardian angels. Not that you could ever truly know for sure." He opened his eyes again, turned his head to the TV, and pressed a button on the remote that was beside him to turn the TV on. Amira was curious. She put down the pen she was playing with, stood up and approached the bed so she could see what was on the TV. She watched Toke select the series 'Vikings', and noticed he was about halfway through the box set.

"Vikings?" blurted out Amira in humorous disbelief.

"Yes, have you seen it? I put it off for a while, but I ended up watching it in the end, it's actually quite good. Kind of reminds me of home."

"Yes, I watched it when game of thrones finished. How is it you can watch it up here?" asked Amira.

"We get unlimited Wi-Fi and very good reception up here, and we don't have to have a supplier or pay for anything. It is fantastic because time has been much easier to pass since these were installed in our realm! A few of the newer twin flames suggested it, and it's brilliant!"

Amira laughed. She found it so funny that in a realm of magic, mystery and love there were TVs in every room, and the King was a series binger.

Toke smiled at Amira and looked at her with joy. "It's nice to hear you laugh." he said.

Amira blushed. No one had ever looked at her that way before. Just then there was a single knock at the door and a note appeared underneath the frame.

"A message, now? Who could that be from?" said Toke in frustration.

Toke walked over to the door and picked the note up to read it.

Toke let out a big sigh. "I have to go for a while and see to this," he said in anguish as he didn't want to leave his beloved Queen Runa again.

"What is it?" said Amira.

"Nothing, I hope. I just have to listen to what some of my subjects have to say and clear things up." he walked over to Amira, sat her down on the bed and put the remote in her hand.

"Watch anything you like, I'll be back as soon as I can." Toke brushed her hair with his hand and looked into her eyes. His expression longed for more, but as he looked into his Runa's lost eyes, which were either shy or scared, he refrained from anything more and left the room to go downstairs.

Amira looked around the room and then at the remote in her hands and started to flick through the TV channels and films. She suddenly felt a little tired 'I wonder what time it is back home?' she thought. Amira looked around the room, and it felt wrong, it didn't feel like home. She missed her mum. 'What will she be like when she finds I'm not there anymore?' This thought made Amira feel very sad and then hopeless. Suddenly she didn't care what was on TV anymore and she let the remote drop out of her hands onto the bed. Before she could begin to cry, another note shot under the door. Amira hesitated at first out of shock 'it's probably for the king,' she thought to herself. She got up anyway and walked over to the note out of curiosity. It had her name on it, her full name and also her grandmas.

'Amira Hardy, granddaughter of Lena Nilsson- Please read.'

Curious, Amira picked it up.

'We can help you get back home. Come to the bottom of the stairs and wait at the ballroom door. Wait there until you hear five knocks then open the door.

From your Friends.'

Chapter 17

The Real Queen Runa

Amira looked at the note suspiciously. She felt it would be stupid to trust an anonymous note in a strange place, and in a completely different realm. Amira was about to screw up the note, but as she looked around the room, she caught sight of herself in the mirror again, and tears were streaming down her face. She looked at herself, at the beautiful dress. 'This isn't me, this isn't home,' she thought. She folded up the note and shoved it down the front of her dress. She plucked up her courage and opened the door slowly to see if there was anyone out there waiting for her. There wasn't, and it was very quiet, which meant the coast was clear. She stepped out and closed the door behind her, and tiptoed quickly down the stairs, taking care not to make any noise, and holding her skirts up with her hands. She reached the door at the bottom of the stairs that lead to the ballroom. She held out a hand to grab the door handle to open it, but then she stopped. She took a second to think before she pulled out the note from the bodice of her dress and read the last part again.

'...wait at the ballroom door. Wait there until you hear 5 knocks, then open the door.

From your Friends'

She waited, tense, her heart was racing and her anxiety was building. She hoped that the authors of this note really were her friends. Just then, she jumped as she heard a quick but sure; KNOCK, KNOCK, KNOCK, KNOCK, KNOCK.

Amira gathered up her courage and opened the door just enough to peak through to see who was there.

A hand suddenly grabbed her and pulled her out into the open, it was wrapped up in one of the black cloaks everyone seemed to have. She was about to blurt something out in shock as the cloak was forced around her head and body. There was a face right up in front of her, an old but very well dressed man put his finger to his lips, signaling her to be quiet. He looked kind, so she stayed quiet 'This must be who wrote the note' she thought to herself. She looked at the man behind her whose hands were gently rested on her shoulders from putting the cloak on her. This man was also rather well dressed and clean-shaven, unlike the other one who had a beard. He smiled to reassure her that they meant well.

"Don't worry were friends. But we need to move you to somewhere safe first." whispered the clean-shaven man.

She nodded. She felt like she could trust them, they had a good-natured manner about them. All Amira could think about was how badly she wanted to go home.

They lead her quickly down along the side of the ballroom and into one of the doors. Amira was careful to keep her bright purple dress from escaping the cover of her black cloak as they hurried through the labyrinth of corridors. They continued on until the bearded man stepped in front, stopped and opened one of the doors along the hallway, the clean-shaven man took Amira inside, and the old man with the beard quickly closed the door behind them.

"Sit down, my darling." said the clean-shaven man.

Amira sat down and panted slightly, struggling to catch her breath.

"I'm Johnny, and this is Thomas."

"You said you would help me get home?" reminded Amira.

"Yes, we will! But we need your help first." said Thomas.

"How could I possibly help?" asked Amira.

Thomas looked to Johnny. They didn't have much time left before the ceremony. It was only tomorrow. It dawned on them both how difficult this could be to explain, especially to a girl as young and as fragile as she seemed.

"Do you know who THEY think you are?" asked Johnny

"Yes, they think I'm Queen Runa, the woman in all the paintings." she said as tears started to run down her cheeks.

"And do you believe it?" said Johnny.

Amira's eyes began to fill with more tears. "No!"

Both Johnny and Thomas sat either side of Amira and put an arm around her.

"Don't worry." said Thomas

"We know who Queen Runa really is." continued Johnny.

"And we know it's not you." finished Thomas.

Amira looked at them both and felt a huge weight lift off from her chest and was able to take a full breath of air into her lungs. This was the best news she had since she arrived in this realm. She looked to her new friends; Johnny and Thomas, to answer "Who is Runa then?"

"It's your grandmother." said Thomas.

Amira was slightly taken aback and then sad. Thoughts of fear went out to her poor grandma Lena.

"What will they do to her?" she pleaded.

"The fact that she is NOT the one here is a major catastrophe." said Johnny.

"You see, no one knows what happens if the ceremony is carried out on someone not of this world like you. You're still without your twin flame! It may have happened in our history before, but no one can know for sure as there is no record of such an event in our archives, but there are small blind spots. But we have a theory." said Thomas.

"Because there is no record of it, it must have wiped us out entirely! Everyone in this realm and everyone on earth, were left to fend for themselves to find their twin flames, creating chaos. The realm might have to start from scratch in such an event until it is eventually rebuilt again over time."

Amira was lost for words. But if everyone in this place were wiped out, that might mean Amira too.

Thomas and Johnny looked over to each other, both uncertain if they should tell her.

"Well, the Queen is supposed to be the same age that we all are now if she lived the full life that she was given on earth. But you see, if she died and came back and was at a younger age than us, then we have to make her the same age as us … for the ceremony."

Terror struck through Amira's heart. "You mean… You mean they'll make me old?"

"Yes, that's why we must all wear these gloves! If anyone from this realm touches you, you will become old like us, for you are of the earth, just as the Queen is at the moment."

It suddenly clicked, she had noticed everyone wearing the black gloves, and Tefnut and Akil were so careful not to touch her without material in the way.

"But the King touched me with his hands." Amira pointed out.

"He is of royalty and still of this realm. He has such privileges. The subjects of this realm are forbidden to interact physically with those still in the life cycle, which is why we have such a detrimental effect to humans if we make physical contact." explained Johnny.

"What about Tefnut and Akil? They were so sure. They nearly convinced me that I was Runa …" she trailed off into her sadness and began to blub again.

Thomas knelt to look at her square on. "They don't care about you, the King, or the realm, it seems. They would have made you old by now if it wasn't for them trying to convince the King you were Runa. King Toke can't see that you're not her, he's so hurt and desperate, so of course he believes them."

Amira looked at him and then had a thought that baffled her. "But why do you think it's my grandma?"

Thomas said, "Well, we tracked her down, basically. Back from where Runa's soul was last known from and then found out that she changed her name, so we followed that and found her at that care home in the little seaside town."

"Lena Nilsson." said Johnny.

"That's her, that's grandma!" exclaimed Amira.

"There's just one problem…" said Thomas.

Amira Paused and shifted her look from both Thomas and Johnny. Amira was beginning to lose hope every second. It seemed to her that every step forward ended up in her taking another two steps back.

"What's the problem?" asked Amira quietly.

Johnny let out a big sigh and began.

"The problem is everyone believes that you are the true Queen already. You look exactly like her, and you have the same first name that she was given when she was reborn to earth. Your grandma doesn't have the same name, and she looks nothing like our Queen, and we can't figure out how to prove it."

Amira stood up when she realized something. "She told me something the other day."

"What?" said Thomas and Johnny, as they stood up and groaned in response their bones cracking.

"She told me that she had plastic surgery after she escaped the holocaust." exclaimed Amira.

"Yes!" said Johnny, punching the air in victory.

"But can we prove it? Do you have any proof?" said Thomas quickly.

Just as Amira was about to celebrate with them with a smile, she stopped as she answered.

"Like what?"

"Receipt for the surgery, a photo of her before she had plastic surgery, anything?" pleaded Johnny as he made dramatic hand gestures.

"No, nothing like that, but I think she must have something somewhere. Can't we just go and ask her?" said Amira. She would be so happy to be back on earth and to see her grandma again.

"Are you close to her, to your grandma?" asked Thomas.

"We've always been close. I think she could give us some proof." exclaimed Amira, desperate to leave the realm.

"Well, it seems to be our only option… but we have to be very quick about this. We had better go, now!" said Thomas in urgency.

"Before anyone notices that you're missing!" said Johnny

"I hope Maria and Antonio are on form today." said Thomas to Johnny.

"Who are they?" asked Amira, who was puzzled?

"Friends who helped us get you out of there." Thomas said.

Amira was thankful that they did get her out of there. She felt a huge wave of relief come over her. 'Finally, someone who believes me' 'I can go home'. Amira then felt the same sense of urgency that Thomas and Johnny were experiencing but for a different reason. If the ceremony is tomorrow, they don't have much time to get to her grandma and get the proof they need. 'I don't want to be turned old or perform the ceremony', Thought Amira to herself. Amira gulped at the very thought of being as old and wrinkly as Tefnut and Akil and jumped up off the bed. She rushed to the other side of the room and looked at Thomas and Johnny who were surprised by her sudden burst of energy and quick but clumsy run towards the door.

"Well, come on then! Let's go!" hurried Amira in panic.

Thomas and Johnny grabbed their black cloaks and fumbled with the door knob, their gloves were slippery, and age was starting to take its toll on their grip strength. Amira, frustrated, opened the door with ease, and they all rushed out. Thomas helped Amira tuck the ruffles of her dress back into her black cloak, and they raced up along the corridors towards the map room.

Chapter 18

The Proof

Thomas and Johnny grabbed the hood of the black cloak that Amira was wearing and flung it over her head. Johnny poked his head out over the corner to check the coast was clear. Then they all went out into the hallway and rushed up the corridor to the map room. Amira stood in-between them both with one hand in Thomas's and one hand in Johnny's. Amira could feel the silk from their gloves. They hurried along the corridor until they arrived at the very end where the big black door was. Thomas was the first to grab the handle and took a few tries to get a good enough grip with the black silk glove before he managed to open it. In the room was an entire wall covered with a very impressive and beautiful map of the world, painted with exquisite detail. Amira looked at the map. It filled her with awe and wonder. All three of them approached it until it was only a step away.

"Close your eyes." said Johnny quickly.

"And keep them closed tight." added Thomas.

Amira did as she was told without question. She really felt a big trust with Thomas and Johnny. They had an entirely different energy to them than Tefnut and Akil did; it was warm and kind. Thomas and Johnny closed their eyes after watching Amira close hers and bowed their heads, whispering a name that she couldn't quite make out. Then their free arms flung up to the wall, and a light showed up on the map which got brighter and brighter until it consumed all three of them in a huge flash, ZAP. Even though Amira had her eyes closed she couldn't help but see the redness from the bright light, almost going through her closed eyelids and made her squint harder. The light consumed all three of them, and then grew dimmer and dimmer, until all three of them had disappeared from the room.

They arrived just outside of the care home where Amira's grandma Lena was living at. Amira recognized it immediately. Amira was speechless. 'Did we just teleport?' she thought to herself. But she was too full of panic and urgency to find the time to ask. She began hurrying toward the entrance when Johnny pulled her back.

"Wait, Amira! We have to tell you that you have to keep the cloak on and the hood up at all times until we get into your grandmas room." said Johnny.

"Ok, but why?" questioned Amira.

"These help us to get around unnoticed, no one can see you when you're wearing one of these, but it won't work if you're loud or clumsy. And don't be surprised if you can't see us, or yourself if you pass a mirror," said Thomas.

"And we don't want Tefnut and Akil to come here and ask people if they have seen someone that fits your description, or they will know for sure that we are on to them." said Johnny.

Amira nodded in agreement. 'A magic cloak' she thought as she clutched the middle together, making sure that the pretty purple ruffles of her dress wouldn't pop through.

They all stood in a single line and began to walk across the car park towards the main entrance. Amira led the way through the entrance, careful not to make a noise and move as smoothly and as softly as she possibly could. Amira saw a woman at the reception desk, and she stopped. She felt a gentle push from Thomas behind her, encouraging her to keep moving. Amira carefully continued to walk. The woman at the reception desk didn't even notice them. They carried on up the corridor, in a very smooth motion; Thomas grabbed Amira's elbows and gently moved her to the side as a staff member rushed by. Amira quietly exhaled in relief and started up the corridor again, turned the corner, passed all the doors of other residents until she reached her grandma Lena's room. They all entered the room, and Johnny quietly closed the door behind him. Amira took her hood off so she could see the room better. 'Where's grandma?' She thought, she looked at the bed, it was empty. She looked at the chair, and that was empty too.

"It's ok! She's in the bathroom." whispered Thomas.

Thomas and Johnny took their hoods off also and made themselves comfortable by sitting on the edge of the bed. Amira sat in the chair next to where her grandma usually sat and waited for a few moments.

There was the sound of a flush and then a tap running in the sink. Finally, the door handle pressed down, and her grandma Lena hobbled out, not noticing Amira until Amira stood up to meet her. 'Will she even believe me?'

"Amira! This is a surprise! What a gorgeous dress! Have I missed something?" said Lena happily.

"Grandma, I'm in a lot of trouble, and I don't know how I'm ever going to convince you that what I have to say is the absolute truth…" said Amira as she started to cry.

Grandma looked up to Amira and wiped away her tears, smiled and said, "Try me."

Just then, grandma Lena looked to her bed and noticed the two elderly gentlemen sat there smiling politely and waiting patiently.

"Are these friends of yours?" asked grandma Lena curiously but delighted to have more visitors.

"Yes, they're trying to save me." said Amira.

Grandma didn't seem fazed by this and said, "Well aren't you going to introduce me?" said Lena as she touched up the bottom of her hair and smoothed out her skirt.

"Yes, this is Thomas and Johnny." said Amira.

Thomas and Johnny stood up and bowed.

"Well, how formal, you'd think I was royalty or Japanese." she said jokingly.

"Listen, grandma, sit down, I don't have a lot of time and I really, really need your help." pleaded Amira as she took her grandmas hand and gently led her over to the chair.

Her grandma's face turned serious as she sat down and listened to everything that Amira had to tell her, from being kidnapped by Tefnut and Akil, to meeting the King, the realm of twin flames, and the lost Queen they had thought was her.

Thomas and Johnny also listened and was ready to add to the story that Amira was telling if needed, but there was no need at all. Amira had done a very good job of explaining and had covered everything.

Grandma Lena sat back in awe as Amira finished telling her everything that had happened to her. After more than a minute had passed, Amira began to look to Thomas and Johnny for reassurance, and then quickly back at grandma, who was still not blinking, her face looked in shock.

"Oh my god, we broke grandma!" cried Amira as she raised a hand to her mouth and sat back into her chair as she began to blub.

Suddenly her grandma came to life and let out a little laugh after she realized what Amira had just told her. She reached over and put her hand on Amira's knee for reassurance.

"You haven't broken me, you silly thing! I'm just speechless... So let me get this straight. You need me to help you. You want me to give you proof that I have had plastic surgery, and proof of my old name, so that I can be reunited with a gorgeous young King?"

She looked to the two men still sat on the edge of her bed, who nodded.

"Yeah, that's correct." said Johnny as Thomas who continued to nod in agreement.

Grandma Lena looked back to Amira as a huge grin started to form on her face that lifted her cheeks and crinkled her eyes.

"Sounds great to me!" said grandma Lena in the happiest and most excited state that Amira had ever seen her in.

"This means that you'll leave and go back to the other realm, if we can pull this off in time before I'm turned old and die." said Amira.

"Yes, yes, I understand you! But I feel … I can't explain it but, it feels right! I remember feeling this way once before! But all of these years have gone by and I had forgotten all about it! As if I was close to finding my destiny." said grandma Lena.

"Oooh, was that when you met granddad?" asked Amira.

"No, it wasn't my dear! I remember now! A very eccentric couple came and asked me questions once. They were oddly dressed ... must have been about 40 years ago now! They asked me if I had gotten plastic surgery, where I came from; they were wearing cloaks just like yours. The conversation never amounted to anything. They just left, but when they were here, I felt a connection." said grandma Lena.

"Egyptian, a woman with braids, a man with no hair?" asked Johnny suspiciously.

"YES! Yes, that was them!" said grandma Lena.

"They have known for 40 years and they never brought you back? All these years, and you could have been with your twin flame. They've purposely robbed you of that so they could try and claim the throne for themselves." said Thomas shaking his head in disgust.

That one seemed to upset grandma Lena. A big missed opportunity was the story of her life. She had known a lot of bad luck in this lifetime. Amira took her grandma's hands into her own.

"Where's that proof we need grandma?" asked Amira.

"I'm afraid I don't have it with me, it's in Switzerland. I don't know if you'll make it there in time." said grandma in a defeated tone.

"We have ways, don't worry, just tell us where the proof is and we will get it and make a case for the King to look at." said Thomas.

Grandma Lena perked up again and focused for a moment.

"Right, I buried everything I valued at the time about my old self, my birth certificate, photos, and a few bits of jewelry. I buried them in a tin, under the tree on the side where the biggest root is sticking out, it's there, and that's where your proof is."

Johnny and Thomas got up from the bed, moved over to Amira and each held out a hand for Amira to take. Amira got up and quickly took both of their extended hands. Instantly, a bright light quickly engulfed all three of them and they vanished from the room, ZAP.

Grandma clasped her hands together and felt the happiest she had felt in a very long time.

***

Amira felt her hair whoosh around her face as the light disappeared. When she opened her eyes she saw a large green covered the land and a little village in the distance, a lake, and next to her was a lovely looking house made of stone. She turned around and saw the tree her grandma had described to her.

She let go of Thomas and Johnny's hands, grabbed her skirts and ran over to it as fast as she could. Her feet were still in the dainty, pretty low heeled sandals and her feet felt cold and wet as she ran through the damp, slightly overgrown grass. At the tree, she crouched down and looked for the root that stuck out the most.

Thomas and Johnny followed behind and reached Amira soon after. They were surprised to see that Amira had already begun digging into the dirt with her hands.

"Darling, we're not animals, for god sake." joked Thomas.

Amira looked up, just as Johnny pulled out a shovel from inside his robe and held it out to her with a smug smile. Amira smiled and grabbed the shovel from him and began digging as fast as she could.

Amira had been digging for 15 minutes and had already dug quite a wide hole. She started to worry she wouldn't find anything. She thrust her shovel back into the soil once again and heard a thud. She froze and stared at the spot where the tip of her shovel was. Johnny and Thomas took a step forward to do the same.

Amira threw the shovel to the side and started to claw around the object until she could get it loose. She heaved a rectangular object out from the earth and sighed in relief.

"Open it then!" said an excited Thomas. Johnny smiled at how excited he was and looked to Amira waiting for her to open it.

She opened it after a brief struggle with the rusty lid. Inside there was maybe 30 photos of someone that looked just like her. The photos got Amira's attention immediately, and she picked them all up and started to look through them. Thomas gently bent down and took the box from Amira's lap to look at the other things. There was some jewelry, a wad of some out of date money, a birth certificate and an old passport. Johnny looked on as Thomas sorted through the objects left in the tin.

"This is it. This is exactly what we need!" Thomas exclaimed cheerfully.

"There's not much proof about her getting plastic surgery though is there?" observed Johnny in skepticism.

"Yes, there is! Look." said Amira.

She handed over three photos that appeared to show a before photo. It was her face with lines dotted all over it. The other two must have been recovery photos after the surgery. The first had lots of bandages and deep dark bruises along the face. It looked painful. The last photo was more familiar to Amira as she recognized it from her grandma's wedding photos, but still with bruises along the eyes, nose, mouth and chin. Amira couldn't believe the resemblance of her and her grandma pre-op, identical. Her mind cast back to the conversations that she had with grandma Lena about her being considered a great beauty when she was growing up.

"This is great! This is everything we need!" said Johnny excitedly. Johnny took the bunch of photos from Amira and put them back into the box. Amira saw two photos of her face looking up from the box smiling. It must have been grandma before she was taken to the holocaust camp. She quickly snatched the top two photos before the lid closed.

"Can I keep these, please?" pleaded Amira.

Johnny smiled and said, "Of course you can."

"So what now, do we go back to the realm?" asked Amira as she held on to the old photographs before the surgery and before the Holocaust, where grandma was young, smiling and happy.

"I don't think Amira should return to the realm with Tefnut and Akil there. We need to keep you as far away from them as possible." said Johnny as he placed a hand on Amira's shoulder.

"I concur. Johnny will go to the realm and show this box to the King. I will take you to your grandmas and wait with you at the care home." said Thomas.

"Ok! I'll bring the King, and we'll meet you both there." said Johnny.

Chapter 19

Ignorance is Bliss

Akil and Tefnut were happily cuddling on their bed watching TV. Akil had his old arm behind his head while his other was around Tefnut's waist. He traced his fingers up and down her skin, every now and then hitting a folded piece of skin. Tefnut was stroking Akil's bare chest. As the loose skin collected up, she smoothed it back out again. They both watched attractive young couples on TV and reminisced on their younger days.

"You know Akil. I don't think we have ever been THIS old before," said Tefnut in a dismissive but joking tone.

Just then, a note swished in from under their door. Akil raised a hand, and the note picked itself up off the floor and hovered quickly into his clutches.

"What does it say, my love?" asked Tefnut.

Akils brows were closed together in concentration. "The King has summoned us." he said, concerned.

Tefnut turned over ungracefully to get up from the bed.

"What could he want? I thought having his precious Queen back would have settled him. He should be busy," she said, frowning in confusion.

"My thoughts exactly." said Akil in a stern voice.

They looked at each other puzzled, but in deep thought. After a moment Akil decided to get up as well. He rolled to the side of the bed and heaved himself upright, sending cracks down his back, he let out a groan of pain.

"This getting old is getting worse." said Akil in pain as he rubbed his lower back.

"You don't think the King suspects..." started Tefnut as she trailed off in thought of the worst.

Akil stood by Tefnut so that they were both looking in the mirror at each other. He put his arms around her thickened waist.

"Whatever is said, just go with the flow and act like we are helping. If we are accused, we play dumb and throw the blame on someone else. Agreed?" said Akil in a loving voice into Tefnut's ear.

"Agreed." replied Tefnut.

Tefnut turned around to look Akil in the face, and she hugged him close to her.

"Anyway, even if they knew everything, they still don't have much time left to do anything about it." she whispered.

"That's why you're so amazing, so positive." smiled Akil, before passionately kissing Tefnut.

"Let us be on our way and see what the King wants." said Tefnut as he pulled away.

Akil and Tefnut entered the ballroom, and then they stopped in their tracks. A rather large percentage of the population of the realm had gathered. They kept their expressions calm and proud and slowly made their way through the crowd of twin flames until they arrived at the foot of the throne, where King Toke was waiting for them.

"What is it, my King?" Akil asked calmly.

"Someone has made a rather alarming accusation against you two." said Toke coolly, but his glare was full of suspicion.

Tefnut and Akil were still holding hands, their grip had tightened in acknowledgement of the information to communicate with each other, but their faces remained unchanged and remained polite and obliging.

"What is it we are being accused of, my King?" asked Tefnut sweetly.

"Endangering the realm, and earth by bringing me someone that is not my twin flame, and doing so intentionally." replied King Toke

Tefnut's heart fluttered in fear at the King's tone, but she remembered what Akil had said to her about playing dumb, and she was determined to stick to the plan. Akil gave her hand a small squeeze to reassure her.

"But that's impossible! Anyone can see that she is Queen Runa, her looks and the same name it's too much of a coincidence not to be her." explained Akil in a calm and polite tone.

The King stood firm, but doubt started to cloud his eyes and he became a little less fierce.

"She does not know me or this life. It has never taken this long for her memories to return before. How can it be my Runa?" argued King Toke.

Akil and Tefnut took a step forward.

"Who has put this doubt into your mind? What if it is they who wish to prevent the ceremony, and they are the ones who are endangering us all?" said Akil.

The King looked to the left of the room where Antonio and Maria were standing. Antonio and Maria looked back at the King and could sense the tables turning. They held on to each other a little tighter in fear. Maria and Antonio then looked over to Tefnut and Akil who were smiling smugly at them. Maria and Antonio shivered as they knew there and then that King didn't believe them.

"Arrest them!" commanded the King as he pointed to Maria and Antonio.

"No, please, you have to let us explain!" shouted Maria in frustration as hands started to grab at her and Antonio.

"I've heard enough!" shouted King Toke as he waved his hand in command to get them out of his sight.

Akil and Tefnut sneaked a smile at each other but quickly turned their attention back to the King. His head was bowed in anguish, confusion and shame.

Akil and Tefnut approached the King and put a hand on either side of his shoulder. As Tefnut looked around the room she noticed that Johnny and Thomas were nowhere to be seen. She hadn't seen Thomas and Johnny for a while now. They would have stuck up for Antonio and Maria if they were here. They had no business anywhere else.

"My King, it has been a while since we have seen Thomas and Johnny." stated Akil, having had the same thought.

The King pulled himself together and said, "Ah yes, well, I hope you're not insulted, but before you brought Amira, I mean Runa back, I asked them to look for her as well."

Akil and Tefnut glanced at each other with intense alarm.

"And they're still not back?" asked Tefnut.

"No, actually, I haven't seen them since they went in search of her… I wonder if they even know she's already here." said the King as he thought out loud.

Tefnut smiled and said, "We will go and let them know she's here. They'll be so pleased! Don't want them to miss the ceremony." suggested Tefnut kindly.

"Would you? It would be nice to have them back, see what they make of all this mess." said the King, who seemed emotionally drained.

Akil smacked the Kings arm in a manly spirit. "Right, we had better be off then! We will be back as soon as possible!"

Tefnut and Akil smiled at the King as he nodded in agreement and dismissed them to go on their way.

They stopped by their room to collect their black cloaks and finally discuss the best plan of action.

"Thomas and Johnny know. They must know! That's why Antonio and Maria spoke up! Those four have always been like that! Thick as thieves."

Tefnut grabbed Akil's hands for reassurance. "What do we do now?" she asked.

Akil thought, for a few moments, as he looked at Tefnut's face, until he had a decent idea.

"The girl is still here, the only people that knew anything are now locked up, and the king won't believe a word they have to say, even if he did interrogate them. All we have to do is to find Thomas and Johnny and put a stop to them." said Akil.

Tefnut nodded without hesitation in agreement, and they tuned quickly to open the door to leave the room. They donned their black cloaks and lifted the hoods up as they walked down the hallway towards the map room.

"Where do we look first?" asked Tefnut.

"Let's trace where Thomas and Akil went to last, shall we?" said Akil menacingly as he and Tefnut placed a hand on the map wall.

Chapter 20

King Toke

King Toke was torn. He felt like he didn't know what, or who to believe anymore. He trusted Tefnut and Akil, but why would Antonio and Maria make all that up? It made no sense to him. He was walking back up the stairs to his bed-chamber thinking, maybe, when he walked through the door it will be his Runa staring back at him, and she would've remembered. The thought gave him hope. Toke reached the top of the stairs and opened the door. He was happy to see that the TV was on; he looked to the bed where he had left his Queen. But she wasn't there. He looked to the rest of the room, the desks, the lounge, but it was empty, no one else in the room but the King himself.

"Runa!!.... Amira!!" he shouted, but there was no reply. His mind raced, his heart pounded, and he paced the room as he tried to think. His mind went straight to Antonio and Maria, and he snapped.

"That's why they accused Tefnut and Akil, to distract me and take her away from me!" Anger and pain filled his body.

He turned on his heels and, in a furious rage, marched out of the room and, with a mighty slam, closed the door behind him as he made his way back down the stairs and back out into the throne room. Some twin flames were in there and all jumped when Toke forced the door open with a loud crash. Toke didn't care what anyone thought. He had to find out what they had done with her. Everyone he passed was smart enough to stay well out of his way. Toke marched through another door leading down to some steep stars to a darker corridor, where the prison was, where Antonio and Maria were now being kept.

"What have you done with her?!" He shrieked as he slammed his fists against the cage bars, making the cell shake, getting Antonio and Maria's undivided attention as they immediately pulled away from each other's arms.

Maria pleaded, "We haven't done anything with her. Please, if you'd only listen, you'd understand!"

"So you admit that you know she is gone!" replied the King, getting more and more furious.

Toke took a breath as he looked at how upset Maria seemed and decided to look past his anger. He observed Maria and Antonio; he was cradling her tightly to his chest, his face looked hopeless and defeated, Maria's expression was full of pain and betrayal. 'These don't look like guilty faces' Toke thought to himself, and he had seen more than his fair share of guilty and dishonest people in his centuries of existence. He was angry, confused and frustrated, and he let out a big sigh. He walked to the edge of the room and sat down on a bench and rested his head in his hands. His instinct wasn't as good as his beloved Queen Runa's was.

She had a sixth sense for knowing if someone was lying or not. He smoothed back his hair to look at them.

"I suggest you explain it to me then." said King Toke in a calm voice.

Antonio and Maria sat upright and faced the King, a little hope filled their faces and they were determined to explain as best and as quickly as possible.

Antonio began to explain immediately "Thomas and Johnny came back from the world to say that they found Queen Runa and that the girl Akil and Tefnut brought back wasn't her. She's the grandchild of Runa, on earth, that was given the same first name at birth."

Toke was deep in thought. He did trust Thomas and Johnny just as much as he trusted Akil and Tefnut. Why would they keep this a secret from him?

"When Thomas and Johnny came back, then why did they not tell me this themselves?" asked King Toke.

"By the time they came back, they saw that the grandchild, Amira, was already presented to you and was believed to be the Queen. They knew they had to make a case to convince you. That's why they asked us to distract you so they could get the girl out of harm's way and get the evidence they needed." replied Maria, drying the remaining tears from her face.

"So who is the real Queen if it is not this child that you say looks exactly like her?"asked the King, who was growing frustrated.

"The girl's grandmother." said Antonio.

The King sat back in thought for a moment and then lent forward again.

"And how do I know that you're telling the truth about all of this? Do you expect me to just believe that Tefnut and Akil have been working against me this entire time?" Toke asked suspiciously.

Antonio let out a sigh and smacked his hands on his lap to show he had no idea how they could prove it. Maria looked down, saddened, but then her head lifted quickly with a brilliant idea.

"Go into Thomas and Johnny's room and press play on their TV." said Amira.

"And then you'll see." added Antonio.

The King sat and continued to stare at them for a moment before getting up without saying a word. He quickly paced to Thomas and Johnny's room, more calmly and more rationally than before. He reached Thomas's and Johnny's room, let himself in, and closed the door behind him. He grabbed the remote, sat on the bed and looked up at the TV. It showed Tefnut and Akil in their bed chambers. Puzzled, apprehensive, but desperate for some clarity and answers, Toke pressed play. He listened to their casual conversation about ruling and taking his place like it was nothing. They talked about the girl Amira as if she was nothing more than a toy to occupy a sulking child.

King Toke had heard enough. He stopped the recording and turned the TV off, he sat in silence. 'All this time I trusted them' he thought. A raging and violent anger began to build up inside his stomach and his chest. Toke launched up from the bed, so he was standing and held his arms out to his side as the light engulfed him and disappeared from the room. He appeared in front of Akil and Tefnut's room and immediately kicked the door with such explosive power it flung of its hinges and splinted into hundreds of pieces around the room. His expression could melt steel and scare off a small army. When Toke realized that Akil and Tefnut weren't there, his rage erupted. Toke picked up everything he could get his hands on, slammed and smashed objects and chairs around the room, and then he squatted down, grabbing the bottom of the bed and flipped it. He stood still and breathed heavily and waited for his breathing to go back to normal now that he had released his anger. When his breathing steadied enough, he took a deep breath and walked back to the prison where Antonio and Maria were. He unlocked the cell and held his hand out towards them both.

"I'm going to need your help." said King Toke.

Antonio and Maria smiled at each other in joy. They both took the Kings hand without hesitation and with great enthusiasm.

"You got it." said Antonio.

***

Akil and Tefnut appeared next to a house surrounded by green land with a village in the distance. They turned to look at the house and couldn't help but notice how familiar it looked to them.

"Isn't that where she used to live before she emigrated to England?" asked Tefnut in dismay.

"Yes, it is." replied Akil disappointedly.

"Then that means we still have lots of time if they have only traced her as far as here, they'll have to find more leads, and then find the next two addresses, will take them much longer to get anywhere. Thank goodness." she said in relief.

Akil pursed his lips in thought while he began to scope the area. As they both turned around, they observed a freshly dug hole next to a tree. They hobbled over for a closer look. It seemed to take a long time to get there even though it was only a few meters away. It seemed they had gotten even older if that was possible. After a slow struggle Akil got on to his knees, on the ground next to the hole, and traced his old fingers around the perfect rectangle-shaped hole inside.

Tefnut bent over with some difficulty picking up a shovel next to the tree as it disintegrated into nothing in her hands.

"Juice. Thomas and Johnny did this. They dug something up." said Tefnut.

"They must have known exactly what they were looking for and exactly where to find it." said Akil.

"Then they know more than we thought they did." said Tefnut. She was in a state of panic and was becoming more and more agitated.

"We have no choice." said Akil in a dark tone.

There was only one thing that could be done.

"Let's go and visit grandma." said Akil.

They held hands with determination and something nasty in the depth of their eyes. A flash of light consumed them both, and they vanished.

Chapter 21

The Edge of Knowing

Amira and Thomas arrived together back in grandma Lena's room at the care home. ZAP. Amira's hair swished about her neck with a warm breeze. She kept her eyes closed until the redness from the light disappeared. Then Amira looked straight ahead and saw her sweet grandma sleeping in her chair with a smile on her face and a book on her lap. She always fell asleep after reading.

"Grandma, wake up! We found it!" said Amira excitedly.

Grandma Lena was in shock for a moment but smiled when she realized it was Amira who was waking her up. She wrapped her arms around her lovely granddaughter for a hug. It was nice to see her again so soon. Grandma Lena saw that one of the nice gentlemen was back with her from before. This one was the one with a beard.

"Oh, hello again, where's the other fellow gone to?" asked grandma Lena cheerfully.

"He is doing a very important errand." replied Thomas politely with a smile on his face.

Thomas looked at how sweet the bond was between this young girl and her grandma. He wondered if the Queen would be just as attached to her when she was fully restored and her memories had returned. Grandma Lena pulled away from Amira as she remembered why they left.

"You found the box under the tree?" asked grandma Lena.

"We did! It had everything, passport, birth certificate and old photographs of you!" said Amira, full of excitement.

"That's wonderful dearest! However did you get there so fast?" said grandma Lena who turned to see what time it was. "You've been less than 40 minutes!"

"Don't worry about that now. Look at these I saved." said Amira as she pulled out the photos from her cloak pocket and placed them in her grandma's hands.

Thomas came around behind them both to look as well. One photo was taken when grandma Lena was still a child; she must have been about 10 years old. The black and white photo showed her wearing a dress with a pinafore wrapped around her middle and she was messing about in a garden somewhere.

"Ah yes, this was when I was still at school, I've always liked gardening, but at that age I used to pretend to make potions from the things I found in the garden." said grandma Lena cheekily.

Amira looked at Thomas and they smiled at each other at the cheeky tone of grandma Lena's voice. Lena brought the last photo to the front, and it was identical to Amira; you wouldn't know the difference between Amira now and her grandma then.

"I was about your age in this one Amira. I must have been 18 there." she said, beaming up at her granddaughter with pride.

Amira looked carefully at the photo. Now she wasn't doing anything she could look at them properly. It was a beautiful photo.

"You know I was considered the beauty of the whole town." continued her grandma smugly.

Amira didn't feel she was the beauty of where she lived, and she looked just like grandma had. Amira had a question for her grandma. She couldn't imagine what answer she would have for her.

"Then why did you get the plastic surgery done? We saw the photos in the box, the recovery photos; they looked so painful." said Amira.

Her grandma didn't speak straight away instead; she looked again at the old photos of herself, in her pretty dress, sat on the car bonnet smiling at the camera, and stroked her old 18-year-old self in memory.

"I was very happy then. I was very well thought of by everyone. I was loved and respected. But then we were put into concentration camps because we were Jewish. Just because we were Jewish…Before my family and I were captured we had hidden away for two years before the neighbor's found out and turned us in." said Grandma Lena.

Amira sat down across from grandma in her usual chair to give her grandmas story her full attention. Thomas did the same as he moved around to sit on the bed getting ready to finally hear Grandma Lena's story.

Just as Thomas sat down, he looked like he was suddenly about to get up. It caught Amira's attention, so she looked in the mirror in front of her, giving her a perfect view of the doorway behind her. There was nothing there. When she quickly glanced at Thomas again, his full attention was on her and her grandma. Like nothing had happened. Amira shrugged it off and began to listen to her grandma's story about how she survived the holocaust and why it led to her surgery.

Chapter 22

The Third Wheel Plan

After ten minutes or so of quick brainstorming and planning with Antonio and Maria in the prison cell, King Toke summoned all his subjects into the throne room. When Toke, Maria and Antonio reached upstairs, a vast crowd had gathered. King Toke led the way to his throne, where Antonio and Maria took care to stay close and keep their heads held high, to show the on lookers that they had been wrongly accused.

"This is an important announcement!" announced the King. His voice rang with authority and power.

"We have all been deceived, for decades now, it seems, my most trusted advisors, Akil and Tefnut have been conspiring to put an end to Runa and me, knowing where she was for decades and keeping it from us, so that they could make a claim to the throne."

There was huge gossip that grew in the kingdom as all the elder twin flames talked among themselves. Toke had more to say, so he raised his hand in the air to silence the crowd so that he could continue.

"They put not only me and Runa at risk, but all of you. Life here could be completely wiped out with such interference. Only the greater power can rightfully decide the royal's fate. As knowledge of such things is inherited only by the royals, I can only tell you that I do know the result of such violations. Although I am forbidden to disclose any of this to you, all I can say is that it would be detrimental, not only to this realm, but for earth also."

The crowd was so silent you could hear only beating hearts and course breathing.

"Antonio and Maria have been wrongly accused and have been loyally helping, not only me, but the kingdom and the balance of earth from disaster. It seems Tefnut and Akil have fled. I and my friends Antonio and Maria will find the true Queen Runa, who is not the girl that Tefnut and Akil kidnapped, but her grandmother who has undergone such trauma that she is unrecognizable. I will go to earth and bring her back. If Tefnut and Akil return in our absence, be sure to throw them in the cells."

The crowd cheered in agreement, and the King humbly asked his subjects if there was anything they wished to say. A voice came from the crowds. "How do you know this girl's grandmother is our true Queen?" asked a concerned subject.

Just then, Johnny burst through the doors at the other side of the room, slightly out of breath and his hair out of place.

"I HAVE PROOF!" declared Johnny across the ballroom.

Everyone in the throne room stopped and stared. Not knowing what to do, Johnny just stood there as all of the old faces stared back at him. He threw his arms up with the box in his hand. He quickly collected himself and smoothed out his hair with his free hand, and quickly made his way to the King with the box. People in the crowd parted the way for him so that he could easily get through. When he got to the King, he looked up to see the King smiling at him, and so were Maria and Antonio. The King was delighted to see Johnny just when they needed him the most. Antonio and Maria were looking past Johnny to see where Thomas was, but they couldn't see him.

"You really went above and beyond this time." said King Toke as he held his hand out to Johnny.

Johnny took it, and the crowd gently cheered and applauded. Johnny opened up the box and handed it to the King to look through.

"This is everything you need to see who the real Runa is." said Johnny to the King.

Johnny walked over to thank Antonio and Maria. He was still slightly out of breath.

"How on earth did you two manage to convince him?" said Johnny in astonishment as he looked to Antonio and Maria.

"Well, it wasn't easy." said Antonio smugly as he put an arm around Maria.

"Tefnut and Akil turned the kingdom against us; we were imprisoned. Then we told the King to go to your room and to watch the footage you took of Akil and Tefnut and now, here we are." said Maria with a shrug.

"In a nut shell." said Antonio in an upbeat manner.

"So where are Tefnut and Akil now? Are they rotting in the cells?" asked Johnny.

"No, they are gone." said Maria.

The King's head jolted up from looking at the old birth certificate. "I don't think they have any idea about us knowing their plot. Why would they leave?"

"They know that we knew." said Antonio.

"And they know we are close friends with you and Thomas." added Maria.

"Akil asked me where the two of you were. They know I sent you and Thomas to look for Runa!" said the King in dismay.

"They know we know? They could be out looking for us right now." replied Johnny.

They all stood with agitated faces and took time to think car fully as it could be a make or break moment. They had hundreds of years' experience and knew that it wasn't safe to act until one obvious realization was spoken, something solid to go by.

"Why go after you two when they can just get rid of the real threat?" thought Maria out loud.

"Runa." confirmed Antonio.

"Where are Thomas and Amira?" asked Maria.

"With the Queen, right now, waiting for us." answered Johnny.

"Then they are in danger!" exclaimed Antonio

"We must go Now!" Ordered King Toke.

Johnny, Maria, Antonio and King Toke all placed a hand in the middle, held on to each other, and instantly vanished from the room in a blaze of light.

***

All four of them arrived in a flash of light outside of the care home that Amira's grandma was staying at. There wasn't anyone around and only three cars in the parking area.

"Johnny and I will go in, you two stay out here!" Toke ordered as he gestured to Antonio and Maria.

"If Tefnut and Akil arrive, don't let yourselves be seen by them. Just let them come in. But if they come back out, disarm them by any means necessary." ordered Toke in a very serious tone.

Antonio and Maria gave a firm and excited nod. They were more than happy to put Akil and Tefnut in their place.

"If they leave, we will take them out." said Maria in a rather deadly voice.

"Wait! You might find this useful!" said Antonio as he took off his black cloak and threw it to King Toke.

King Toke took the black cloak without a second thought and smiled in gratitude at Antonio as he made his way towards the main entrance. Toke put the cloak on as he walked, Johnny followed closely behind him, and at the same moment, Toke and Johnny threw their hoods to cover their heads and disappeared into their surroundings. They entered the building and crept up along the hallway. They had to dodge a few staff members along the way who were completely oblivious to their existence and going about their day.

Johnny, who was leading the way, stopped and gestured to an open doorway. King Toke observed the name beneath it.

'Lena Nilsson '

Toke looked at the name for a moment and remembered that it was the new name that Johnny had mentioned, the name of the girl's grandmother, his Runa.

King Toke walked in and looked on at the old woman sat in the chair across the room from him. She looked nothing like his queen. It made him sad. Maybe there was a mistake. He remembered the photos in the box that Johnny brought him with the new face that was changed through surgery. It was strange, to see his Runa in such a way. He then noticed Amira sitting opposite the old woman in the chair with her back to him. 'The Similarity really is uncanny' He thought to himself. As Toke edged closer into the room, he noticed Thomas was sat on the edge of the bed with his hood down, listening in the same manner Amira was. Thomas caught sight of King Toke, 'How odd that the king was wearing a black cloak' thought Thomas to himself. . He was going to get up to greet his

King but Toke quickly gestured at him to stop. Thomas did so immediately and watched as Toke put a finger up to his mouth asking for his secrecy. Thomas continued to act like nothing had happened, as if no one else were in the room.

Johnny tapped King Toke on the shoulder and gestured him to go into the bathroom with him, where they would wait for Tefnut and Akil to arrive, as they obviously hadn't been there yet.

Toke and Johnny both edged into the bathroom and stayed out of sight from the entrance for when Akil and Tefnut arrived. This was ideal for Toke as he could not only pounce on Akil and Tefnut when they came in, but also in view of the old woman sitting in the chair, he could hear everything that she was saying. Johnny knew he had to tell Thomas of the plan so he got his phone out to text Thomas, he kept his fingers crossed that his phone would be on silent. Johnny pressed send. Thomas felt a little buzz in his cloak pocket, he kept forgetting he had a phone, he took it out to peak at it and found a message from Johnny had popped up. He clicked on it.

'Were planning an ambush on Tefnut and Akil, we think they are going to try and kill Queen Runa and Amira. Stay out of sight from the doorway!'

After Thomas read the text from Johnny, he shuffled along the bed up against the wall. From here, no one would know he was in the room until they reached the corner, and then it would be too late. Meanwhile, Johnny and Toke were still in the bathroom; they both had enough of a view to see Lena and listen to her telling her story as they waited for Tefnut and Akil to arrive.

***

In the shadows of the bushes about ten minutes down the road from the care home where Amira, Lena, Toke, Johnny and Thomas were, lurked Tefnut and Akil. They were extremely hunched over; their skin more sagged and wrinkled than before. They had finally reached the very limit of how old the human body could possibly go. They looked extremely exhausted but were still determined to get what they wanted by any means necessary, even if that meant murder. They had arrived some time ago and had managed to walk some of the way. They had used up every last bit of juice they had. They wouldn't have any left to even make it back home to their realm. It was all or nothing now. They couldn't move quickly, their bodies were terribly stiff and they found it incredibly difficult and awkward to move at all. Their joints creaked, cracked and ached terribly, but they were determined. They continued to drag their withered bodies towards the care home. Tefnut's breath was extremely hoarse as she moved along. Gasping for breath, she began to slow down even more.

Akil noticed quick enough and urged in a croaky raspy tone, "Keep going!"

Chapter 23

Grandma Lena's Story

Amira sat patiently waiting for her grandma to tell her story, she could see that her grandma was agitated, and it was going to bring back many traumatic memories for her. Finally, grandma Lena looked at Amira, found her courage, leaned forward, and told Amira everything.

"I was born and raised in Hungry, and I had a wonderful childhood, I loved my parents, we weren't particularly rich but we had everything we needed and lots of friends. When I got to about your age." said Lena as she pointed to Amira. "I started to get a lot of attention from boys. I got asked to go for walks, to go to dances. I even got given little gifts like fruit or chocolates. I was very happy, but no one in the village took my fancy, however, I still got along with the boys despite that."

Grandma smiled in memory of such happy and simple times and how sweet living used to be then.

"Then around 1940 or 1941 when I was about 19 years old, we had to go into hiding because we were

Jewish. Some very good friends of the family hid us for a long time until one of the neighbor's must have turned us all in. I don't know what happened to that lovely, brave couple that hid us. I never saw them again." said grandma Lena as she trailed off in to sad assumptions about what might have happened to them.

"So what happened to you next?" asked Amira in an encouraging manner and placed a hand on top of her grandmas.

"When I was 21, we were put into a concentration camp, and I was separated from my mother and father. For months I didn't know what had happened to my parents until one day I saw my father again....he was bone thin... I asked where mother was, and if he had seen her, he said he had, but that it wasn't good."

Grandma's voice quivered a little, and her eyes were watery "She was dead," said Lena as a few tears fell down her cheeks

"He said mother was among a group of many others who were taken into the gas chambers. He never saw her come out. He was so thin. I had three more days with him, we were kept outside in the cold, and one day he just didn't wake up..."

Amira began to tear up just at the very idea of going through such things that no person should ever be put through. She squeezed her grandma's hand to give some small comfort. Lena sighed deeply after feeling her granddaughters hand on hers and carried on telling her story. Amira knew that it was going to get worse.

Thomas leaned forward to listen more closely to his Queen's most recent earth-life story. He had known what it was to be tortured, beaten, and hungry, but he had never heard of such neglect, brutality, and disregard for human life on such a scale as this before. In the bathroom, Johnny looked in sympathy to the King, whose attention was fixed upon this old woman sitting and crying in the chair, still telling her story. He still found it difficult to believe she was his Queen. He pulled out the two photos he had taken from the tin that Johnny had brought back for him. He noticed how badly bruised her face was after the surgery. It was hard to believe any kind of face was accomplished after such butchery. He was saddened most of all that his beloved and fierce Queen had gone through so much. He felt useless and helpless, but he felt a warm flutter of hope, and he couldn't wait to be reunited with her finally. The thought brought a small smile to his face. Toke continued to look upon his Queen in the chair and listened carefully to the rest of the story. But he still braced himself so that he would be ready to put a stop to Tefnut and Akil and beat them to a pulp as soon as they reached his sight.

Grandma continued on with her story.

"After my father died and many, many more, the rest of us were taken to a different part of the camp. We got to stay indoors this time and I made some friends. One day a few of the guards were staring at me. They began taking me away from the group regularly. They said I was the most attractive woman they had seen for months…they did a lot of things to me… as horrible as it all was, they granted me certain privileges, such as extra food. I still get flashbacks of what they did to me to this day…" said grandma Lena as she scrunched up her eyes.

Amira put her hand to her mouth as she realized the levels of abuse her grandma had gone through, now realizing that the biggest one was sexual abuse.

"Fortunately, the guards were too happy and stupid ever to suspect foul play from me", continued grandma Lena. "I began helping people in the camp escape. It was always the person who needed to escape the most if they were being picked on by the guards or would soon die if they didn't get out. They were the ones next to leave, but one day, one of the guard's saw me and what I was doing, but he ended up helping me then, and every day after that. He looked out for me as much as he could. The only time he couldn't was when the other guards wanted me for their own amusement. He was a lower rank than them and he would have been severely disciplined if he ever did anything like speak out of term or raise a hand to them." said Lena.

King Toke listened on and smiled at her bravery and selflessness in putting others first. That was the Queen he knew and loved. Toke admired his fierce and beautiful Queen as he continued to listen on.

"Months went by in the same way. The other guards continued abusing me, and my sweet guard kept comforting and looking after me whenever he could."

Grandma Lena let out a sigh of exhaustion from telling her story but continued on anyway.

"Then, one day, my guard came rushing up to me before the other guards had arrived. He told me it HAD to be my turn to escape this time. He heard the guards say what they were going to do to me. He never told me what they had planned for me. I just remember looking into his eyes and know that it would be the worst, most horrifying thing. I was terrified. I told everyone that mattered to me in the camp. I told only my closest friend the new name I would take so she could find me in the future. And I left that night with my guard."

Amira and Thomas both sat back and felt overwhelmed by what Lena had told them both. There wasn't much you could say after hearing such horrible real-life terrors. Amira's mind went to the guard, and she thought about how thankful she was for him and wondered what would have become of her grandma if he had not been there.

"But what happened to the guard?" asked Amira, who was puzzled and curious to know what became of the man who had saved her grandma.

Grandma smiled sweetly. "Well, I married him. He was your granddad."

Amira's heart fluttered with affection, and she smiled.

"Yes, he arranged all the documents for both of us, we began our travels, but we heard that the guards had sent out a search party for a guard and a Jewish woman that fitted my description. They even had photos of me. We were found once in the street by another guard, and your granddad had to beat him to death. So I decided that I had to have plastic surgery if I ever wanted to feel free again, invisible to the guards' that did all those things to me. I told your granddad, and he would do anything I asked. He arranged it all for me. I got it done just one week later. After that we hid out at my childhood home in hungry for a few weeks while I recovered. I found a few of my old things, jewelry, photos and documents that were still there from when my father had hidden them away under a floorboard. So I put everything I had of me in a tin box, along with my plastic surgery photos, and buried them outside by the tree. After a few weeks, we fled to Switzerland and eventually got married and began a new life together. By then, the war was over and we felt we could finally breathe."

Grandma Lena let out a huge sigh of relief as she had gotten past the worst of her story and began to relax a little. She wiped away the tears from her cheeks.

"We tried for many years to start our own family. By the time I was 40, we just gave up, but then I had your mother, Sharron, when I was 46! It was a surprise I'll tell you," Grandma Lena laughed. "We moved to England in 1980 when your mum was 14, your granddad died in 1992, and your mum was all grown up and suggested that we moved up here and, here we are." said grandma Lena.

Just then, Lena's gaze suddenly shot up behind Amira, her expression full of horror. There was a loud bang. Lena's face went to fear as she slammed her hands down onto the sides of the chair and stood up. Amira couldn't respond quickly enough to see what was happening around her.

Chapter 24

Double Edged Knife

Akil led the way up the corridor of the care home with Tefnut close behind They both had their cloaks on with their hoods up. When the door to their 'beloved' Queen was insight, Akil slowed down so Tefnut would go in front of him. As Tefnut went to the front, both her and Akil slowly took off both of their gloves and placed them in a pocket in their cloaks. Akil unsheathed a small very fine, slightly curved blade from a pouch that hung on his side. Akil was careful to keep the knife from moving beyond the protection of his cloak. Tefnut paused for a second to analyze what the situation was inside the room. 'Perfect', she thought. Amira was in there too and had her back to the door. Akil peered over her shoulder into the room, as Tefnut glanced at him from the side; he gave her one small nod with his head. That was it. They hobbled as smoothly, and as quietly as they could, their bodies were terribly stiff and achy. Tefnut was very close to Amira now, close enough to touch. She began to extend her arm, and reached for the back of Amira's shoulders with her naked hand, another few inches, and she will be drastically aged. Akil edged just beyond Amira towards the old woman sitting in the chair. Akil began to position himself so he could slice her throat when he was suddenly yanked back by the scuff of his neck. Suddenly Tefnut was forced back too. They were both dragged back by something extremely strong. It picked up Tefnut by her old sagged throat and threw Akil to the other side of the room, causing Akil to drop his fine knife to the floor. Johnny quickly edged out from the bathroom, grabbed Akil's hands from behind, and pressed him against the wall to restrain him. Akil let out a groan from the cracking it caused, he was unable to move. Toke had flung his cloak off as he had acted and had one large hand around Tefnut's throat against the wall she gasped in surprise and in pain. Toke was in such a state of anger and rage. He could have killed them both himself with one swing. Thomas left his old Queen and Amira's side and wandered over to the blood thirsty King and put a gentle hand on to Toke's shoulder. The King looked angrily at Thomas for a moment.

"Allow me, my King." said Thomas gently.

The King's anger subsided and he graciously allowed Thomas to hold her down instead.

"My, my! You've both let yourself go, haven't you? You both look like you're at death's door." said Johnny smugly.

"But don't worry, they'll be something worse than death in store for you two back in the realm."

Fear sank into Tefnut and Akil's old and weathered faces, and their minds began to race in panic. Johnny quickly opened the door to the hallway, and Thomas gave a powerful shove, slamming Tefnut into Akil out of the room and into the hallway. Johnny and Thomas observed how quickly they moved. They couldn't help but cringe at the clicks and cracks their bodies made getting up off the floor, scurrying away as fast as they could, in the clumsiest and most awkward way possible. Johnny closed the door without a second thought and turned to their King who was looking at Thomas and Johnny in an amusing manner. Toke knew they were going to get themselves a front-row seat to that show, the one that was just chucked out of the room.

"We'll leave you to it. We will be back in a few minutes." Informed Johnny to the King, as he grabbed Thomas's hand and in a quick blaze of light, they vanished.

Toke took a deep breath and turned around to face his Queen. She was completely stood up. Her old unfamiliar face was in shock and bewilderment. Amira backed away from them to look at them both, looking at each other, figuring each other out. They had been waiting for each other for a hundred years, but they were just stood there. Amira decided her grandma needed some encouragement, so she took her grandma by the hand and led her towards the King. Amira extended her other hand to the King, who smiled and gave his hand to her in response. When Amira had both their hands in hers, her eyes began to water, and she brought both of their hands together. They held on to each other instinctively, and their hands slowly explored the other gently. Amira stepped back again, sat on the bed, watched, and tried to fade into the background. Toke looked at Grandma Lena for a while, searching her eyes. He smiled when he found what he was looking for.

"Runa" he spoke softly, as he smiled and his eyes slightly watered.

The old woman holding the King's hand stood to attention and beamed up at him at the sound of her name. Her eyes began to well up as her memories came flooding back to her.

"Toke!" she exclaimed as she threw her arms around him, and they hugged each other so tightly.

Amira could feel their love for each other and it was overwhelming for her to experience. Toke wrapped his arms around Runa lovingly as he held her body and cradled her head with his hand.

They drew back to look at each other, and then they kissed while in each other's embrace. For a moment, Amira was slightly taken back and ready to look away before she could see a bright glow emitting from her grandma. As she continued to watch them kiss, her grandma glowed brighter and brighter until it hurt to look. She quickly covered her eyes with her hands and turned away. After a few moments, it became incredibly dark. Amira thought it safe to look and took away her hands from her face. She turned back to see if her grandmother was still there. But she wasn't there anymore. In her place stood a woman with light blond, long flowing hair in the King's arms. The woman and the King pulled away and finished their kiss. The King cupped his hands to her face and looked at her as if it was for the first time.

"Grandma?" said Amira in a mousy uncertain voice.

The woman tuned around, and it was as if Amira herself was looking back at her, like a mirror, only the hair was lighter, and her face seemed more mature.

"Yes, it's me." She said in a beautiful voice and in a different accent to what her grandmas had been. Queen Runa walked over to Amira, and they held hands.

"Does this mean you're not my grandma anymore? Have I lost her?" Amira began to cry at the new beautiful face that stood before her, her mirror image.

"No, that part of me will always be your grandma. I still have every memory of you that I had in that life, Amira. And I always will." She reached up and wiped the tears that had fallen from Amira's eyes.

Knowing this made Amira feel better, and she also realized that every life Queen Runa had lived must have meant she had to leave many loved ones behind back on earth, and if Amira knew one thing, they have lived hundreds of lifetimes.

***

Meanwhile, outside of the home, Thomas and Johnny were leaning directly opposite the home's front entrance, watching patiently with little excited smiles on their faces. Johnny had told Thomas that Antonio and Maria were outside somewhere and were given orders to stop Tefnut and Akil by any means necessary. They hadn't seen Antonio and Maria yet, but couldn't wait to see what would happen when they finally did. They were both eating and sharing a little tub of popcorn as they waited. Thomas kept finding bits of popcorn in his beard and picked them out and ate them anyway. Just then, Tefnut and Akil rushed as fast as they could out of the care home, clawing their way along the walls. Johnny threw away the popcorn instantly and hurried to get his phone from his pocket so he could film it all straightaway. Akil and Tefnut had made it just a few yards outside when suddenly Antonio and Maria appeared out of nowhere. They both charged at full speed at an incredible pace and strength, screaming. Akil and Tefnut had no time to react at all before they were violently tackled to the ground by Antonio and Maria. They flew in the air after impact, and the sound they made from contact was impressive. Thomas and Johnny howled with laughter. Thomas couldn't stand still and had collapsed to the floor in laughter. Johnny's eyes were watering with laughter but he tried to keep still so he could catch every moment on film using his phone; he clutched his rib cage as he began to get a stitch from laughing so hard.

Chapter 25

The Invitation

King Toke still had his arms wrapped around Queen Runa in the little room in the care home. Amira was so happy for them to be back together again, and it was nice to see how much her grandma looked like her now that she was young again, even though the whole thing was very peculiar 'Will I come back in the next life and look the exact same?' she thought to herself.

"So every time someone is reincarnated back into the world, they look the same every time?" asked Amira assumingly.

"No, that's only our privilege as royals. Because we found our twin flame and we are King and Queen of the realm, how you see us now is our permanent form. The subjects like Thomas and Johnny grow old in the realm but always keep their form from the life they first met each other. And when you meet your twin flame, you will keep that form when you move on to the life after, in our realm." replied Toke; his voice was soothing and warm now that he had Runa back in his arms.

"So, how does it work, when I die, what happens?" asked Amira.

"Well, you remember everything your soul has ever experienced or learned about, from all your previous lives when you die. Most like to stay around for a while if they are attached to their recent life. But sooner or later, they must move on to their next life." replied Toke.

Amira was glad about that, to have some small control for what happened afterwards, to stay for a while then move on to the next life when you were ready; she wondered exactly how much control they could have about where they went in the world.

"Can we choose who we get to be in the next life?" asked Amira.

"After a few lifetimes, you can. Usually, in the first 20 lives (depending on how much experience you get from them), you can choose your next life. You can choose where in the world, male or female. You will also get to see your spirit guide to talk things over with. When you are ready for your twin flame, your spirit guide asks you if you are ready and sends you around where they are for your next life. Whether or not you meet them in that lifetime is 50/50."

"Spirit guides? Like a guardian angel?" asked Amira.

Queen Runa pulled away slightly from King Toke to look at Amira properly. She smiled and wanted to reply to that question, still very much remembering that she is still Amira's grandma.

"Yes, every soul has a designated spirit guide. They're with you from the very beginning, from when your soul is born into existence. They're with you your whole lives, helping and comforting you in any way they can. Then when you die, you can finally meet and talk with them about everything that happened. They are the best friend you will ever have. Until, of course, you meet your twin flame when you die after that, you say farewell to your spirit guide, and you move into our realm, and spend eternity with the love of your life, your twin flame." said Runa.

"If you can do what you want before you're reincarnated into the next life, how long can you stay around and can you communicate with people from the life you left?"asked Amira.

Amira thought she might have pushed her luck on that one. Toke pulled a face but then looked to Runa, to let her decide. Runa pulled a sweet face at her King and he gave away to it instantly.

"Well, I will tell you, only because I know that I can trust you to keep it a secret." Runa walked across the room to crouch on the ground in front of Amira and held her hand.

"Those who stay too long can become ghosts, and I would not wish that on anybody. Many souls feel pressure to stay when the grief is very strong when those they had loved and cared for still remain, but it does not do them any good. It's best for them to give a sign that they are ok and then leave and move on with their next life." said Runa.

"What about after they're gone, do they still get a sign?" said Amira.

"Well, a soul's spirit guide can sometimes take action, if it is in their soul's best interest, and they are incapable of happiness until a sign is given to them, they will intervene when they see it's necessary. They hope the person they are looking after will find comfort in thinking it's the person who died, and then they will hopefully move on with their lives. The new souls have a harder time with death than the older souls." said Runa, in the manner that her grandma would have said it.

Amira was intrigued by the idea of an old soul and a new soul. She wondered how old her soul was. Was it older than her classmate's souls?

"So, how do you know if someone is a new soul or an old soul?" asked Amira.

"Have you ever met someone with no common sense at all? They can be quite intelligent but are completely devoid of all common sense." asked Runa instantly.

"Yes." Replied Amira, she could think of a lot of people like that.

"That's how you can spot the newest ones. It's actually quite a common phrase used on earth; old soul and new soul, but they don't seem to take the meaning of it literally for some reason." said Runa.

Just then, there was a blaze of light at the opposite end of the room. If Amira had blinked, she would have missed it. The appearance of light was followed by giggling and a raspy cough that was probably from laughing too much. Runa and Amira stood up to look over to where the giggling was coming from. Toke turned around to see too. It was Thomas and Johnny. They were both leaning on each other so they wouldn't fall over from laughing so hard. A big smile appeared on all their faces; their uncontrollable laughter was very infectious.

"What are you two so happy about?" asked Toke, who was smiling broadly and eager to know what the joke was.

Thomas tried to explain but couldn't get past the first few words from laughing. Johnny, without saying anything held out his phone with a video recording on it. Amira took it and held it so that Toke and Runa could watch it also. Amira pressed play. It was only a 10-second long video. Two extremely old and rigid people were hurrying out of a building.

"That's Tefnut and Akil." pointed out Amira.

"Just watch." said a smirking Thomas who has stopped giggling in suspense.

Just then, two people sprinted at such a speed, collided and tackled them to the ground. The running couple took Akil and Tefnut out, flying a few feet before crashing on the floor in such a thump. You could hear the groans, clicks, and cracks. It's made Amira lift her hand to her mouth in surprise. Runa laughed at the video, but no one in the room was laughing quite as much as Toke was. His face was lit up and was howling uncontrollably; it made his eyes begin to stream with happiness, his face becoming red.

"We must play this on the big screen at the ceremony tonight." exclaimed the King as he laughed loudly.

Runa seemed to be laughing more at Toke laughing, Thomas and Johnny were off laughing again, too, and they were finding it hard to stay up as their legs were giving way from laughing so much. Amira was stunned, such a violent video and all those cracking noises their body's had made from the impact. 'These people are sick' Amira thought to herself as she looked around at them all in stitches. Still, she couldn't help but smile and laugh a little about how much the 'higher beings' were laughing at it. Once the laughing had died down a little, Runa looked like she had an idea, so she tugged the top of Tokes shirt and stood on her tip toes to whisper something in his ear. Toke smiled and gave her a loving stare. "Why not" he said happily.

They both looked and beamed at Amira.

"What?" Amira said, rather paranoid.

"We would like to invite you to the ceremony tonight as our guest of honor." said Runa.

Amira was flattered and very taken back. She didn't know what to say.

"Do you do this for all the loved ones you leave behind on earth?" asked Amira jokingly.

Toke scoffed, "It's never been done in our lifetime."

Amira was very surprised by this. "So I'd be the first, but why?" She wondered.

"Not only have you been caught up in this, but you stayed true to yourself the whole way. You knew Toke wasn't meant for you, you followed your feelings. That, and we have a sneaky suspicion about you, Amira. But we will have to find out more about it before we can tell you." Runa gave Amira a little wink, just like her grandma did whenever she was up to something. It reassured her and comforted her immediately.

Johnny and Thomas gave each other a quick look and then looked back at Amira.

"We might have something to tell you too. Later though." they said as the King glanced at them both as if he knew that they were up to no good. Thomas and Johnny looked very mischievous indeed.

Amira smiled and started to get excited about the 100-year ceremony.

"So what now?" asked Amira without a care in the world. She felt fantastic all of a sudden like anything was possible, and nothing seemed so serious anymore.

"Back home for us, back to the realm, get some decent clothes." sighed Runa as she tugged on the clothes she was wearing and pulled a face.

"Thomas and Johnny, will you take Amira home?" asked Toke.

Thomas and Johnny replied together "Of course." and they beamed with happiness to be given such a lovely task. In such a short time Amira felt like family to them both, like their very own niece.

"They will collect you again tomorrow night for the ceremony as well." added Toke as he patted his hand on Amira's shoulder.

Amira smiled at the thought of finally being able to go home. She was also happy to see Runa with her beloved Toke, and they looked at each other with unconditional love, happiness and hunger. She liked to think she had played a big part in helping to bring them both together. It filled her with such fulfillment and pride. Amira felt mixed emotions as she looked at Runa, she was, after all, her grandma, but she seemed to be something more than that now; it was a nice feeling.

Chapter 26

Home and Inspiration

Thomas and Johnny had decided to walk Amira home from the care home, they both enjoyed Amira's company, and something about her that they saw potential in. She asked them both lots of questions. They didn't mind at all. In fact, it proved that the opinion they had about Amira was right, and this knowledge would be essential for her if their hunch was correct.

"What if your twin flame is 50 years older than you?" asked Amira out of the blue as she walked beside them both down the street. There was no one around, and the sun was nearly fully set. The sky was filled with deep purple and flourishes of pink.

"It's not uncommon. But if one of them hasn't reached sexual maturity, then they won't find each other. Anything before sexual maturity is a violation. Most humans think such an age gap as big as 20 is out of the question and never entertain the idea. If it doesn't happen in that lifetime, they will both keep living and dying until one day they find each other." explained Johnny.

"What if thousands of people are out of sync with their twin flames?" asked Amira curiously.

"Ah well, after many centuries, our archives have shown that humanity is thrown out of balance when not enough twin flames are united each year. This reflects in what we call human errors such as wars, terrorists, serial killers; everything horrible that happens with humans resulting from not enough twin flames meeting. But the lives taken are always of those who were out of sync with their twin flame." said Thomas.

"So how likely it is that all those people who died from human error will be reunited with their twin flame?" asked Amira.

"It depends on the current life experience and whether the people are in the correct mental state to allow you to see your twin flame if you ever met them. So many souls have missed many such opportunities." continued Thomas.

They wondered around the corner of the street and the road was busy, a few cars passed by. There wasn't much further to go before Amira was back at home, and she couldn't wait to be back at home again. They walked in silence for a while and Amira's mind wondered more about reincarnation and twin flames.

"Do you know how many lives I've lived?" asked Amira curiously.

"Don't know. We could always check later and tell you tomorrow at the ceremony." Suggested Johnny, he stroked a loose hair strand back into place with his hands and weaved his finger through his grey hair.

This whole new world had opened up for Amira. She had a great idea, and she felt like she finally knew what business idea she would present in 1 week at college. She felt so amazing, relieved, happy and excited. She couldn't wait to get started on her presentation, but it would probably have to wait until tomorrow. She suddenly realized how tired she felt. Amira looked at Johnny and Thomas, and it clicked, that they were two men and twin flames. She wondered if they had always been men in their past lives or had they been women also 'wonder if I was ever a man in a past life' thought Amira.

"I have another question, and it might be a bit personal." said Amira sheepishly.

"Ooh, our favorite kind." Said Johnny as he rubbed his hands together, Thomas smiled in reply to Johnny's cheeky tone.

"You're both twin flames, and both men. Are souls always reincarnated as the same sex?" said Amira.

"When humans die, they will meet with their guardians and talk, remember and reflect everything about every life they ever had. They will make decisions about their next life, or they can opt for a random life. I very much doubt that you have been a woman in all the lives you have lived. Besides, the first bunch of lives will be randomly selected to gain a broad range of experiences." said Thomas.

"So if I die without meeting my twin flame, I meet up with my guardian, my guardian angel? Like Runa talked about with the spirit guides?" asked Amira, full of interest.

"Yeah, we just call them guardians or spirit guides." summed up Johnny.

"And I talk to them when I die and decide if I will come back as a woman or as a man?"

"Exactly" said Thomas. He linked on to Johnny as they continued walking.

"So why are they called guardians if they're only there for you when you're dead?" asked Amira, frowning and slightly in confused.

"My darling, they are with you all the time, every moment of every life you have lived, even now. Whenever you have asked for help from them, they have always answered. You should invite your guardian to help more often. They are terribly respectful of your free will and privacy. If you want their help, you have to let them know. It's the code they live by." said Thomas.

They had finally reached Amira's house. Amira was very happy to see it, and she could feel all the stress, adventure, and excitement finally leave her body as she stood in front of her home.

"I don't have my keys with me." said Amira in frustration.

Johnny moved past Amira and opened the door, just like that, on the first try. Amira was puzzled at first thinking maybe she didn't try the handle hard enough, and then she remembered that they were higher beings after all.

"Did you use your magic for that?" asked Amira, a little unsure and confused.

"Just a little juice, hardly matters now with the ceremony being tomorrow." said Johnny shrugging.

"Why do you both do things the long way around all the time, like walking here? If I had powers, I'd use them all the time." said Amira as she opened the door up fully.

Amira went inside and both Johnny and Thomas followed her in and closed the door behind them.

"Well, it's not very practical to use it all the time. Did you notice how much older Tefnut and Akil looked?" said Johnny.

Amira lead them to the lounge room next to the kitchen and sat down on the sofa. Thomas and Johnny sat down also and got comfortable.

"So using magic is bad for you?" asked Amira, as she rested her head on her hand and leaned on the arm of the sofa.

"In a way, we all have the same amount of juice allocated to use to last for the next 100 years, which will soon be fully replenished at the ceremony for everyone in the realm tomorrow night." said Thomas as he snuggled up next to Johnny a little more.

"And we find other ways to do things so that we don't have to keep using up our juice. Like with modern technology for example, it's fantastic! Saves so much magic and we don't become so old that way!" said Johnny.

"Being old is terribly uncomfortable you know." added Thomas.

Amira couldn't imagine being old. She shuddered as she remembered the cracking noises Tefnut and Akil's bodies made when they were tackled in that video that Johnny and Thomas had filmed outside of the home. She squeezed her eyes shut at the thought of it being Tefnut's and Akil's intention to turn her old. Amira got rid of the thought at once. It didn't feel good. She wondered about her grandma instead and how she wouldn't be at the home anymore.

"Won't they be suspicious at the care home? That grandma isn't there, that she has completely disappeared? My mum won't understand." Said Amira as she was getting herself worked up.

"Don't worry, we've taken care of it, nothing a bit of juice and a favor from an old friend won't sort out." said Thomas with great ease.

Amira was relieved instantly at Thomas's sweet but passive tone, and she relaxed her shoulders again. It hit her again how very tired she was. It'd been the longest day ever.

Thomas and Johnny noticed how worn out Amira was; she had had a very long day, especially for a human.

"What day is it?" asked Amira as she yawned.

"It's Saturday night, and you were kidnapped in the early hours of this morning." answered Johnny as he was playing with Thomas's beard.

Amira suddenly felt exhausted. "I think I need to get some sleep." She said.

Thomas and Johnny both understood and saw Amira upstairs to her room. Amira slumped down on her bed despite her blanket not being there. She then remembered that her duvet was back in the twin flame realms huge dressing room.

"Was that your purple duvet in the dressing room, my dear, back at the realm?" asked Thomas.

"Yes, it was. That's where I left it." said Amira sleepily.

Thomas quickly left the room.

"We'll get it back to you tomorrow." said Johnny as he took the black cloak off from around her shoulders and hung it on his arm.

Thomas came back in with her mother's duvet, threw it on top of Amira, and tucked her in. She fell asleep instantly. Johnny and Thomas smiled and agreed to leave a note for her in case she woke up.

'Dear Amira,

We will call on you tomorrow at 10pm. You can get ready over here.

Your friends T & J '

When they were happy with the note, they placed it on Amira's desk next to her college notes. The notes on the desk caught both Thomas's and Johnny's attention as they read;

'Business Plan Presentation'

They both observed the presentation date and time and made a mental note of it.

"Potential indeed." whispered Johnny to Thomas.

They left the room and turned the lights off. They went down the stairs, pulled the curtains shut and went over to check if the door was locked, and it was. They clasped their hands together and closed their eyes as a mass of light expanded and absorbed them and they vanished. ZAP.

***

Some hours later, Amira woke up. She looked around her room and saw, through the gap in her curtains, it was still dark outside. She allowed her head to slump back on the bed. Her mind went back to her grandma, King Toke, Thomas and Johnny. 'Was it a dream?' she thought to herself. She laid there for a while and felt so thirsty and hungry she decided to get up. It was so dark, she fumbled around for her bedside lamp switch and switched the light on. The light hurt her eyes, so she looked away to let her eyes adjust. She saw that she was wrapped up in her mum's duvet. 'That's odd', she thought to herself. She threw the duvet off and stood up, and gasped when she felt and saw what she was wearing. She looked down to see the beautiful purple dress from her dream. She moved quickly to the mirror and stared at herself in disbelief.

"It wasn't a dream. It was real!" she exclaimed happily.

She carefully took the dress off; her body had creases left from sleeping in the dress. She gently placed it on a hanger on her wardrobe door and she stood back to admire it.

"They will probably want that back." said Amira sadly.

She sighed and changed into her comfy, baggy clothes, wrapped herself in her fluffy dressing gown and went downstairs into the kitchen. She turned the light on when she got to the bottom of the stairs and looked at the clock; it was quarter past four in the morning. Amira went to the fridge and saw a pack of sliced ham, she quickly checked the bread to see if it was ok, and it was. "Bingo," She said to herself.

When she finished rehydrating herself and had eaten her sandwich, she still felt so tired and decided to get back to sleep. She wandered back upstairs and sat down on her bed and was about to turn her light off when something caught her attention on her desk. It was a note with very fancy handwriting.

'Dear Amira,

We will call for you at 10 pm tomorrow. You can get ready here.

From your friends T & J.'

"Thomas and Johnny, the Ceremony!" She said as she remembered.

The thought made her so excited and happy. She couldn't wait to see her grandma again and Toke, Thomas and Johnny. She was full of wonder about what would happen at the ceremony. She couldn't wait. She closed her eyes and imagined being back in the realm. She felt dizzy with how tired she still was. She laid on her bed, wrapped her mum's duvet around her and turned her lamp off. She felt the warmth build up in her little self-made cocoon and went to sleep in less than a few minutes with a smile on her face.

Chapter 27

Coming of Age

Amira was woken by the harsh light that appeared from the side of her bed, ZAP. She flinched at the brightness and covered her eyes.

"Wake up, sleeping beauty!" said two male voices.

Amira was startled for a moment, and she opened her eyes as best as she could. She was relieved to see Johnny and Thomas.

"Your back." she said sleepily as she rubbed her eyes.

"You haven't been asleep since we left, have you?" said Thomas jokingly.

"Course she hasn't. She's changed out of her dress and into her nightwear." said Johnny as he looked at Amira's clothes as she sat herself up.

"I woke up, got changed, had something to eat and then went right back to bed. I thought I dreamt up most of what happened until I saw the dress and your note on the desk." said Amira.

Amira reached out for her phone on her bedside, she had a missed call from her mum, she would have to call her back later.

"What? I've been asleep all this time?" exclaimed Amira, glancing at the time. It was 10 pm.

"Please, darling, you needed it! Now get up. It's time to get you ready!" said Thomas.

"Oh, we brought this back for you!" said Johnny, who gave Amira her own duvet back.

"Oh, thank you!" she said as she clutched it and hugged it tight, that was one less thing she felt she had to explain to her mum when she got home.

Johnny beamed and grabbed Amira's mum's duvet. "I'll put this back where it belongs".

"Right then, ready to go?" asked Thomas.

Amira got up and swapped her fluffy dressing gown for a long cardigan, and Johnny came back in from making Amira's mums bed.

"I'm ready." announced Amira.

Johnny and Thomas extended their gloved hands to Amira, and she instinctively took them and closed her eyes, ZAP. She could feel the light surrounding them and blowing her hair about her face. When her hair stopped blowing, and the light went away, she opened her eyes again, and she was in the grand dressing room, back in the twin flame realm. It was just as amazing as she remembered.

"The sooner you get ready, the sooner you can see the Queen and King." said Thomas.

Amira longed to see her grandma again, although maybe she shouldn't call her grandma anymore, though, she thought. She felt so excited and wanted to be ready as soon as possible, but she didn't know where to start.

"Go on and find something you want to wear! The Queen has told us that whatever you choose, you can keep!" said Thomas excitedly.

Amira was shocked and happy and even more excited to pick something, then she remembered the pretty purple dress she left hanging on her wardrobe door.

"Oh, I forgot to bring the purple dress back!" said Amira guiltily.

"Don't worry your pretty little head about it. That's yours to keep, too." said Johnny happily.

Amira couldn't believe how lucky she felt to have two gorgeous dresses from a world no one knew about. She still had so many questions about this place and how it all worked. Then she remembered that she had asked Thomas and Johnny to find out how many times she had been reincarnated.

"Did you happen to find out how many times I've been reincarnated?" reminded Amira politely. "Pick you're your dress first and then we will tell you." said Johnny smiling.

Johnny thought she would find it hard to find a dress if she was thinking of other things, and he was right. She was grateful, so she smiled in defeat, turned and walked along the nearly endless stream of formal dresses. She couldn't have imagined more beautiful dresses if she tried. She didn't know how she would ever pick. Her hand trailed along the dresses so she could feel how the fabrics felt to her fingertips, just as she had the first time. She felt all the ruffles, glitter, and sequins, satins and silks glide past her fingertips. There were beautiful colors, purples, pinks, reds and then she saw the dress that stood out from all the rest. A brilliant peacock blue dress, that was so elegant, beautiful and magical. The purple dress she picked last time was beautiful, but this one seemed slightly more grown-up and sexy. She took the hanger off the rail and held the dress out to properly observe it. It had a satin corset bodice that was a brilliant peacock blue. It had thin straps that would hang beside her shoulders with little gems hanging off of them. The dress's brilliant blue satin fabric continued on past the corset top and into a sleek, elegant full-length skirt with a split going down both sides. Over the skirt was a very thin fabric that was a slightly deeper shade of blue that glittered and twinkled so subtly.

"This is the one." announced Amira to Thomas and Johnny.

They both came down to have a look at the dress that Amira had picked.

"It's perfect." said Johnny.

"It will look amazing on you." added Thomas.

When Amira took her eyes away from the dress to look at Johnny and Thomas, she noticed that they had already changed their clothes. Both of their outfits were indeed stylish, and very dapper, but were much suited to much younger gentlemen. Johnny had cut his hair to a very fashionable and trendy short back and sides. He wore a dark, and slightly baggy, shirt with a waistcoat with some smart trousers and shiny black shoes. Thomas had changed his beard style and was now stubble with very clean cut edges, 'very modern' Amira thought. Thomas wore a simple long-sleeved dark green shirt, with what looked like skinny black jeans, that he was trying his best to hold up, as they were a little baggy on him, he wore some causal brown loafers to finish off his outfit. Amira was slightly taken back and couldn't help but remark on this sudden change and how ill-fitted the clothes were compared to what she had seen them in before.

"You've changed your style all of a sudden." remarked Amira.

Johnny and Thomas shot each other a knowing, cheeky glance.

"We know it's very young, but that's sort of the point." said Johnny.

"Besides, we love the new fashion for men that's starting to come out." added Thomas happily.

"What do you mean 'that's the point'?" asked Amira curiously.

"All in good time, but right now, we need to finish getting you ready!" Urged Johnny.

They both ushered Amira to sit down at the dressing table. Thomas immediately, skillfully shaped Amira's hair while Johnny hung her beautiful blue dress in the changing room.

"I'll find you some shoes that will match. I promise you'll love them. Size?" said Johnny.

"Size 6. Can you promise that I can walk in them too?" Shouted back Amira after Johnny was already mincing down to the shoe wall.

"So we saw your assignment about presenting a business plan, on your desk. Do you have an idea for it yet?" Said Thomas casually, and he continued to weave through Amira's hair.

"I've decided to set up a dating agency, all of this has really opened my eyes, and I want to help." said Amira.

Johnny had arrived back in time to hear Amira's idea. Amira looked at them both in the dressing table mirror and they were smiling at each other. Johnny put a hand on Thomas's shoulder and nodded.

"We both have a proposition for you, Amira." said Johnny.

"A proposition for me, what is it?" Amira's mind filled with wonder and curiosity.

"We both had a feeling about you as we got to know you more." said Thomas.

"As you know, we like to save our juice as much as possible. We have been waiting for such an opportunity for some years now. We would like to create an alliance with you as our point of contact on earth." said Johnny.

"What do you mean?" asked Amira, puzzled.

"Well, if you follow through with your business idea and start up a dating agency, we will assist you in making it successful, and we will supply you with twin flames to match up." said Thomas.

"And help maintain the balance?" followed Amira.

"Exactly!" confirmed Johnny excitedly.

Amira didn't need to think about it at all, she already loved the idea of starting her own dating agency, but now she would have the support of Johnny and Thomas, too. It was a no brainer.

"I'd love that!" beamed Amira.

Thomas and Johnny clapped and grabbed Amira by the shoulders and shook her with playful excitement. It made Amira laugh at how excited they were about it, and she was excited too.

"Don't let on to the King and Queen just yet, though! We need their blessing first." said Johnny.

Amira nodded in acknowledgement but was still excited and extremely flattered that they would even want to work with her.

"We will come to your PowerPoint presentation too." said Johnny.

"Cloaked of course, but we will find you later that day for a talk. Ok?" asked Thomas.

"Agreed!" confirmed Amira.

Johnny finally remembered the shoes he had selected for Amira and presented them to her for approval. They were the same blue as the dress, they had many straps, with sparkles dotted around them, and they would show off her toes, they had a kitten heel that was big enough to add shape to her posture but little enough to feel comfortable in, for at least 2 hours of standing anyway.

"They're perfect." said Amira approvingly.

"I told you they would be." Replied Johnny confidently.

Johnny strapped the shoes onto Amira's feet while Thomas finished styling Amira's hair.

"Now for a little makeup!" said Johnny as he did a flourish with his hands.

Johnny took charge of the make-up and quickly brushed and blended Amira's eyes. The brush tickled a little, but she kept her eyes closed and stayed as still as she could. When she felt him stop, she listened to him rummage around for something and then felt Johnny applying some more products on her face again. After only a few minutes, he was done. Amira opened her eyes and saw that both Johnny and Thomas were staring at her with approval and awe. She began to look in the mirror, but Johnny and Thomas flailed their arms to stop her and practically forced her into the changing room. She obliged, of course, she was actually having a lot of fun. She took off her comfy clothes and slid the dress over her head, when it was on she realized doing up the back of the dress would be extremely difficult, but she was decent. Amira opened the dressing room curtains and asked for help. Johnny held the corset together while Thomas laced up the back. It felt comfier than Amira had expected. Thomas and Johnny finished helping Amira into her dress; she turned around to face them both to see what they thought. Both Thomas and

Johnny had their hands over their mouths as if to say they had outdone themselves this time. They stepped aside so Amira could step onto the platform to look at herself now that she was fully ready.

"Oh my god." said Amira, as she looked at the beautiful woman in front of her.

Amira's body had an elegance and maturity that she hadn't seen before. She had curves and a bust. Her hair was half up, half down, with some curls coming down and hanging over her right shoulder. Her eyes popped with blue and black that was shaped to emphasize her best features to stand out. Particularly her hot red lips made them look like they should be on the front cover of vogue. She was not so much taken back by how beautiful she looked but more about how grown-up she looked. Her mind went back to the girls at school and how self-conscious she had felt around them. The thought made her laugh. 'I'll never feel like that ever again now that I've seen myself like this' she thought to herself.

"Shall we take you to see the King and Queen now?" asked Thomas.

"Yes! … She is still my grandma, isn't she?" said Amira as she hesitated slightly.

"You were a big part of her most recent life. Of course she is still your grandma. In fact, there's some news for you about that." said Johnny.

Amira remembered that she had asked them to find out how many times she had been reincarnated, and anticipation filled her mind. Would she have been anyone famous? a man even? a war hero?

"What did you find out?" asked Amira impatiently.

"We promised the Queen that she would be the one to tell you." said Thomas.

"Are you ready?" said Johnny.

Amira gave a very decisive nod and smiled, she was having a great time, and she couldn't wait to find out about how old her soul was and see her grandma again.

Chapter 28

A Gift from the Royal Twin Flames

Amira followed Thomas and Johnny towards the royal chambers. She was very aware of her body in a room full of old people, she could feel eyes on her, but she didn't feel judged or shy, she felt empowered and confident. In just one day she felt that she had changed so much. Amira passed through the rest of the old people that were beginning to fill the ballroom more and more. She noticed that they all were as oddly dressed in a similar way that Thomas and Johnny were. Everyone's clothes and outfits didn't fit properly, and some looked more questionable than others, in rather revealing outfits that showed off stomachs, chests and legs. All the outfits were in some ways inappropriate, Amira thought, especially for a royal ceremony that happened once every one hundred years. Was this not considered to be a very formal event? Some of the outfits were of the finest material, mostly smart and beautiful. She couldn't decide if it was the clothes that didn't suit the old people or if it was the old people who didn't suit the clothes. Amira felt herself judging, but then she thought that if they were all dressing in uncharacteristic clothing, perhaps there was a good reason for it, even though she couldn't think what that reason would be.

They walked casually through the crowd of oddly dressed twin flames. They walked past the grand throne and carried on to walk through the doorway that lead to the royal room. Amira's eyes cast around the familiar room with the endless amount of portraits of King Toke and Queen Runa. She remembered the scared, unsure girl that didn't know herself well enough to know that Tefnut and Akil had been lying to her about who she was the whole time. She felt she had come so far in such a short time. As Amira started to walk up the spiral staircase after Johnny and Thomas, she stopped to look at one of the portraits of Runa and Toke. Runa was wearing a similar color dress to the one Amira was wearing now. As she looked at the portrait, she felt sad. In many ways, she felt that her dear grandma didn't exist anymore but was merely one of many lives lived by Queen Runa.

Thomas noticed that Amira had stopped, so he called after her. "Are you coming, Amira?"

Amira glanced halfway up the stairs to find Thomas and Johnny patiently waiting for her. She grabbed the sides of her skirts and ran up the stairs until she had caught up with them and continued up the rest of the pretty spiral staircase. When they reached the top of the stairs, Thomas and Johnny opened the top door, entered and announced Amira's name to the King and Queen.

"Amira, your majesties." said Johnny.

Amira walked through the door wondering if she should bow or courtesy, but instead she was lifted into a massive bear hug by King Toke and then a tight hug back on the ground from Queen Runa. Amira was shocked but yet so smitten with the lovely personal greeting as if she had known them both her whole life. She was stuck for words, and she was too busy laughing from the lovely greeting.

"We're so glad you could come." said King Toke in a warm, friendly manner.

Queen Runa pulled away from Amira, holding her by the hands, and said, "We discovered a few things that we would like to share with you."

The King and Queen gestured towards the sofas at the other end of the room to invite them all to sit down.

"So what is it you wanted to tell me?" Asked Amira as she glanced to the King and Queen to her left, and then at Thomas and Johnny to her right.

Runa leant forward and said "We're related." And then she leant back to wait for Amira's reply with a big grin on her face.

Amira was at a loss and slightly confused.

"Well, yes, you were my grandma." Said Amira with confusion written across her face, looking at Runa like she was mad.

King Toke then leaned forward and said, "And we're related." He said, pointing to himself and to Amira.

Amira was even more confused, but no one was giving her any clear answers. She looked to Thomas and Johnny, who quickly said, "We're not related."

Amira was still confused and was getting slightly impatient, for she had no idea what any of it meant.

Runa leant forward again and said, "Not only am I grandma to you from my previous reincarnation, but you are in this current life, a direct decedent from us when we first met as humans."

The information slowly dawned on Amira. She was taken back, and for a few moments, she was speechless. But then she found a question that she thought would help make things clearer.

"You mean from when you were Vikings?" said Amira.

King Toke replied, "That's correct. Great, great, great, great and even more great-granddaughter."

"So that's why I look like you. I'm a direct descendant from all that time ago?" gasped Amira.

"Remarkable, isn't it?" said Johnny in amazement.

Thomas added, "The chances are so remote. Honestly, you can't make this stuff up."

They all chuckled together. Amira felt so happy, she knew now that she'd never lose her grandma. Now it seemed Queen Runa had been her grandma in more ways than one, that made Amira feel so grounded and warm hearted 'she'll be my grandma no matter what now' thought Amira.

Johnny leant forward and clasped his hands together, and said, "Now, you wanted to know how many times you have been reincarnated?"

"Yes." said Amira as she leaned forward to hear more.

"And you still want to know?" checked Thomas.

Amira gave a sure nod and scooted forward a little in anticipation.

"This is your 70th reincarnation." Said Thomas

"Wow, 70th?? I've lived 69 other lives?" exclaimed Amira.

"That's right." replied Johnny, who found Amira's astonishment slightly amusing.

"How many times had you been reincarnated when you met each other?" Amira asked Johnny.

"I was in my 120th life when I met Thomas."

"And I was on my 112th life when I met Johnny."

They gave each other an affectionate stare and looked back at Amira, who was consumed by thoughts and trying to get her head around the idea. Amira looked to Toke and Runa and waited for their numbers.

Toke went first, "I was on life 77."

"And I was on life 80." said Runa shortly after.

"Gosh, so different from Thomas and Johnny's." said Amira.

"Yes, the number of reincarnations before the meeting of a twin flam has risen over the centuries." said Queen Runa.

Jonny followed on and said, "We believe that is because the world is much more heavily populated now, and there are so many more experiences and things to learn about these days, compared to when we first met."

Amira felt nourished with knowledge as she listened, but as her mind wandered, more questions came to her.

"What happens in the ceremony exactly?" asked Amira.

Runa, Toke, Johnny and Thomas all exchanged looks before Queen Runa answered.

"We want it to be a surprise, but what we can tell you is, that it's a reset button for our subjects. The source of our power is completely replenished." said Runa.

King Toke continued, "Most use it up by the time it gets to the end of the 100 years."

"How do you know if you've used it up or not?" asked Amira.

Johnny answered this time, "Every time we use the source or as we call it 'juice', we age at the same rate that you would age on earth, some people age quickly and some more slowly. Up here, we age depending on how much of our juice we use up."

"I should have known Akil and Tefnut were up to something." Said King Toke in a low key fury as he clinched his fist.

"They had defiantly used up every last bit of juice they had, looking at them now." said Thomas.

Amira remembered how incredibly old they looked when she last saw them at the care home. When she looked at Thomas and Johnny, they looked so young in comparison.

"So it's been a hundred years to this date? How is it Thomas and Johnny have done so well?" asked Amira.

King Toke replied with tones of respect and appraisal, "It's astonishing, isn't it? Since the technologies have come about, they've really taken advantage of what's available in the human world."

"If technology continues to evolve, it could become a great asset to this realm." added Johnny smugly. He and Thomas gave each other a proud and slightly smug look of pride to each other.

The Queen glanced at the time and gave the top of King Toke's hand a gentle tap.

"Now, Amira, the Ceremony starts soon, and we wanted to thank you properly before it starts. Now we would like to give you your gift." said King Toke.

"But you have already given me this dress and the shoes and the purple dress and shoes from before." said Amira in a pleading tone.

"No, we insist." said king Toke kindly.

"The gift will be of your choosing, Amira. It can be anything you want. Anything in the whole of existence." added Runa sweetly.

Amira sat and thought for a moment and couldn't think of anything she wanted. She tried to remember what mattered to her back home. She could only remember the

PowerPoint presentation for her business idea. Then it hit her. She knew what she wanted as a gift.

"You won't be offended, will you? For what I ask for?" said Amira.

"We won't be offended." confirmed Toke warmly.

Amira felt better after their reassurance and opened her mouth to speak her gift into existence.

"I would like to know as much as possible about what gets in the way of people finding their twin flames and how to unite them." said Amira.

"You want THIS as your gift? Why?" asked Toke as he lifted an eyebrow.

Amira shuffled a little. She thought maybe that was crossing the line or perhaps asking too much.

"Well, I have to put together a business plan to present back home, and I've decided to create a dating agency. I thought perhaps, I could be of some help, real help." Said Amira sheepishly, bracing herself for rejection.

Amira sat and waited for a response, but silence was all she got. She started to feel uneasy. Maybe she had said the wrong thing. She glanced about the room to look at their faces. King Toke looked across to Thomas and Johnny and shook his head at them, then leant back and smiled. Amira didn't know what to think; she looked over at Johnny and Thomas, who had not moved but were wearing very smug faces.

"What?" demanded Runa, clearly in the dark.

Toke whispered something to Runa too quiet for Amira to hear. Toke had finished whispering and pulled away to look at Runa's face and see if she had got all the information. Runa smiled and looked over to Thomas and Johnny.

"Talk about landing on your feet. This is the only circumstance in the world where we would ever allow this, do you two understand?" said Runa in a serious and teasing tone.

Thomas and Johnny nodded seriously, unable to hide their smiles as the sides of their mouths began to curl up at the sides. Amira was still confused. However, Runa could see this and decided to give her sweet granddaughter some peace of mind and tell her what had just happened.

"Your gift is granted! Thomas and Johnny will tell you the rest after the ceremony." said Runa.

Amira felt her whole body relax and smiled back at Runa in relief and joy.

"It's Time for the ceremony." said King Toke.

Chapter 29

The Twin Flame Ceremony

Queen Runa wrapped her arms around Amira and held her close as if to say goodbye.

Runa said quietly to Amira, "When the ceremony is finished, either me or the King will be reincarnated into the next one hundred year cycle. It's completely random, we never know who will be the one to stay or go. So just in case, it's me, I'll say goodbye now." said Runa as she hugged her sweet granddaughter a little bit tighter.

Tears started to form in Amira's eyes, and she hugged tightly back. They pulled away and looked at each other for a moment. Just then, King Toke, like some brutish bear, grabbed Amira and lifted her into another bear hug.

"And this is in case I'm reincarnated; it's been an honor to meet my great, great, great, great, great-granddaughter." Boomed King Toke like a playful farther.

He gave a big hearty laugh, and Amira couldn't help but laugh too. He placed her down back on the floor.

Toke turned to Runa, held his Queen by the waist, led her out of the room, and closed the door behind them.

"We will wait here for a few minutes just so they can say their goodbyes in private before the ceremony." said Thomas.

Amira realized that in 100 years, Toke and Runa only had a day together. She couldn't imagine what that must feel like, and for one of them to leave again so soon. Amira wondered if it was unusual to rush around to find Queen Runa. Was she supposed to be up here years ago instead of last-minute like this?

"When was Runa supposed to come back to the realm?" asked Amira.

"The minimum age the Queen was to be before being fetched by someone up here is 25." said Johnny.

"So they could have spent 75 years together? But instead have spent 100 years apart. But they've only just found each other." Said Amira becoming sadder for them both the more she thought about it.

"Yes, it's been very unfair this time, no thanks to Tefnut and Akil. But they had one full day together at least. All they can do is hope it will be as quick as possible before they are reunited again, which should be easy now Tefnut and Akil will be out of the picture." said Johnny.

"What will happen to them? to Tefnut and Akil?" asked Amira.

"None of us know. Only the King and Queen of the realm know, and are forbidden to speak of it as part of their royal burdens." replied Thomas.

Amira thought about imprisonment, but it seemed somewhat unlikely in a place like this.

"What do you think happens, Thomas?" asked Amira.

"Johnny and I have shared a bunch of theories about stuff like this over the years, but we think they get the worst of the worst if they are indeed reincarnated, and would be destined to never find each other again, or maybe reduced down to a creature at the bottom of the food chain." said Thomas darkly.

Johnny added, "Or perhaps they will be wiped completely from existence, eliminating any trace they ever left behind, and are only remembered by those who rule."

"You mean the rest of us would forget they ever existed, like we never met them or anything?" said Amira checking to see if she had fully understood Johnny's theory.

"Yes. But of course, we will never know for sure, unless we become the rulers of this realm someday." said Johnny as he looked at Thomas. They giggled at the silly thought.

Just then, they heard a roar of an audience coming from downstairs. Thomas opened the door and glanced down at the bottom of the spiral stairway where the King and Queen were.

"Let's go. Follow us, and we will show you where your place will be for the ceremony." Said Johnny as he took Amira's hand, and they all quickly tiptoed down the spiral staircase. Amira followed closely behind as she held her skirts out of the way so she wouldn't trip. They got to the bottom of the stairs, and before she knew it, she was through the doorway and had frozen in place. The crowd of old couple's dressed in odd outfits that were far too young for them was vast now and surprisingly loud and energetic. Johnny led Amira by the hand and gently moved her to the right-hand side of where the thrones were placed for her to stand and watch. The beautiful youthful King and Queen were stood in the middle of the platform of the throne and looked on at each other with deep concentration.

As Johnny let go of Amira, he said "Pay attention and keep watching!"

When Thomas and Johnny were together, they turned to face each other in the same way the King and Queen were. Just then, the noise of the crowd stopped all at once. Amira could hear nothing but the gentle shuffling of feet as the rest of the thousands of old couples in the crowd turned to face their twin flame too. The silence became deafening but Amira stayed very still and very quiet and looked around, waiting for something to happen.

As Amira looked out into the vast crowd a light caught the corner of her eye. She quickly turned her head toward where the King and Queen were stood and realized the light was growing around them both. When the light had covered their entire bodies, they moved towards each other to kiss. Amira had never had her first kiss yet, but she felt that this was the perfect kiss as she looked on. A few seconds later, the light burst and spread to the rest of the kingdom, making Amira flinch at the dramatic yet beautiful display. All of the couples began to kiss. The light brightened more as it filled the room. Amira could see that something was beginning to happen to all of the old couples. Before she could get a good look, she had to shut her eyes tight and flung her hands up to help protect them. Then it went pitch black behind the protection of her hands and the light that Amira sensed from behind her closed eyes had gone. She opened her eyes and slowly opened her hands to look through her fingers. There weren't any old people anymore. She gasped over the huge crowd and observed that all the odd outfits didn't look odd anymore. They weren't too baggy or too tight; they fitted perfectly, like they were hand made for every person. Not one person had a wrinkle on their face anymore. Amira's attention went over to Thomas and Johnny. But they were gone, instead there in their place stood two very handsome and muscular men. Their youthful, modern clothes were filled with muscular bodies. She remembered Thomas had his beard shaped and trimmed, and it suited him very well now, he had dark brown hair that was gelled back with a timeless quiff at the front. Johnny's hair was pitch black, and his jaw line was so prominent it would put any male model to shame. Amira remembered how silly she thought they looked in their clothes before and shook her head in disbelief at how stunning they looked now. They could be the world most beautiful male models. In fact, as Amira looked around, everyone in the entire kingdom, everyone looked painfully beautiful. Everyone in the crowd had moved away from the kiss, had a quick cheer, then turned to face the King and Queen again. Amira followed their gaze and saw that it was only the Queen stood there now, on her own.

The crowd in perfect synchronization said together;

"May his reincarnation be swift and quick; may he be reunited with his Queen soon." chanted the crowd of twin flames.

The Queen lifted her head and acknowledged her subjects with a grateful but sad smile.

"I and my twin flame wish you all a happy 100 years. Use your source wisely and keep the earth in balance with the love of all loves. There are jobs to be done. Thank you." Said Queen Runa gracefully, and very much rehearsed, but very sincere nonetheless.

The crowd rejoiced, and the sounds of laughter and steps began to fill the room from the couples leaving the ballroom. Queen Runa had tears in her eyes as she turned to go through the door. She stopped just before and turned to Thomas and Johnny, who were getting rather hands-on with each other and said "You two may go. I'll take Amira home."

Thomas and Johnny bowed to the Queen and minced off quickly. It made Amira laugh. When they left the ballroom, there was no one left but Queen Runa and Amira. Runa turned to face Amira, she smiled gently and held her hand out to her. Amira walked quickly up to her and took her hand in hers. Runa led Amira back up the spiral stairs and back into the royal chamber. When they were back in the room Runa let go of Amira's hand and slumped face down onto the bed.

"Why is everyone in this realm so beautiful?"Asked Amira.

Runa looked at Amira and was happy for the distraction. "It's sort of like a reward. At the end of graduation you get a diploma, or people get a knighthood. Everyone is at their most beautiful when they meet their twin flame. Many were never as beautiful on earth as they are now. However, that's because we are at our peak of health up here, with no damage that humans can do to themselves back on earth." replied Runa.

"Like drinking and smoking and stuff." said Amira.

"Yes exactly, and negativity, don't forget that one." said Runa as she smiled and gave a wink. This reminded Amira that part of her was her grandma who she loved so much.

"Think I'll find my twin flame in this life?" asked Amira.

"I couldn't tell you. I haven't looked. But I will say that it's more likely for you to find them in another life. Your soul is still rather young. Even if you don't meet your twin flame in this life, you should always find a way to be happy, happiness in its purest form like when you were a child. Souls grow, develop, learn and thrive at their brightest when they're happiest. That's the true point of life, to learn and do what you love to do, to be as happy as possible."

"So why is it not soul mates? Why do you call yourself twin flames?" asked Amira.

"It's always been twin flames, since the very first. Soul mates are a common misconception amongst those of your life, still. Your soul mate could be anybody, people that help you grow, and you have things in common with similar goals and care about each other. It's still love. It could be a friend or your grandma." She smiled and winked again.

Amira sat and absorbed the information, and she felt a sense of peace within her that life's aim was to be happy and learn as much as you could. All of a sudden, all the things Amira had ever worried about seemed so unimportant and small. She thought back to earlier and remembered that Thomas and Johnny were supposed to tell her something when the ceremony finished.

"What is it Johnny and Thomas were supposed to tell me? After the gift I asked for?" asked Amira.

"Oh well, I'll let them tell you, but what I can say is that they will have a proposition for you. I honestly can't believe how lucky they are sometimes." She laughed to herself.

Amira knew what that was. Thomas and Johnny had told her that they wanted to be an ally of Amira's for when she opened up her dating agency, but she didn't want to get them both into trouble, so she kept it to herself.

"Where did those two go anyway? Where did everyone go?" asked Amira.

"Ha, well, if you and the love of your life have been so old for what feels like a long time and are then regenerated to the peak of their youthfulness, it is very hard to resist each other." Runa looked down and smiled at her most recent memories of her and Toke.

"Toke and I were remembering what it was like going from old to young again the first few times it happened to us. They were simpler times."

"So you two weren't always King and Queen here?" asked Amira.

"No, there's been many before us, but we are the longest raining so far." said Runa boastfully.

246

Amira decided to lie back on the bed, like Runa, and stared at the ceiling for a while.

"What will you do while Tokes is gone?" asked Amira.

"We leave each other a letter and a list. There's a lot on Tokes list this time. But what do I expect, after 100 years of being away?"

"A list?" asked Amira.

"Yes, after our day together of catching up and talking, he has left me a list of TV series and films he thinks I will like."

Amira laughed at how very average that was and, for royalty, of a twin flame realm too.

"I bet Vikings is on it." Said Amira as she remembered what Toke had put on the TV before the big mess made by Tefnut and Akil had been resolved.

"Is that a series?" asked Runa.

"Yes, a drama based on history and legends about Vikings." replied Amira.

"I think I'll watch that first, It might feel just like home, it will be nice to have that while Toke is away."

Runa turned on her side to look at Amira, and Amira did the same.

"As your grandma, I want you to start living your life the way YOU want, don't be so shy, and don't over think so much. If it feels good, do it. As for your mother, I think you might be able to help her a little." said Runa.

"What do you mean?" asked Amira.

"Thomas and Johnny will tell you soon enough. Now then, let's get you home." said Runa.

Runa jumped up with no trouble at all. Amira heaved herself up, but it was very difficult to get up. Her corset was very tight. Runa extended her hand out to help Amira up, and she took it. When Amira was standing, Runa had kept hold of her hand and closed her eyes. Amira knew it was time for her to go home, so she closed her eyes too, ZAP. She could sense the light surrounding her, and a breeze lifted her curls from her shoulder, and the light faded away. She opened her eyes, and she was back home, in her bedroom. She was alone. Runa was gone. She looked around her room and saw that it had been cleaned, organized and tidied. She looked to her bed that now had a very grown-up set of covers on it with a pretty silver pattern. In the middle of the bed was a small pretty box with a ribbon wrapped around it and a letter underneath that had 'Amira' written on the front. She looked at the box and the letter and decided to open the letter first. As she sat down she felt the tightness of the corset and decided she had to get herself out of it before she could read the letter comfortably. She jumped up and turned her back to the mirror so she could get a better idea of how to undo the corset. She fumbled at the ribbon until it was loose enough to wriggle out of and she let out a large sigh of relieve when it came off.

She flung her shoes off her feet and gently placed the beautiful peacock blue dress over the top of her desk chair; she would find another place for it tomorrow. She grabbed one of her oversized T-shirts and slipped it on, and got into her bed and felt instantly comfy as her warm legs stretched beneath the cold bed sheets. She reached forward and grabbed the letter, and opened it.

'Dearest Amira,

This trinket will help you and is part of the gift you requested. Thomas and Johnny will visit you sometime this month with the rest of your gift, and they will tell you about the trinket in this box.

P.S. Hope you're happy with your fresh and organized room and new bed covers.

Lots of Love, Grandma'

She put the letter aside and picked up the pretty little box and untied the ribbon to open it. Inside was a beautiful silver ring with intricate detailing along the band itself. In the center was a clear, smooth stone. It looked very antique and very expensive. It looked timeless, and it could be hundreds of years old or be brand new and shop-bought from a designer. She put the ring on her middle finger and admired how it looked on her hand. She looked at the letter again and re-read it. 'This trinket will help you'. She looked at the ring again in case it had done something or changed since she put it on, but nothing had changed. She kept looking anyway, admiring all the tiny details of hearts, flowers and leaves that ran along the rim.

She caught the clock in the corner of her eye and couldn't believe the time. It was 3:30 am. Her mum would be coming in a matter of hours. She decided it was time to go to sleep. She flicked off the light switch and curled up in her fresh new bedding, and fell asleep instantly.

Chapter 30

Life Goes On

Amira woke up and took a deep breath in, and smelled an unfamiliar fresh scent. Curious about the smell, it motivated her to open her eyes fully so she could see where the smell was coming from. When she had finally opened her eyes fully, she saw the pretty patterned bedding she was wrapped up in, and then the whole evening came rushing back to her. She smiled at the memories. She looked to her clock by the side of her bed, '8:35am', which was early for Amira. She felt wide awake and restless, so she got out of bed and opened her wardrobe. All her clothes were neatly arranged, folded and hung, and her shoes were all clean and in order along the bottom from winter to summer. She looked for her jogger's and found them on a shelf, neatly folded. She gently slid them out from the middle of the pile and put them on. A large stylish box caught her eye at the bottom of her wardrobe, so she picked it up and opened it. Her beautiful purple dress and matching shoes were inside, and a note was placed on top of the dress;

'Put your new dress and shoes in here too'.

She looked behind her and found the stunning elegant peacock blue dress draped over the top of her desk chair and the shoes tucked under the chair on the floor. She picked up the pretty blue shoes and put them neatly beside the purple ones. She observed how the purple dress was folded up in the box, tried her best to fold her blue one in the same way and carefully placed it on top of the purple dress. She grabbed the letter and box her grandma had sent and buried them at the bottom of the box under the dresses. When she put the lid back on top of the box, she caught sight of the beautiful ring that she was still wearing that her grandma Runa had given her. She lifted the box and placed it back where she found it in the bottom of the wardrobe and closed the doors. She stood and admired her ring in the light for a moment and wondered what the stone in the middle was. Her phone pinged, she looked over, and she saw it was from her mum. She picked up the phone and read the message.

'I will be home at about 2 this afternoon x'.

Amira quickly replied

'Ok see you soon x'.

She wondered what she would do with herself until her mum came home. She looked at her clock again, and it was 9:00 am now. She looked at her tidy desk and saw the neat pile of papers stacked into one pile for her PowerPoint assignment. She felt a new lease of excitement and felt some inspiration about getting started with her assignment. So she sat down at her desk, and she opened her laptop, sorted the stack of papers into three smaller piles, and began making notes on them while her computer loaded up. When she had finished making notes, she pulled her laptop closer; opened up the template of her PowerPoint she had made a few days before and began to type.

Three and a half hours had passed and Amira continued to type on her laptop and with a flourish of her hand, she added the last full stop to her PowerPoint. As she finished, she sat back, put her hands behind her head, and smiled at her work. She took a big stretch, and began to flick through the slides to check them all before she saved it and turn her laptop off, it looked pretty good to Amira. When she'd absorbed her finished work she clicked save and closed her laptop. She brushed her hands through her hair but her fingers got stuck. She remembered that she never took her hair out of the curly up do that Thomas had styled for her. She stood up and went over to the mirror to see what the damage was. It wasn't as bad as she thought. It was still quite pretty but it was certainly messy, it had managed to stay intact pretty well considering she had slept with it in the whole night. She felt around her head for the hair grips and pulled them out one by one until she couldn't find anymore. She was in awe of the glorious tangle in which hair now lay in, but decided it would be a good idea to wash it all the same. She grabbed her dressing gown off the hook from the back of her door, went into the bathroom, turned the shower on and closed the shower door so it could get warm and water wouldn't go everywhere. While she was waiting for the water to get hot she undressed and wiped the makeup off her face with some makeup removal cream and a damp face flannel. She rubbed her face until all the makeup was gone and then she got in the shower, she closed her eyes as the warm water rained over her. It was exactly what she needed. When she'd got her hair completely wet she shampooed and conditioned it, it felt much silkier already. She ran her hands up and down her legs and decided she would give them a shave. She took the razor from the shelf in the shower and run it up and down her first leg and then the second. When her legs were glossy and smooth she finished her shower off by shaving under her arms. She felt completely refreshed and relaxed. She turned off the shower, got out and dried herself off with a towel, then used the towel to squeeze most of the water out of her hair. She flicked her hair up and wrapped herself into her warm dressing gown which she had left on the radiator while she showered and went down stairs to see what was in the fridge. Amira pottered down the stairs and saw the curtains where shut in the living room so she walked over to open them and then looked to see how the weather was. 'It's chucking it down' she thought to herself as she saw a little stream of water flowing down the street and the dots of ripples that filled up the puddles. She turned and power walked straight to the fridge and quickly opened the door. There wasn't much in there; the more she looked the more she lost her appetite by observing that the sell by dates had all expired on the packets of food. With a look of disgust and disappointment she picked out all of the out of date foods and threw them in the bin. As she stood and observed the rather empty fridge she checked the time and decided to wait for her mum to come back home before having something to eat. She hoped her mum would suggest a takeout again. She went back upstairs to her bed room, took her dressing gown off and found her comfy jogger bottoms and a baggy thick black jumper and put them on. Her hair was still wet so she plugged in her hair dryer and tipped her head upside down and began to blow-dry her hair. After about 10 minutes of constant hair drying, she ran her free hand through her hair and decided it was dry enough. She switched off her dryer and plonked it on top of her desk then flipped her hair back while she stood upright again. She looked in the mirror and was impressed by the amount of volume she managed to get in her hair from drying it that way. As she looked in the mirror and looked at herself, even in her baggy, comfy clothes and no make-up, this was the first time she truly loved and appreciated her own natural beauty. The more she looked the more she found it hard to remember why she used to always be so self-conscious. 'I wonder what mum sees when she looks in the mirror without makeup on' she thought to herself. She turned on her heels, grabbed her phone, and trotted down the stairs again, walked up to the sofa and slumped onto her usual spot and switched on the TV with the remote. Then, her phone vibrated next to her. It was a message from her mum.

'Just gotten some sad news, will tell you about it when I get home, love you lots x'

Amira sat and looked at the message for a while and started to think about what the news could possibly be. She looked at the last part of her mum's message, *'it's bad news'*. She remembered that her grandma wouldn't be at the home anymore and that Thomas and Johnny said they had friends who would take care of it all so that it wouldn't look suspicious to humans. Amira knew what the news would be 'mum must have gotten a call saying grandma is dead' Amira thought to herself. She wondered how sad her mum would be when she came home. Amira knew her grandma would always be okay and was royalty of another realm, but her mum wouldn't and could never know about that. As she sat and thought, she started to remember that Runa had said that they always leave a sign behind for their loved ones to let them know they were ok. Amira wondered what the sign would be and decided not to worry about that. But she was a little worried about not acting sad enough. She decided that she would worry about it when the time came.

Amira went downstairs, got comfy on the sofa and turned on a film. Halfway through the film, Amira heard a car pull up in the driveway 'mums home', she thought to herself. She tried to not over think or anticipate what her mum would say, so she did her best to act like nothing new had happened. She heard a rustle of keys as her mum unlocked and opened the front door, heaving in a large luggage bag onto the hallway floor. She closed the door behind her and took off her wet coat. She looked over to the TV that was on and then saw Amira curled up on the sofa.

In a soft, sad tone, Amira's mum Sharron said, "Hello sweetheart."

Amira saw the sadness in her mum's face. "Hi mum, how was your trip?"

Her mum was in a pair of jeans and a Blue jumper. She walked over and slumped down on the sofa next to Amira.

"I got a phone call on the way home from your grandma's care home."

Amira could see tears filling her mum's eyes, so her eyes began to fill with tears too.

Sharron took a breath as she began to cry and managed to say "Grandma died."

Amira began crying in response to her mum and the pain, so she uncurled her body to hug her mum. Amira flung her arms around her mum, and they cried together until the film that Amira was watching had finished.

After a while Amira and her mum had stopped crying, and were rubbing their red puffy eyes with tissues and then threw the used ones on to the floor, with the rest of the other used tissues, there was quite a big pile now.

When they'd calmed down, Sharron looked at Amira and asked "Do you fancy a take out?"

"Yes please." replied Amira.

Sharron got her bag and fished out her purse, and gave it to Amira "You pick and get it ordered, you know what I like. I'm going to go unpack, get washed and settled."

Sharron kicked her heels off at the bottom of the stairs, picked up her luggage bag, and went up the stairs.

Amira went to a kitchen draw, pulled out many menus, and started to look through them all. She decided that Chinese sounded the most appealing, plus it was her mum's favorite. She selected a combo box of starters with prawn toast, spring rolls, dim sum, seaweed and spare ribs. Two mains; Beef in black bean sauce, a chicken chow main and egg fried rice with a side of salt and pepper chips. She picked up the house phone and dialed the number for the takeaway. She proceeded to make the order to a very obliging Chinese lady on the other end of the phone and made a last-minute decision to add on two fortune cookies at the end. She picked out the money from her mum's purse and put it next to the door ready for when the takeout would arrive.

"So what did you pick?" asked Sharron, sitting back down on the sofa beside her.

"Chinese." said Amira with a knowing smile.

"Ooh my favorite!" she said as she smiled at Amira.

As Amira looked back at her mum, she realized she didn't have any makeup on at all. It wasn't often Amira would see her mum without the stuff, and her mind went back to when she looked at herself in the mirror earlier and what it was like. How she saw how beautiful she was without even trying for the first time.

"What do you see when you look at yourself in the mirror, just as you are now, with no makeup?" asked Amira.

Sharron thought for a second but answered quite quickly, "Well, I prefer how I look with makeup on. Why?

What do you see when you look in the mirror?" asked Sharron to her not so little girl anymore.

"When I looked at myself today, I thought I looked beautiful." said Amira confidently.

Sharron brushed a stray hair behind her daughter's ear and looked at her with a proud, envious expression. "And so you are, sweetheart."

The doorbell rang, and Amira instinctively jumped up.

"That's the food!" said Amira excitedly.

She grabbed the money beside the door and opened it to find a friendly-looking man with a bag that had her name on it. She gave him the money, took the bag and wished him a good night. She placed the bag on the floor in front of the sofa for her mum to sort through while she got two plates and two sets of chopsticks and brought them back to the sofa. They picked out the food they wanted and ate without talking as they watched the TV programs that Amira had picked. The whole time both Amira and Sharron ate, they both felt that the meal hit the spot. It was just what they both needed after the days they have had, and the loss they felt for grandma being gone, even though Amira knew different, it was still a little sad. When they had finished eating Amira put all the rubbish in the bin and put the dishes in the dishwasher. She went back to the sofa and saw that her mum held out both of the fortune cookies for Amira to choose from. Amira picked the one in the red packaging, and her mum had the blue one. They both unwrapped the cookie and crushed it at the same time.

"Mine says; this is the perfect time to learn and achieve. What does yours say?" said Amira.

"Mine says; the purest beauty is the beauty within." Said Sharron as she squinted slightly to read what the small piece of paper said.

They then proceeded to eat the broken bits of their fortune cookie and chucked the little pieces of paper with fortunes on them to one side.

"Do you have college tomorrow?" asked Sharron as she crunched on a bit of fortune cookie.

"Yes." Amira then had a flash of memory about Monday and pulled out her phone to look at her calendar. "Oh, and dads coming over to take me for lunch tomorrow after college."

"Oh, that's good actually. I'll get the funeral all done and sorted tomorrow if I can. How is your dad? Still seeing Sophie?" Said Sharron sadly, but she was determined not to let herself get worked up.

"Yeah, I think so." said Amira as she observed a look of jealously in her mum's eyes.

Amira had thought she would have gotten over it by now. Sharron and her dad Paul splitting up was over ten years ago, but she didn't want to go down that road just now.

The TV switched channels, and it was on the last thing Amira had picked, which was her mum's favorite chat show.

"Oh good, I like this show! Who's on it tonight?" said Sharron.

They watched as the presenter read out the names of who they were interviewing, and Amira couldn't believe her eyes. Darren Wilson was one of the star guests on the show, Amira winced, and she knew she would have to tell her mum sometime. Sharron was getting very enthusiastic about him, saying how glad she was to see him on the show and how amazing he is. Amira thought that she had to tell her about college. She braced herself, and she began to speak.

"Mum? The rest of the class and I have to think of a business idea and present it at the beginning of next week." She said as carefree as she could manage.

"Can you tell me after this, darling?" Said Sharron, who was eager to listen and watch Darren Wilson.

"We will be presenting it to parents and to the guest of honor…. Darren Wilson." Amira shut her eyes tight as if she was bracing herself for impact. Sharron's jaw dropped, she looked at Amira and then back at the TV.

"WHAT!?" blurted out Sharron in disbelief.

Amira didn't hear the end of it for the rest of the night and was very glad when it was time to go to bed.

Chapter 31

Why I Left Your Mother

Amira woke up the next morning and got up straight away. She switched her laptop on, and while it was loading, she got dressed. She decided to wear a pleated mini skirt with tights and a slightly long jumper that stopped just below her hips. The sleeves were long enough to fully cover her hands. She brushed through her hair and left it as it was. She saw her laptop was ready, so she picked up her USB stick, saved her PowerPoint presentation, and then placed it into her bag. She looked in the mirror to see what was left to do and decided to put a little eyeliner and mascara on. Happy with her small efforts, she flung open the wardrobe and picked her trusty knee-high black boots. Her attention went to the box placed away in the bottom corner of the wardrobe that held some of her most prized possessions and memories inside. As she put her boots on, she wondered when Thomas and Johnny would turn up. She caught sight of her beautiful ring as she reached for her bag for college and admired it. She looked at how detailed and unique it was. Amira was about to take it off so her mum wouldn't see it and ask questions but then remembered that she had it on when her mum got home, and Sharron didn't notice it all day yesterday, which is unlike her. Amira's mum was usually good at pointing out new things, but maybe that was because she was upset from grandma passing away. Amira put it out of her mind; she was running late for college. She grabbed her coat and ran downstairs. She saw her mum was up with some papers and had the phone in front of her, ready to plan grandma's funeral.

"I'm off to college, mum, and dads picking me up after, at 1 pm, so I should be home by 4, ok?" announced Amira.

"OK, sweetheart. You look nice today." She smiled and looked on proudly, she wasn't used to seeing Amira in a skirt or a dress, but she thought they suited her very well.

"Thanks, mum, so do you." Amira edged close to peck her mum on the cheek.

"I'll have this in case you need me. Bye, love you!" said Amira as she waved her phone so her mum could see it. She speedily walked grabbing her keys and ran out of the door. She gently jogged half of the distance so she could walk for the rest of the way and be on time. She observed all the familiar faces as she got closer to college she noticed that some people were staring at her, but looked away when she looked back 'That's odd' she thought, as people usually didn't notice her. She got inside, climbed the stairs and found her classroom that Mr. Clark had just opened. When she was inside, she saw that Tammy and Rose were there. Rose beckoned Amira to sit in the empty seat next to her. Amira did so and was glad for the invite.

"How was your weekend?" asked Rose.

Amira sat down and fished her USB out of her bag to be ready for when class started.

"Was ok, didn't get up to much. What about you?" said Amira in a confident but casual way.

"Went out again, didn't we, Tammy?" said Rose.

"Yeah, was ok." Said Tammy rather unenthusiastically as she avoided eye contact and carried on staring at her computer screen.

Amira looked to Rose for answers, and she mouthed 'tell you later' back to Amira. She nodded subtly in reply so that Tammy wouldn't notice.

Mr. Clark got the attention of the classroom. "Who's done their presentation then?"

The class moaned but the boy called James shot his hand up, which the class expected and laughed a little.

"Yes I thought you might have James. Anyone else?" said Mr. Clark jokingly.

Amira put her hand up too, without any hesitation. The classroom stared with suspicious faces, but Mr. Clark looked pleasantly surprised by Amira's enthusiastic hand raise.

"Very good! Now the rest of you will use this morning to keep adding to your PowerPoint's and for those who have finished, bring them over, and I will give them a look through and give you feedback about any improvements that can be made."

Amira got up and walked over to Mr. Clark's desk straight away, holding her USB stick in her hand. She noticed James was fumbling about on the computer trying to save his work and download it to his USB stick before Amira could get to Mr. Clarks desk, but it was too late. Amira smiled at the betrayed look that James gave her and held out her USB stick to Mr. Clark.

"I'm excited to see what you've done. Pull up a chair, and we will go through the slides together." said Mr. Clark.

Overall, Mr. Clark was impressed with the business plan Amira had decided to go with and couldn't find much wrong with the PowerPoint at all, so there wasn't much work left for Amira to do. It was finished. Mr. Clark congratulated Amira on her good work but decided to give her some advice.

"Amira, writing a good PowerPoint is half the battle. My advice to you would be that now you have a head start against everyone in this class, you should begin practicing presenting it. This time next week, you could tick all the boxes and not just because you wrote a great PowerPoint, but because you would give a flawless presentation." encouraged Mr. Clark.

Amira felt a warm pride flush over her and she took back her USB that Mr. Clarke had handed back to her. Amira had a big smile on her face; she thanked Mr. Clark and went back to her seat.

The boy James quickly walked towards Mr. Clark's desk and sat in the seat Amira had been sitting in, giving Amira a dirty look. When Amira got back to her seat she saw that Tammy wasn't there anymore and her bag was gone too.

Amira asked Rose out of curiosity, "Where's Tammy gone?"

Rose finished typing a sentence on her computer then turned to Amira to unleash the gossip.

"Well, that's what I wanted to tell you about. We went out at the weekend and that boy she kissed last week is actually a boy I really, really like. Not that I'd ever try anything because, Tammy was there first. But this weekend, he and I just got talking while Tammy went somewhere else in the club, probably chatting up some other guy. Anyway, we just sparked, and we had so much to talk about! It was amazing. Anyway, we ended up leaving the club for some food and ended up kissing, and Tammy happened to find out about it." said Rose.

Amira understood how awkward it all must be for them both, 'Wonder if that guy is Rose's twin flame' Amira thought to herself as she nodded along sympathetically. She felt the ring on her finger that was hidden away under her long sleeves.

Amira looked at Rose's computer screen. "So, how is your PowerPoint coming along?"

"Oh, it will be finished in a few days, I'm sure. Well done you, for getting it done so quickly. What did Mr. Clark say about it?" asked Rose excitedly.

"He said there wasn't much left to do apart from practicing presenting it." Replied Amira modestly.

"That's great. Are you nervous about presenting it? I am, especially in front of Darren Wilson." said Rose as she clenched her teeth nervously.

"I'll be too worried about how my mum will act around him for me to worry about actually presenting" Said Amira as she gave a light-hearted laugh.

"So what is your business plan for? You didn't know last week." asked Rose.

"It's a Dating agency." Replied Amira Proudly.

For the rest of the lesson, Rose worked on finishing her PowerPoint while Amira began to write a speech out for her presentation. She managed to get her speech fully written out by the time the class had finished. Amira put her USB stick, notepad and pen back into her bag, and then she stretched her fingers out that were aching from writing for the last 2 hours. She stretched so much that her long sleeves came up her arms revealing her hands. Rose noticed the ring immediately and Amira had thought she had just seen the ring flash.

"What a gorgeous ring. Where did you get it from?" asked Rose.

Amira looked at the ring and thought about what the note had said about it being a part of the gift she had asked for. The last two days she had worn it Rose was the first to notice it. Amira thought about the flash and decided it must have been the light reflecting on it.

"Thanks, it was a gift; I don't know where it's from." said Amira.

Just then, Amira's phone pinged, so she checked the screen and saw a message from her dad saying:

'Parked outside'

Just then Rose grabbed Amira's phone and put her number into it and said "We should do something sometime! Remember to message me back so I have your number too!" She said as she had finished adding herself into Amira contacts and gave her phone back to her, and went on her way home.

Amira felt touched and had a feeling that she and Rose would become very good friends. She smiled and went downstairs and then outside into the car park to look for her dad's car. She saw the blue roof of a BMW and made her way over to it, her dad was sat in the driver's seat. She gave the passenger side window a little tap to get his attention and waved to say hello.

"Hello, scrunchy!" Said her dad as she got in the car and they kissed each other on the cheek.

"Hi, dad! So where are we going?" asked Amira.

"I thought we would go for some noodles?" said Amira's dad as he quickly wrapped an arm around his little girl for a quick hug.

Amira loved noodles and nodded violently in agreement. Her dad chuckled and started up the engine to his car, and set off.

Amira looked at her dad, it had been a while since she had last seen him, but he looked very well. He was tanned, his hair didn't have greys in it anymore, and instead it was a rich chocolate brown color. He was wearing some trendy jeans, Chelsea boots and a casual top with a warm grey puffer jacket over the top, he looked quite stylish. They drove into town and parked up in the car park closest to the noodle bar and they both got out to walk the rest of the way

"So how're things at college scrunchy?" said Amira's dad as they walked.

"It's ok, we have to write a PowerPoint and present it to Darren Wilson." confessed Amira to her dad, Paul. Paul was much more easy-going and relaxed than Sharron, but he was just as loving and caring.

"Heck. How did they manage that? Bet your mum would like that." He said with a chuckle.

"Yeah, she's tried to 'butt in' and said she wanted to see what I'd be presenting, but I told her it was something I wanted to do on my own." said Amira. She put her hands in her pockets and looked at her dad's facial expression.

"Very impressive young lady. Well, I'm sure it will be great. Do you think your old man can get a seat to his daughter's presentation?" He said as he swung an arm around his daughter's shoulders.

Amira laughed and said, "Sure, I'll pull some strings." They laughed together and carried on walking until they got to the noodle bar.

As Amira opened the door to the noodle bar she immediately smelt the spices, the sauces and the meats they were cooking. The warmth that hit her made her want to take her coat off as soon as possible. She found a table and sat down. Her dad followed her and sat down across from her. They both took their coats off and hung them on the back of their chairs. Amira felt much better but rolled up her sleeves as far as they would go, which helped cool

Amira down instantly and felt much airier. They both picked up a menu to study what delights it contained.

"Wow, what a beautiful ring!" said Paul.

Amira could have sworn that the ring flashed, but only for a fraction of a second, but she thought it was probably just the lighting again.

"It's so detailed. Where did you get it?" asked her dad who was still admiring the ring.

Amira paused for a moment and said, "Got it on eBay last week. So what have you picked for lunch?"

Amira's dad's eyes shot back to the menu and said, "I'll have the seafood noodle stir-fry. What about you?"

"Black bean noodles, please." said Amira without hesitation.

"Shall we get some of these boa buns as well?" asked Paul.

Amira nodded quickly in agreement.

Her dad got up to order their food at the bar, and Amira sat and looked at her ring. 'That's the second time anyone has noticed you since I put you on' she thought as if speaking to the ring. It was a very unusual and very distinct ring, she thought it would have gotten a lot more attention than it had, and by her dad's reaction to it just now she thought that it should have gotten lots and lots of attention, it was after all very distinct and impressive. 'Maybe it is a special ring, after all, it was a gift from the queen of the realm of twin flames' she thought to herself.

Paul had returned to the table with two drinks and set one down for Amira. She took it in her hand and took a large sip through the straw, and then a bigger sip after, she had no idea how thirsty she was until just then, and the cold fizzy coke zero felt so fresh and nice. It cooled her down instantly.

"I'm sorry to hear about Grandma Lena dying Scrunchy. I know you both were close." said Paul as he put his hand on Amira's arm.

Amira smiled at her dad's concern, but she knew better than to be sad about it now. Besides, she was intrigued about the ring that Runa had given to her. Why was it that Rose and her dad had been the only ones to notice it? Amira thought it must mean something, something to do with the twin flames. She decided to do some digging to find out.

"Dad, what made you leave mum?" asked Amira.

Her dads face dropped and shame filled his expression.

Amira quickly added, "I'm not saying it's wrong or anything, dad. I just wanted to know that's all." reassured Amira.

"I felt so terrible about doing that to your mum, truly I did, and I still do." He held his hands up to emphasize his point.

"But when I went to your mum's birthday all those years ago, all her friends were there, there was one I had never met before. But when I saw this mystery friend of your mums, I knew that she was the one. We talked most of the night. I even forgot it was your mum's birthday party." said Paul as he pulled a guilty face.

"Sophie?" Asked Amira to double-check her dad were definitely talking about his current girlfriend.

"Yes, Sophie", Answered her dad.

Amira took another gulp of her coke zero, she had heard her mother talk badly about Sophie and her dad, with much bitterness in the past, about how Sophie was her best friend, and it was a huge betrayal.

"So, as far as you know, Sophie feels the same way about you?" asked Amira.

"It sounds so stupid. But somehow, I know it's exactly the same for Sophie as it is for me and that there is no one else in the world I could ever feel like that with. She's just the one, and I'm the one for her."

Amira listened to what her dad was saying and could see that he had doubts that Amira wouldn't believe a word of it, or think he was making it up, or was delusional. Amira might have done before her little adventure at the weekend 'Maybe he found his twin flame' she thought to herself. It sounded just like how Runa and Toke had described it to her back at the realm. Amira concluded that, that must be the case.

"I believe you dad." said Amira as she put her hand on top of her dad's hands that were clasped together tightly as he anticipated that she wouldn't understand and get mad at him.

Her dad looked up in disbelief for a moment. His eyes teared up slightly, and he felt a huge relief that he hadn't lost someone as important to him as his little girl was. He was used to being shouted at or ignored after he had found Sophie. He had felt so guilty about how the whole thing came about, but he couldn't go against every cell in his body when it came to Sophie, nothing else in life could compare to life without her. He took Amira's hand and gave it a sweet kiss and then the food arrived. The atmosphere eased and became a very happy one. Amira's and her dads' noodles arrived in cute little oriental boxes. Amira opened her box up and began to salivate as she smelled the spices and the black bean sauce. She picked up some chopsticks, pierced them into the noodles to get a big bite and had a mouthful immediately. She closed her eyes so she could appreciate how amazing the noodles tasted. When Amira had finished eating her first bite of food she decided to ask her dad another question.

"How did you end up telling mum about Sophie?" asked Amira curiously.

Her dad was just about to put food in his mouth as Amira asked but put his chopsticks back down in the box to answer.

"It sounds crazy and heartless, but because me and Sophie spent hours talking that night and we had such strong feelings so quickly, I couldn't bear the idea of going home with your mum, on her birthday, to pretend. So …" Said Paul hesitantly.

"You told her that same night? Well, no wonder mum has a grudge. She must have thought you two had been seeing each other for ages before then." said Amira as she thought out loud.

"That was just the thing. People just didn't believe that we had met that night, me and Sophie lost a lot of friends and fell out with a lot of our family too." He said sadly.

Amira felt sad for her dad at that moment. Amira knew what her mum thought of him and Sophie and had heard gossip from her mums other friends. But Amira knew they wouldn't think that way if they knew what Amira knew now.

"Well, you haven't lost me. I'm really happy you found the one, dad." said Amira.

Her dad's heart filled with warmth and gratitude for his little girl at that moment. They both continued to eat their noodles and Boa buns and talked about life until they had eaten everything they had ordered, and their bellies were full.

Chapter 32

Life after Death

Later in the week, Amira and her mum attended grandma Lena's funeral. The cremation ceremony was itself very sad, and Amira began crying whenever she saw the sadness on her mums face build up, but it was the get-together afterwards that was so lovely. So many people came up to Amira and her mum and told such lovely stories about their grandma. It made Amira realize she would probably never see her grandma again for the version she knew and loved so much.

A few days after the funeral Amira and her mum had continued to move on with their lives, and things started to go back to normal. Her mum started working again, and Amira was working on her speech-giving skills for her PowerPoint presentation that would be due at the beginning of next week. She paced in the room, keeping her voice down as she didn't want her mum to hear her, as Sharron was downstairs doing her own work.

When she turned to pace the other way, ZAP. She jumped back and put a hand over her mouth so she wouldn't scream. Two beautiful men with rather familiar faces had appeared out of nowhere and were there and staring at Amira with kind smiles.

"Thomas? Johnny?" said Amira in disbelief.

"That's right, darling. We're finally here." As Johnny said this, Amira put a finger up to her mouth, then pointed downstairs and said in a quieter tone "My mum is downstairs."

They both shuffled past Amira and sat on the bed. Amira sat on her desk chair that was directly opposite so she could give them her undivided attention.

"We're here to give you the rest of your gift." said Johnny.

"To tell you the secrets of finding a twin flame and what prevents it from happening." said Thomas.

Amira moved her chair closer and listened as intensely as she could.

"We will touch on the most obvious things and then answer any questions you have. OK?" asked Thomas.

Amira nodded with a focused look on her face.

"Now, appearance, people who alter their appearance risk altering their perception of their true selves. Sometimes altering an appearance can help improve perception of a person's true self, but that is very rare." said Johnny.

"Makeup is a big one. These past few decades' especially, people prefer how they look with makeup on, but that's not them. If this is the case, then they have a bad relationship with their true looks, and this is what creates a barrier." said Thomas.

"Yes, there is actually a correct way to wear makeup." added Johnny quickly.

"There is, How?" asked Amira.

"It's very simple. To work with your features and not against them, to not add anything that isn't there." replied Johnny.

"Basically, it's so you still look like you, simple as that." said Thomas.

"I have a question about that." said Amira in an alerted whisper.

"Yes, go on." said Thomas smiling.

"My mum wears a lot of makeup. Is she doing it right?" asked Amira.

"Well, from the photos we saw of her in her bedroom, we would say no. She's putting too much on, and she's trying to look like other women, big lips, massive eyes lashes, thinner face. We've done some research on her, actually." said Johnny.

"Her twin flame is alive and is 5 years younger than her. He lives just in Newcastle. Can you believe it?" added Thomas.

"Newcastle? She's going away there this week for two days! So if she sorts her makeup out and has a better relationship with herself, she could meet him?" summed up Amira.

"It would definitely improve her chances, but we don't know much about him yet." admitted Johnny.

Amira made sure to store that in her mental filing cabinet for later.

"So what else gets in the way?" asked Amira to help Johnny and Thomas get her back on track.

"People have ideas about what they want from an ideal mate and it is common that they don't match who their twin flame is at all. These ideas can come from being around a group of people that just want looks or money. These people can be in denial about having a real connection with someone, thus prevents them from seeing their twin flames even if they were right before their very eyes." said Thomas.

"Also, many people's previous experiences, that they form their opinions from, can massively get in the way. Humans find it difficult to be open-minded as they get older, or if they've had a lot of bad experiences." said Johnny.

This made a lot of sense to Amira, in fact it reminded her of a conversation she had had with Rose at college.

"So ego, pride and prejudice get in the way a lot" Said Amira.

"Yes, essentially." said Thomas as he rubbed his stubble.

"So we see that your business plan is for a dating agency." Said Johnny very out of the blue, so out of the blue that Amira didn't know what to say for a moment, it seemed so off-topic.

"Yes, that's right." said Amira suspiciously.

"Well, we made the proposal to you before the ceremony. Are you still game?" said Johnny.

"Is this the thing you were talking about with me, then when Runa and Toke were throwing you looks?" asked Amira.

"Yes. So we want to form an alliance with you." said Johnny.

"We would give you some twin flames to match up, and this will help your business flourish, and we keep the numbers up, and the balance of the world upheld." said Thomas.

"Oh, that ring Queen Runa gave to you can come in very handy." said Johnny as he pointed to Amira's hand.

'Finally!' Amira thought. She's been wondering about it since she had gotten it.

"This helps you distinguish people and where they are concerning finding their twin flames." explained Johnny.

"I have worn this since I was given it, and only Rose and my dad had noticed it for the entire time I have had it on. What does that mean?" asked Amira.

"That means they are in the perfect state to find their twin flame." Said Thomas

"What about if dad has already found his twin flame?" said Amira.

"It would act in the same way but only with a very subtle flash within the gemstone. Did you see a small flash from the ring when they had noticed it?" asked Thomas.

"I thought it was just the lighting, but yes, I think it did flash." said Amira.

"You could be surrounded by twin flames!" said Thomas excitedly and in disbelief.

"Must be a sign, two matchup's already." added Johnny happily.

"I think we are in for a prosperous century, don't you, Johnny?" said Thomas as he looked at Johnny.

"I think so, Thomas!"

They laughed together. Johnny and Thomas told Amira the rest of the secrets about finding a twin flame in the perfect state. She discovered that not only would the ring appear very obvious, to people in the correct state, and flash if they have already found their twin flame, but when others attention is brought to the ring, the gem in the middle would appear as a different colour concerning what state that person was in. 'Just like a mood ring' Amira thought. After about an hour of learning, Amira snuck downstairs to get herself, Thomas and Johnny a drink. Luckily her mum had fallen asleep on the sofa, so she grabbed herself a can of coke from the fridge and poured two glasses of wine for Thomas and Johnny. She tucked the can of coke under her arm and grabbed the glasses of wine, and went upstairs as quietly as she could. The can of coke was very cold under her arm.

She talked for another hour or two with Thomas and Johnny and kept their voices down so that her mum wouldn't hear them. They talked about twin flames, the dos and don'ts, methods, and how to use the pretty mystical ring. Amira was confident about using her ring a bit more now and felt that she would be able to discover a lot about people without having to ask Johnny's and Thomas's help all the time. But she was their ally after all, and they assured her they would stop by for a meeting every month with updates, a list of names, and a general catch-up, which Amira liked the sound of very much. Although this was technically work, she loved Thomas and Johnny's company. They were such good fun. Thomas and Johnny finished their glass of wine, stood up and placed their empty glasses on the desk.

"Now, when you're setting all of this up and if you have any difficulty, technical or financial, we might be able to help you, so be sure you ask." added Johnny as he brushed a strand of hair behind Amira's ear with his glove hand.

This gave Amira a lot of comfort to know, it was always nice to have a plan B, but she would only see them once a month for an unannounced meeting 'what if I need help when they're not around?' she thought.

"What do I do if I'm stuck or need help or have a question and you're not here?" asked Amira.

"Ah well, we already thought of that. You need to get yourself a set of angel cards. Not tarot cards, Angel cards." replied Thomas.

"Why? What do angel cards do?"

"They're good for getting answers, comfort or clarity. They're basically a form of communication between you and your guardian angel."

"They're terribly respectful of privacy, so if you want help or answers, you have to invite them by asking them." added Johnny.

"Can't you guys just tell them for me?" asked Amira.

"We can't see them or hear them. We only know they exist because of our deaths from our past lives. Your guardian angel is exclusive to you." said Thomas.

"But if you guys have nothing to do with twin flames, then what are they?" asked Amira.

"We can never be a sure what happens to US when we die, just like humans on earth they don't know what happens when they die, until they die. But when we die as twin flames, we die together, at the same time, as one. So we think that we are either an explosion of new souls or we bind together and become a single guardian angel." replied Johnny.

"So guardian angels are twin flames that have merged as one being of some kind?" Said Amira hoping it would help to make sense of Johnny's answer.

"It is one of many possibilities," Said Thomas.

"Do I ever get to meet my angel?" Asked Amira, who was very frustrated that she had gone all this time not knowing something that seemed very important was around her all the time. All those times she cried and felt alone or angry, she had her personal guardian angel by her side the whole time. Didn't seem believable to Amira, but then it seemed that they wanted to remain an unknown secret from what she had found out from Johnny and Thomas just now.

"Every time you die, you have a huge catch-up and reflect on your experiences. They are with you until you find your twin flame and die. They're technically your oldest and dearest friend who knows everything about you." said Thomas.

Thomas and Johnny told Amira that they had to leave, so Amira gave them both a big hug and closed her eyes at the bright light that emerged and took them both away, ZAP. She sat down at her desk, opened her laptop and began searching for angel cards until she found a pack that she liked. She added them to her basket and fiddled around with her bank card to pay for them online. She went downstairs and saw her mum was sat upright and back on her laptop typing. Amira sat next to her and saw she was editing a new video she had made about some new makeup products. She thought about everything that Thomas and Johnny had told her and decided it might be good to put some of it to the test.

"Haven't you noticed my new ring?" said Amira, who flashed her hand to her mum.

Sharron tore her face from her laptop to Amira's hand to look at the ring.

"Oh, very nice is it supposed to be a pearl?" said Sharron dismissively as she continued to focus on her laptop.

Amira looked at the clear, see-through gem in the middle 'Pearls aren't see-through,' thought Amira.

"It was advertised as clear on eBay, you know." Replied Amira carefully.

Her mum looked at the ring on Amira's hand again, only a bit longer this time.

"You should get your money back. It's not clear at all; it's all dull and cloudy looking." Replied Sharron as she clicked and scrolled on her laptop. Amira thought to herself for a moment and tried to see if she could remember what Thomas and Johnny had said about the colors to see if she could figure out what that meant. 'If clear was the optimum, then cloudy could surely not be too far from being clear' she thought to herself

Amira looked at her mum and the make-up that covered her face from the video Sharron had made advertising the products for her social media. Amira thought perhaps all of that make-up and how she sees herself and what Sharron believes is acceptable is most likely the main reason why the stone isn't clear to her yet. That made it very simple for Amira if that was the case. All she had to do was to make her mum see it differently. The hard part would be thinking of the best way to phrase it to her mum without offending her. Amira decided to give it a go.

"Do you think makeup gets in the way of women finding the right man?" Amira said as passively as she could manage.

Her mum closed her laptop screen and turned her body to face Amira.

"What do you mean?" asked Sharron.

Amira felt a little scared that she might have offended her mum already.

"I read somewhere that men are more attracted to a woman's natural face, instead of applying makeup to hide their features its more effective to work with those features. Men apparently respond to it better." said Amira, keeping her tone playful and off-hand.

"What's the point of wearing make-up if you're not hiding your worst features?" said Sharron in a sassy manner.

"That's just in your head mum, you don't have any worst features, and you're just masking your true and very authentic beauty." Replied Amira as she fluttered are eyelashes sweetly.

Amira's mum appeared to be in thought but impressed nonetheless, that gave Amira great relief, as she was scared her mum would have made it into an argument. Amira didn't have the energy for an argument; she had been working the whole day on her PowerPoint and then had that visit from Thomas and Johnny.

"You know, a few people are coming out saying similar things, you might be onto something, you know." Said Sharron smugly as if she had taken credit for what Amira had just said. But as long as it worked, Amira was happy. Amira didn't say anything else; she didn't want to press her mum to change there and then. It was completely up to her mum at the end of the day if she wanted to make changes or not. They chatted for a bit and watched something on the TV before Amira said night to her mum and then went upstairs to get ready for bed. Amira went into the bathroom, brushed her teeth, brushed her hair, got into bed, and turned her light off. As she lay there she hoped her mum would change enough by the time she went on her work trip to Newcastle, then she might meet her twin flame. Amira shut her eyes and thought about her future business, her mum, Thomas and Johnny and grandma Runa. She went to sleep and dreamed about happy possibilities.

Chapter 33

Practice Makes Perfect

A few days had passed and it was the last lesson before the big PowerPoint presentation which would be on the following Monday afternoon. As Amira followed everyone into the classroom she felt very confident about her PowerPoint. She had been practicing for the last few days and couldn't find any fault with her performance anymore. She looked around the room as she sat down next to Rose and saw a few nervous faces that looked like they still had a lot of work left to do.

She turned to Rose and asked, "Have you finished your PowerPoint?"

Rose turned back to her to reply, "Yes! I finished it the other day, and I've gone over it a few times. I'm pretty pleased with it. How do you feel about tomorrow?"

Amira tilted her head to the side and said, "Pretty good actually. I've done everything I can for it, I think."

Mr. Clark stood up at the front of the class and looked around the room, and in his usual excited and happy manner, he asked the class how they all felt about Monday. Half of the class cheered and the other half grumbled with little enthusiasm.

Mr. .Clark continued, "Well, I have some exciting news about the presentation day. Darren Wilson will pick his favorite business plan and offer them a partnership, he will help get the business started and even invest some money towards it."

The class replied with "Ooo's" and gasps of delight and surprise.

Suddenly everyone turned to the computers and began clicking, scrolling and typing very quickly.

Mr. Clark kindly added, "If any of you want feedback or help, this is the last day to do so, and I'll be here until 5'Oclock."

Two students got up immediately and went over to Mr. Clark's desk for his help, the first one there was the boy called James that Amira beat to the desk last time; he shot Amira a daggered look as he was the first one there but looked defeated when he saw that Amira was sat relaxed in her chair. Amira felt there was nothing more she could do. She looked to Tammy who was sat next to Rose and thought she would ask her how her presentation was going.

"Have you nearly finished yours yet, Tammy?" asked Amira.

Tammy was slightly stressed by the question but replied, "I don't have much left. I will be able to finish it today, though."

Amira could see that Tammy was in a rush to finish her work, so she decided not to ask her anything else. Instead, she asked Rose something.

"Do you want to see if there's a spare classroom and we can practice our PowerPoint's on each other?" asked Amira.

Rose was all for it, they both wanted to ask Tammy, but she shooed them away so she could finish her work in peace. Amira and Rose managed to find a room that was only a few doors down the corridor, and they began practicing their presentations. Amira went first, and her PowerPoint was within the 10-minute limit. Rose gave an encouraging clap when Amira had finished and said how impressed she was and that she couldn't think of any way to improve it. Amira was flattered and felt very pleased with herself. Rose presented hers to Amira, and she stumbled over some of her words and had a few long pauses, but Amira thought the content and the things Rose had to say were very good. Rose was grateful for Amira's feedback and said she would practice a few times tonight and over the weekend before the big day. Now that they had finished their PowerPoint's, and had given them a practice, Amira and Rose decided to chill out for a few minutes before returning to the classroom.

"So what happened with you and that boy Tammy was mad at you about?" Asked Amira who was eager to get to the bottom of why Rose had noticed the ring just like her dad had all those days ago.

"Oh, well, Tammy is on to another guy now and has sort of given me her blessing." said Rose.

"So, have you seen the guy since? What's his name?" asked Amira.

Rose's expression had a dreamy smile, and she replied "Josh. He's called Josh, and we've been talking all week. We met up on our own the other day, after I had finished my PowerPoint and gone over it a few times, and we kissed. It was amazing, and we talked none stop. I can't wait to see him again." Said Rose excitedly as she placed her hands on top of her heart, almost like she was making sure it wouldn't leap out of her chest.

Amira saw the look on Rose's face, and it reminded her of how her father looked when he was talking about his girlfriend, Sophie.

"Think he's the one?" asked Amira.

Roses face had some doubt in it as she looked to Amira. Amira could see that maybe it would be her response that would put Rose off answering her, so she decided to add something else.

"I think you have found the one." said Amira.

Rose beamed a smile instantly and agreed with overwhelming romantic excitement, it made Amira smile to see how happy Rose was. Amira thought that from all the information she'd found out, it must mean that this boy Josh must be Ross's twin flame. Not only that, but she could sense it by how Rose had looked when she talked about Josh, and she could sense it when her dad talked about Sophie. They went back to the classroom and looked through their work until it was the end of the lesson. Many of the students stayed to finish or improve their work, eager to win the partnership with Darren Wilson. Amira couldn't care less about the prize as she already had two very handsome and almost angelic partners. Amira got home and found her mum in a very chipper mood. Amira's mum had gone to Newcastle for a few days and had just come home. Amira closed the door behind her as she came into the house and walked towards her mum cooking in the kitchen. Amira stopped dead in her tracks when she saw her mums face.

"Do you like my new look?" asked Sharron.

Amira had never seen her mum this way before, her lips were a neutral color, and she had subtle eye shadow and eyeliner with very little mascara. She looked so natural and elegantly pretty. She just looked like herself. All the features that Amira had never seen or noticed before were now out in the open. It had hugely enhanced how pretty her mum actually was.

"Mum, you look gorgeous. What happened?" said Amira in bewilderment.

Her mum blushed and relished in the compliment "Well, I decided to take your advice! So on my first day in Newcastle, I decided to try out a new look. I got so many compliments about it and social media loves the new look! The business has boomed for the products too. So that will be a big commission for me!" Her mum said excitedly, just like a kid at Christmas.

Amira was very surprised by such a quick result; she knew that Thomas and Johnny said that her mum's twin flame was in Newcastle so she decided to test her ring again. She lifted her hand up and tucked her hair behind her ear so her mum could see the ring. But her mum didn't notice it despite looking directly at the ring on her hand;

there was no flash from it at all. Instead, Amira's mum carried on talking about all of the success she had received on her social media platforms and the commissions she had made from showing off her new look. Amira knew then that her mum had not met her twin flame yet. Amira was at least glad that her mum had listened to her advice for once though, and she did look great. Her mum gave her a hug and had cooked Amira a bowl of spaghetti bolognese with meatballs and cheese on top. It smelt good. Amira plunged her fork and twirled up some spaghetti with half a meat ball on the end. Amira stared at the sauce covered meat ball and spaghetti before putting the whole thing in her mouth in one go. She sunk her teeth into the meatball and could taste the garlic in the tomato sauce. Amira finished eating her mouthful and began to twirl some more on the end of her fork. She thought now was as good as any to tell her mum about the news that Mr. Clark had given the class today.

"By the way, Darren Wilson will apparently offer a partnership and some money for his favorite business plan." said Amira quickly.

Amira didn't want to make eye contact with her mum as she said this. She had another fork full of food ready for when she had finished speaking and shoved it into her mouth as quickly as possible.

"You mean.., you're in with a chance to be business partners with Darren Wilson? Thee Darren Wilson?!" exclaimed Sharron, who was energetically enthusiastic about the whole thing.

Amira made sure to make this bite of food last as long as possible. She looked up to see her mother's jaw dropped expression and nodded while still chewing her food.

Amira swallowed her food and calmly said, "Mum the presentations are on Monday. I'm well prepared for it. All I'm worried about now is you having a giddy-fan-girl meltdown in front of Darren Wilson and embarrassing me." She grabbed her drink and took a sip of it to allow her mum to process what she had just said.

Sharron calmed herself down and thought about her daughter and her having to deliver her PowerPoint presentation in front of major celebrities, and realized it must feel like a lot of pressure to do well, even though Amira was acting like it was no big deal all.

"I promise I shall be calm and respectful. You're just much calmer than I would be in your position. I can't help but fret and get excited, sweetheart." Replied Sharron thoughtfully.

"I know you mean well mum, but everything is done, finished and sorted. Nothing else can be done. All I need now is to chill out before I have to actually present my business plan." replied Amira.

Sharron smiled at how grown-up, independent and organized her little girl was becoming and looked proudly at Amira. They both continued to eat up the rest of their spaghetti and meatballs. When they had finished and put away their dishes in the dishwasher, they both sat down to watch a game show together.

"Aren't you even going to tell me what your business plan is?" asked Sharron impatiently.

Amira sighed, she wasn't surprised by this request, in fact she was expecting it, she was surprised how long it had taken for her to ask, a whole 5 minutes at least.

"You'll find out what it is on Monday." Said Amira and she gave a sassy look to her mum and they both continued to watch the game show and went to bed shortly after.

Amira brushed her teeth, brushed her hair and sat in her bed. She turned to see what time it was, it was only 9pm. She looked at the beautiful detailed ring on her finger and decided she wanted make sure she would remember everything that Thomas and Johnny had told her about it, and about the barriers that blocked people from seeing their twin flames. She jumped out of bed again and opened her bottom desk draw and rummaged around. She pulled out a journal she had gotten a few Christmas's ago that she hadn't justified using yet, 'Perfect', she thought. She took a pen off her desk and jumped back into bed pulling the sheets up and placing the journal on top of her lap. She began jotting down everything she could remember about what Johnny and Thomas had taught her. By the time she had finished a third of her journal was now covered in writings, scribbles and notes. She looked at the clock and to her surprise it was 11pm so she put her journal in the draw next to her bed, switched the light off, and curled up to go to sleep. Her mind filled with excited thoughts about the presentation in a few days' time and when she could see Thomas and Johnny again. But most of all she couldn't wait to begin her very own successful business and to be able to use the ring to its full potential to unite as many twin flames as she could.

Chapter 34

The Day of the Big Presentation

The weekend had passed and now it was Monday, the big day. Amira had been up since 8 am, running through her PowerPoint once more and taking her time to indulge in a hearty full English breakfast that her mum had made for them both. Amira enjoyed all of her full English breakfast and sat very satisfied chatting to her mum for a while. When it got to 9:30 am Amira and her mum went to their rooms to get ready. When they got to the top of the stairs, Sharron asked Amira to wait for a second; she had something for her and went into her room to get it. Amira waited patiently for a few moments and saw her mum come out with a pretty dusty pink long blazer with gold military buttons down the front.

"Saw this the other day and thought you might like it for the presentation today. If not, I can always return it tomorrow." said Sharron.

Amira looked at it and thought it was very pretty and smart. She didn't have any idea what she would wear to do the PowerPoint, but it made perfect sense to dress smart as Darren Wilson was going to be there. Amira was glad that her mum had thought of this. Amira had been so wrapped up in finishing and perfecting the presentation that she had completely overlooked that there was probably a dress code.

"Thanks mum its perfect." beamed Amira.

Amira took the pretty pink blazer, gave her mum a kiss on the cheek, and turned to go into her bedroom to get ready. She laid the blazer on her bed and went over to her wardrobe to pick out the rest of the outfit. She found some three-quarter length smart black trousers, a casual navy T-shirt and put it next to the rest of the outfit on the bed. She was very happy with how the outfit looked. She turned and sat down at her dressing table to put a little bit of makeup on her eyes, found a light pink lipstick that would go nicely with the pink blazer her mum had given to her. She curled the ends of her hair and put it into a midway ponytail; she pulled and adjusted it to give her some volume; it looked very 60's. She put on her outfit that she had laid out on the bed and went over to the mirror to see how she looked. She looked sophisticated, classy, but girly and pretty. She was glad her mum had bought her the blazer; she didn't even own one until now. She looked at her bare feet in the mirror and stood up on to her tiptoes. She went over to her wardrobe to look for a pair of black shoes. She pulled out a pair she had worn once before to her grandma's funeral. They were black and shiny with a pointed toe and a small block heel. She put them on and looked in the mirror 'That's it' thought Amira smiling at herself in the mirror. She grabbed her tote bag, put her USB stick and notes inside it, and went back downstairs to wait for her mum. To Amira's surprise her mum was already downstairs and sitting on the sofa waiting. Sharron looked up and saw her very grown-up daughter coming down the stairs and could see the confidence radiating from her. Sharron relished how good her taste was in clothing as she admired how well the pink blazer looked on Amira.

"You look perfect. You'll be the most fashionable one there!" praised Sharron.

Amira beamed at her mum but asked, "How is it you're ready before me this time?"

Her mum laughed. "I have no idea. I think it's the new look, it just doesn't take so long to get ready now. That and I'm not going back and changing everything over and over again anymore. Honestly, it's such a time saver." said Sharron with a cheeky smile.

They shared a laugh, and then they looked at the time; it was 10:30.

"Perfect timing, let's get going." said Sharron.

The college was packed.

"Word must have gotten out about Darren Wilson coming." remarked Amira.

They eventually found a parking space and walked over to the college presentation room. It was already pretty full. Amira saw her dad across the room who had already found some seats. He looked up and saw Amira and Sharron, so he beckoned them both over.

"Hello, Amira, you look so grown up! Hi Sharron, I saved you a seat." said Paul hesitantly.

Amira looked at her mum, half expecting to see a bad look on her face, but she was surprised to see Sharron kindly smiling back at him.

"Thanks that's really considerate." replied Sharron.

Amira relaxed a little and saw that her dad was happy and smiling as well. A loud clap and a cough got everybody's attention; they turned to look at the front of the room where the noises were coming from. The college manager Mrs. Hill stood at the front trying to get everyone's attention.

"Take your seats! Students, who are presenting today, please come down to the front!" She said.

Amira looked at her mum and dad and told them it was time for her to go. They both wished her good luck and gave her a hug and a kiss on the cheek. She found Rose and Tammy when she reached the front of the room. Tammy was wearing a plain shirt with black trousers and a pair of very high heeled shoes. Rose wore a pretty but classy blue wrap dress and some heeled boots.

"You guys look nice. Are you both ready?" asked Amira to both Tammy and Rose.

"Urgh, I wish we had been given more time." said Tammy.

"I'm ready, but I think I should have practiced a bit more. What about you?" replied Rose.

"I did everything I could. I'm actually quite excited." said Amira as she rubbed her hands together.

Mr. Clark walked past all of the students and lined them up facing the audience at the front of the room.

Amira, Rose and Tammy were in the middle. Mr. Clark went up to the microphone and announced Darren Wilson into the room

As Darren Wilson came into the room everyone cheered and clapped. He wore a grey and silver matching three-piece suit, waved confidently to the crowd, and then turned to the students. When Darren Wilson had finished greeting all of the students he turned to the audience that was full of friends and family of the students. He worked his way down the line shaking all their hands and saying things such as; 'hello it's great to meet you' and 'can't wait to see your presentations'. The most excited boy there was obviously James who had given evils to Amira for completing the PowerPoint first in the class. He was blushing and shaking with excitement, when Darren Wilson had finally reached and had shaken his hand, he was officially start struck.

"Now, I am sure some of you have heard, but I shall announce it to you all now anyway. Whoever has the idea I like the most will be offered a partnership with me, and will be given a start-up fund to kick start their business. They will also have daily one to one time with me to help them run their business." announced Darren.

The audience gasped and applauded. Darren Wilson then raised his hand to quiet the audience. Amira could see her dads mouth gaped open, she'd forgotten that she hadn't told him that, her mum who was sat next to him clapped frantically and crossed her fingers.

Darren asked the students to take their seats in the front row and proceed with the first presentation. Darren seated himself at a lone table right at the front, with a notepad and pen and the entire printed out PowerPoint presentations in front of him, with the student photo stapled onto the top corner. There would be 15 presentations in total; Amira was assigned to the 10th presentation. The first few students that went up gave pretty standard presentations; they read carefully and sounded rather toneless as they read off the screen that their PowerPoint's were on. One of the business presentations was for a café; another was for a delivery platform for sweets and drinks and another for a night club that sold alcoholic ice-creams.

It was soon Tammy's turn to present after 45 minutes had gone by from the other students. Tammy's business plan was for small cosmetic treatments that were very mainstream at the moment. They involved hair removal, fillers, Botox and lipo. Another few went up after Tammy, who were a little quieter, but they were gently prompted by Mr. Clark, who was tucked in the corner of the room. It came to Rose, who gave a great presentation. She was the most confident by far and explained her business idea that included therapy and psychology programs for many day to day things that perhaps shouldn't be normalized, and how her service providing business will be of value to a wide range of people. It put her friends Tammy's presentation in a bad light as cosmetic treatments were given as examples of why people don't live up to be their best selves. Not that Tammy cared; she had been busy picking at her nail varnish as soon as she had finished giving her own presentation. Amira wasn't sure how people in the audience, or how Darren Wilson, viewed Roses presentation, but it all made perfect sense to Amira. The more she thought about the things Rose was saying, the more it sounded very similar to the information that Thomas and Johnny had given to her about barriers to finding a twin flame. Things such as people never being able to see themselves clearly and keep burying themselves in things they think will help them or make them feel better. 'I wonder if Rose and I could end up working together somehow' Amira thought to herself. Then, it was Amira's turn to present. She got up and swept her curly ponytail off her shoulders, she walked to the front of the room to face the audience. The room looked much fuller from the front of the stage than it had before. Amira stared for a moment, but then her mind went to how well she knew this presentation. She smiled and began. She had an out of body experience; it was like she was back in her bedroom oozing with confidence, and the words came out with charisma and passion. Amira paced around the space and used hand gestures as she talked. She found herself improvising and ended up asking the audience a few questions, to which they all responded by raising their hands. Amira even made a witty joke, and everyone laughed, even Darren Wilson. When she had finished, she got a healthy round of applause, and her heart began to race frantically with elation. She smiled and sat back down next to Rose

"That was amazing." whispered Rose.

"I can't believe how well it went." whispered Amira.

. This time last week Amira would never have been able to do what she just did, she could barely find the nerve to answer questions in the classroom before. Her belly filled with warm pride for her small accomplishment.

Then finally all the presentations were finished, and all the students in the front row breathed a sigh of relief that it was all over. Darren Wilson and Mr. Clark went to the front of the podium and announced that it was time for an intermission.

"If you would please leave the room and get yourself some refreshments, there is a buffet and drinks down the hall." said Mr. Clark.

Darren Wilson continued on after Mr. Clark, "I will be staying in here with Mr. Clark, we will both be going over all the notes I've made about your PowerPoint's. When you come back here in one hours' time, we will announce the winner." said Darren Wilson.

Everyone gave a brief clap and began to make their way to the exits. Amira went to find her mum and dad, they were already in the hallway outside, waiting eagerly.

"What did you think?" Amira asked as she ran into her mum's outstretched arms, and then to her dads.

"You were so amazing. You were the best one there!" said her dad, as he made awkward eye contact with one of the other parents by accident.

"Out of all the things I pictured you picking for your business plan, the last thing I thought you would pick is a dating agency." exclaimed her mum.

"Does that mean you liked it?" asked Amira with a quizzical face.

"I loved it, but I'm just not so sure it's Darren Wilsons sort of thing." said Sharron honestly.

"I'm not bothered if he wants to invest in it or not. I think I'll just go ahead with it anyway." said Amira confidently.

Amira linked arms with her mum and dad and they began walking to where the food and drinks were. They went in and found a table to sit at while each went up in turn to get some food. Her dad got a pork pie with a few sandwiches with a coffee. Her mum came back with pasta salad, a boiled egg and a single mini sausage roll with a cup of tea. Amira got up and wondered around to see what there was, it was a great little buffet. Amira grabbed a couple of mini sausage rolls, a sandwich and a small serving of the pasta salad. When she was pouring herself a glass of juice she noticed there were a few cakes as well. She got another plate and put a flapjack, a chocolate nest and a slice of lemon cake on it and stacked it on top of her own plate so she could carry them back to the table.

"I brought you both a cake." said Amira as she sat it down on the table.

"I didn't see them." exclaimed her dad who was delighted by the site of the cakes.

"Yes, that's what I thought." said Amira jokingly.

They sat and enjoyed their food. Amira was so happy with how well her mum and dad were getting along, just like old friends. Her dad complemented Sharron's new look, and she remarked how much leaner he looked. Amira clocked Mr. Clark whizzing around the room, getting plenty of food, and grabbing one of the jugs of juice from the table. As he was quickly leaving the room, he spotted Amira and quickly tiptoed towards her and her parents.

"You were amazing, Amira, the best presentation by far. If you don't win the prize, don't be discouraged, it is the personal preference of Darren after all. But I'm sure something good will still come of it, though." He was grinning and his face was pink with excitement, and he winked to her parents before he left.

"What a great guy." said Paul as he put the last piece of pork pie into his mouth.

"So sweet of him to say, I wonder what he meant though." said Sharron.

Amira was on her last sausage roll and her mum and dad had started on their cakes. Her dad picked the flapjack and her mum had gone for the lemon cake. Amira was happy, she loved chocolate nests.

"So mum, because you know Darren so well …" Said Amira sarcastically. "Who do you think he will pick to be a partner?"

Her mum's brow creased in thought as she finished her slice of lemon cake.

"I think it would be that boy who wanted to deal in luxury cars … what was his name?" said Sharron.

"James?" answered Amira.

"That's it. That sort of thing is right up Darren Wilson's street." stated Sharron.

"Well, if that's the case, there isn't another person in the college who would be as happy as James would be to get that partnership, I thought he was going to launch off like a rocket when Darren shook his hand." said Amira.

Amira began picking off the chocolate cornflakes into bite sized chunks, her dad looked at the time and decided there was enough time to have another flapjack, and he was kind enough to bring back her mum a small cup of coffee too. When they had finished eating it was time to go back into the presentation room to find out who the winner was.

Chapter 35

And The Prize Goes To …

Everyone was back inside the presentation room now. Mr. Clark and Darren Wilson had each popped their very last mini sausage roll into their mouth. Mr. Clark quickly scooped up the empty plates and glasses and stepped out of the room to put them away. Darren Wilson was shuffling through his notes and adding a few things to them with his pen. Amira was back sitting at the front of the room with the rest of the students. She looked around the room and saw that everyone was gossiping, talking about who they thought would win. She looked over to where her mum and dad were sat, and they were in deep conversation; it worried Amira for a moment, but then she saw that they were sharing kind gestures and friendly expressions between themselves, which settled her worries of them having a fallout. 'Whatever they're talking about, at least it's about something good,' she thought to herself. It was a nice change. Her mum always used to be so bitter towards her father, but who could blame her, as far as Sharron was concerned, he cheated on her with her best friend and left her on her birthday. Not that it mattered anymore, in fact, it seemed as though all of that was well behind both of them now, looking at how well they were getting along together. Mr. Clark was back in the room; he cleared his throat, stood at the front of the room and got everyone's attention.

"Thank you for coming back. I hope you all enjoyed the refreshments. Now for the moment you have all been waiting for." said Mr. Clark as he stepped back to allow Darren Wilson to continue on with the speech. Darren took a step forward.

"I have been very impressed by all of the presentations here today, but sadly, there is only who I will offer my partnership with today along with a start-up investment." said Darren who left a long pause for effect.

Everyone was silent in anticipation; a few of the students were all leaning forwards in their seats except Amira, who was comfortably leaning back into her chair.

She was happy with her work and effort she had put in, she already had two business partners lined up after all; Thomas and Johnny. She looked down the line of seats to her left at James, who her mum had said might win. He had his face in his hands with his eyes peeking out; his right leg was bouncing up and down.

Darren took a breath in and said "James Owen."

James took his hands away from his face instantly and looked up to Darren Wilson in shock. The crowd applauded, and then all of a sudden, James jumped up and threw his hands in the air shouting, "Yes, yes, yes!" The applause began to quickly die down after that. James strutted up to Darren Wilson and they shook hands. Darren

Wilson handed him a small glass trophy and a piece of paper. They posed for some of the photographers who were there from a few newspapers who had been tipped off about the visit, they had moved up to the front to take their pictures. James had an incredibly broad grin on his face. Darren Wilson gestured him to sit back down. James hesitated and looked at Darren to make sure he understood him correctly. He was surprised to be sat down again so quickly, surely it was all over now and there was nothing else to say. Darren Wilson went back to the podium and looked at his notes again. It looked like he was getting ready to make another announcement.

Rose leaned in to whisper to Amira "Wonder what this is about, I thought it was over now."

Amira looked back at her, made a face and shrugged her shoulders, as if to say 'neither do I', they both looked towards Darren for more information.

"Now, Mr. Clark and I both agreed that one more prize should be awarded today." announced Darren.

The room filled with hushed tones and whispers, all the students suddenly perked up from their slouched positions. Amira was very curious too.

"In recognition of this person's flawless presentation, who was well prepared, well-rehearsed and captured all of our attention. I have decided to award £1000" Said Darren.

The room went silent and most of the students lent forward, they were almost off their seats.

"To Amira Hardy!" shouted Darren Wilson smiling and gesturing to Amira.

Amira's jaw dropped, and she sat upright. The crowd applauded, Amira could hear the cheers from her parents in the crowd. Rose nudged Amira, making her stand up, and she began to walk towards Darren Wilson and shook his extended hand. Darren seemed delighted by how shocked and grateful she was. The noise of the crowd filled the room, and Amira was just beginning to realize that she had won £1000 from Darren Wilson. She began to smile and laugh with joy, she didn't expect anything to come of this, yet she had just won £1000 out of nowhere.

Darren took her by the shoulders and spoke in her ear, "One of the best presentations I have ever seen! Something tells me you'll do just fine on your own. But you deserve this. Well done!"

Amira thanked him and shook his hand again, the crowd was still applauding. Darren gave Amira a check for £1000, and the photographers came up to take more photos. Amira looked to the audience and saw the boy James sulking with his arms crossed. She looked further up to find her parents who were jumping up and down and cheering. Somehow things worked out better than Amira could have ever expected.

When all the fuss had died down and all the students had reunited with their friends and family they started to leave. Amira was back with her parents again.

"Why don't we all go to dinner?" said Sharron.

Amira was confused. "What us three? Now? You, Dad and Me?" She said in disbelief.

"Yeah! We thought you might like it. A meal with your parents." said Paul.

Amira looked at her dad and her mum, 'they're both in on this together,' she thought to herself, which if that was the case, she was very happy to go to dinner with them both.

"Ok, then sounds great!" exclaimed Amira.

"Pizza or steakhouse?" said Paul.

"I haven't had steak for ages." Said Amira as her tummy rumbled.

"Me neither." said Sharron.

"Right then, I'll meet you both there." said Paul.

Amira saw her dad get into his car and leave. Amira got into her mum's car and in a few minutes they were at the steakhouse car park. They saw her dad's car already parked up, but it was empty, so they knew he must be inside. When they walked in they saw that he had already gotten them a table. They got settled and began to look through the menu. Amira's dad got a burger with fries, Sharron and Amira got steak with fries. After they all gave their orders over to the waitress, Amira's mum and dad both leaned into the table to look at Amira. Amira looked back at them both, puzzled.

"What?" asked Amira confused.

Amira watched her parents look back and forth to each other, until her dad nodded to Sharron and Paul began to open his mouth to speak.

"Sophie and I are getting married, and we want you to be the bridesmaid," Said Paul as he looked at his daughter.

Amira was shocked, but a smile appeared immediately. "Yes, I would love to." She said.

"Good! Now your mum won't feel so lonely when she's there." said Paul as he took a sip of the beer that was just delivered to the table with the rest of the other drinks.

"Mum? You're going to the wedding too?"

Her mum was looking happily back at Paul and Amira. She extended her hands and placed them on top of Amira's and Paul's.

"What? I was invited." Said Sharron very casually with a little smile on her face, it was nice to have her old friend back, and Amira was happy too.

The food arrived, and they all began to tuck in and chat about the wedding and about Amira's success from the presentation.

***

Amira and Sharron arrived home. They were so full from their steak dinners. Amira said good night to her mum and went up to her room, where she undressed from her smart outfit, and changed into her comfy baggy clothes to let her full stomach breathe, and then she collapsed onto her bed, ZAP.

"Hello, stranger!" said a deep American voice.

Amira sat up immediately in shock and saw two beautiful men standing at the end of her bed. She recognized them immediately, of course.

"Hi Johnny! Hi Thomas!" She shouted in a whispered voice as she hopped off the bed and gave them

314

both a hug. She felt a little sick from getting up too quickly. Her belly was still very full.

"We watched your presentation today." said Thomas as he and Johnny sat at the end of her bed.

"Wait. You saw that? You were both there?" Asked Amira, who was pleasantly surprised.

"Of course, we wouldn't have missed it!" said Johnny.

"We were cloaked of course." Said Thomas as he tugged his black cloak

"Well done, by the way, that was amazing, £1000! That other kid that won was not happy about that, was he?" said Johnny in a very gossipy tone.

"He has issues" Laughed Amira. "By the way, I'd like to ask you guys something about an idea I've had." said Amira.

"Is it about that girl Rose?" Said Johnny as he looked to Thomas and then towards Amira with a quizzical expression.

Startled by their response, "Yes … Yes it is. How do you know that?" asked Amira in utter astonishment.

"We liked her presentation too." said Thomas happily.

"Yes, I want to go into business with her. Everything she was saying about human psychology fits in with what you say gets in the way of a person finding their twin flame. That and I actually get on really well with her." said Amira.

Johnny playfully nudged Thomas, as he shoved a hand inside his robe to fish something out from one of the inner pockets. He found what he was looking for; it was a leatherback journal.

"All the steps for you and Rose for your business are in there. Even if Rose says 'no' to you two being partners, the steps and phases all still apply," Said Thomas as he tapped the top of the journal he held in his hand.

"So we have got a head start for you, my darling." said Thomas.

"What do you mean?" Asked Amira as she leaned in to listen closely, making sure that she was paying attention.

"We have been researching starting up a business and all the things you will need to think about and organize. Everything we could think of and get our hands on is inside this journal." said Johnny.

They both handed over the journal to Amira and placed it into her hands. She opened it at the first page that said phase 1. It was a to-do list followed by all the steps, and reasons why, for each point on the list. She flicked through the rest of the book, there were 10 phases in total. There was even a Q & A section at the end of each phase; it was extremely detailed and very self-explanatory.

"We put everything we could think of in there in case you got stuck and we weren't around." said Johnny.

"Wow, thanks guys. It looks like you have saved me a lot of work." said Amira as she continued to flick through the pages.

"You're welcome" Said Johnny in a sassy tone, as he stroked a loose strand of hair back into the rest of his flawless hairdo.

"Well, we have to get going my dear." said Thomas. "We will be back in about one months' time, and by then, we hope to see you on phase 2." said Johnny as he pointed bossily at the journal and then playfully on Amira's nose. Amira laughed.

They both came over to hug Amira goodbye. Thomas and Johnny held hands as the light grew to consume them both, and they vanished from the room, ZAP. Amira's hair gushed about her face as they vanished; she looked back to the journal they had given her. As she flicked through, she noticed that all the notes were handwritten and not typed. It was very impressive and clean, it must have taken years of practice to write this way.

She studied the first page carefully, which had the list for phase 1. Most of this phase was to do with social media platforms, some things to research, and asking Rose to be her business partner, 'seems easy enough' Amira thought. She closed the book and put it in the draw next to her bed, turned the light off and closed her eyes to go to sleep.

"I'll begin tomorrow." Amira said to herself.

She pictured what her business would be like with her friend Rose as she drifted to sleep.

Chapter 36

The End of College

It was Amira's last week at college, and she had grown very close to Rose. Amira had asked Rose, a few days after Thomas and Johnny had stopped by for a visit in her room, and handed over the journal of lists, notes and tips for her business. Rose was skeptical at first, not quite seeing how a dating agency and human psychology could possibly go hand in hand, but after a little convincing from Amira, she became very excited about the idea and had already helped Amira tick off more than half of the list for phase one. They both decided to divide the handlings of the social media platforms. Rose handled Twitter and YouTube, Amira dealt with Facebook and Instagram. Of course, they didn't have much content posted, but they had made a start at least. It was all so new to them, but they both had a really good feeling about it. They already had over a thousand followers. They were really excited to see how it would progress in the future. As the very last lecture finished, Mr. Clark expressed how proud he was of everyone and said his goodbyes to the class.

Amira clapped her hands together like everyone else and waited for everyone to say thanks and goodbye to Mr. Clark before she had an announcement of her own to make.

"You're all invited to my 18th birthday this Saturday! Bring anyone you like." Amira announced to the classroom.

The class was filled with voices of excited gossip and cheers. Everyone was more than happy for an excuse for a night out, plus it was a great chance to have fun after all the work they have done. James who'd won the competition took the trouble to make a group chat for the occasion, which surprised Amira, but she was happy with the kind gesture after all the angry glances he had given her when she began doing well at college. Amira and everyone else were excited, even Tammy, who had been in a mood for about three weeks, was now smiling and already planning what she was going to wear.

It was soon Saturday, the day of the party. A few days ago Amira had searched online for outfits to wear on her 18th birthday and her first night out. After looking in her wardrobe, she was certain that nothing in there would do at all. Amira had decided to go with a pretty, sparkly pink mini dress that was off the shoulder, with a frilled hem. Amira's mum begged her for a preview of the dress, so Amira tried it on. Not only was the dress just as nice as the picture had shown, but it fit like a glove. Amira was getting excited for the night out, her first night out ever, and everyone in her class was coming to it too. She messaged Rose and Tammy to see if they wanted to get ready at her place. Rose said she would love to, and it made sense as Amira's house was the closest to town, Tammy however, said no as she hadn't decided what to wear yet and she didn't want to be rushed, she would meet them later. So because it would be just Amira and Rose they decided to meet up earlier for bite to eat and to talk about their business before they let loose and had fun. They decided to go to a very popular food place known for its reasonable prices and good Wi-Fi. They met at the entrance; Rose got there first and was wearing some casual trousers and a simple black top. Around her arm was a large tote bag with all her things in it for later that night. They waved at each other and found a nice booth with a window seat to sit at. They decided to order something light so they wouldn't feel too full for the night out, they ordered three light bite dishes to share. They ordered spicy chicken wings, a bowl of cheesy fries with bacon crumbs and battered fish bites. They decided to get stuck into their business talk while they waited for the food to arrive.

Rose started, "I've finished the list you gave me, and I've also made new posts for my social media platforms for the next two weeks." She said confidently.

Amira was impressed and glad that Rose was not only taking this all seriously, she also seemed to be having fun with it all too.

"Wow, that's great. How many followers do you have at the moment?" asked Amira.

"About two thousand, which isn't bad in just over three weeks! What about you?" asked Rose.

"I'm at nearly at two thousand on mine as well. We've done everything on the phase 1 list, and it hasn't even been a month yet." said Amira excitedly.

"Do you think we should move on to phase 2?"

"I think we might as well."

Just then their three plates of food arrived; Rose and Amira lined them all in the middle of the table so they could help themselves. Amira grabbed a chicken wing and Rose grabbed a few fries covered in cheese with bacon crumbs, and they gorged themselves without speaking for a few minutes. Amira finished picking all the chicken off the small bones and placed the remains on a napkin. She licked her fingers to get all the sticky, spicy sauce off; it tasted good. Rose took a big gulp of her drink before she resumed the conversation.

"So, because I'm staying at yours tonight, why don't we start the new list for phase 2 tomorrow when we wake up?" suggested Rose.

Amira had just shoved a few fish bites into her mouth, so she thought while she chewed. 'Does sound like a good idea, it's so nice and easy to work with Rose, and we will get this business up and running in no time', she thought to herself while she ate. When Amira finished and swallowed her fish bites, she took a big gulp of her drink to help swallow them down so she could answer.

"Sounds perfect." We should get this up and running pretty soon. It's been kind of easy so far, don't you think?" asked Amira.

"It has been easier than I thought it would be. At least it is at the moment. I think it helps that there's two of us though. I like that I will have my own part in this shared business, and you will have yours, but that we are still a team too." said Rose thoughtfully.

"Yeah, same here! Hey, is that guy you're seeing coming out tonight as well? "

Amira was curious to meet Rose's guy, mostly because she wanted to see how twin flames on earth would interact with each other.

"Yes, I think so. I can't wait for you to meet him! He's been so supportive of our business, you know. He says it's inspired him maybe to start something of his own." said Rose.

Amira took a sip of her cold coke zero and said, "That's so sweet. So being with him doesn't get in the way of doing what you want to do?"

Rose smiled "No, not once. He's just happy to see how excited I am about this. He wants to find something that makes him excited too. So when I am working on our business, he makes lists of his passions and does a bunch of research alongside." said Rose as she rested her head on her hand while still feeding herself fries with the other.

Amira's mind flashed back to overhearing couples arguing in shops, restaurants, and in the movies about how they were too busy and they never made time for each other, 'guess that's a big sign if they are a twin flame or not' she thought to herself.

Amira decided to confess a very small fraction of the truth to Rose but was careful about how she would put it.

"You know, the reason why I wanted to go into a dating agency is that I can tell if people have met the one or not." said Amira.

Rose looked skeptically at Amira for a moment. "I suppose that would make sense about why you are so confident about it all. When did you first know you could tell?" asked Rose curiously.

Amira replied in truth, "My dad met his, and it was my mum's best friend; he felt so guilty about it, but he said that when he met Sophie he knew straight away, and it was unstoppable. And I knew it was true that Sophie was the one for him." said Amira.

"Oh gosh, doesn't your mum hate him for that?"

"I thought she did, but now she doesn't. In fact, they seem pretty good friends, almost like they had never been out with each other. Dad and Sophie have invited my mum and me to their wedding." said Amira.

Rose was excited about a wedding, they chatted about Amira being a bridesmaid and what she hoped her dress would look like if they let her pick it. Rose seemed to like the idea of a wedding a lot. They carried on chatting until they had finished all of their light bites. It filled them just enough to satisfy their hunger.

"Shall we go back to mine and get ready then?" said Amira as she drank up the rest of her drink.

Rose nodded and took a last, long suck of her drink until she started to suck air up through the straw. They picked up their bags, Rose heaved her large bag over her shoulder and they walked back to Amira's. It was only a 10-minute walk, and it wasn't long before they were both at Amira's house. They looked at the time when they arrived home; it had only just gone six O'clock.

"At least we have plenty of time to get ready." joked Rose.

"Yeah, we do. We could put a film on while we do our hair and makeup. I've never had a night out before. I want to dress up but not be too over the top." said Amira.

"Trust me, if you want to see over the top, wait until you see Tammy tonight." comforted Rose.

"Why? Does she dress to impress?" asked Amira.

"You could say that." They both laughed. Amira couldn't wait to see Tammy on a night out, she always seemed so dull and gloomy in the classroom, and it would be nice to see her having some fun for a change. Amira put on Charlie's Angel film while they started to get ready.

"I haven't seen this film in ages." said Rose.

Rose and Amira were in a giddy mood as they started to get excited about the night out. Amira offered the dressing table chair to Rose as she was starting off with her makeup. Amira sat by her full-length mirror on the floor to curl her hair. They chatted and gossiped while they got ready, and Amira's mum gave them both a glass of wine half-filled with lemonade to start off their evening. Rose thanked Sharron and took hers, Amira took a sip, and it was sweet, refreshing and cold. Amira had finished with her hair and looked over to see how Rose was getting along. Rose looked stunning. Her eyes popped and shimmered, the makeup intensified and defined the natural shape of her eyes, and the pale lipstick made them pop even more.

"You look gorgeous." said Amira.

"Thanks. I just worked with what I have." Said Rose in a joking and yet smug way.

"Would you do my make-up? I'll do your hair?" proposed Amira.

"Deal." agreed Rose.

Amira sat very still and patiently while Rose gently applied makeup to Amira's eyes. Rose would often ask Amira to look up or close her eyes, and she did so without question. When Rose had finished doing Amira's eyes she started going through all of Amira's lipsticks and lip-glosses in her makeup draw.

"You have so much make-up! I've never seen you wear much. Most of these have never been opened." said Rose as she rummaged.

"Yeah, mum gets a lot of free stuff with her job." admitted Amira.

Rose picked out a pretty sparkly lip gloss and started applying it to Amira's lips. Rose pulled away and stepped back to get a better view of her artwork.

"Done." announced Rose.

Amira turned her chair to look in the mirror and here blue eyes were piercing and bright. Rose had applied mostly black eye shadow and eyeliner that gave Amira a very intense but sexy look. There was a very light high shiny blue highlighter subtly applied into the inner corners of her eyes that helped make the whole look pop, so did the glitter lip gloss, which helped it all not look so harsh. It was very pretty, girly and 'slightly sexy, if I do say so myself' Amira thought.

"That's amazing. You just thought of this?" Asked Amira, who was impressed by Rose's makeup talent.

"I saw a YouTube video tutorial with a model that had similar features to you. She had blue eyes as well.

"Now my turn, do as you please." said Rose as she offered up her hair.

Amira looked at Roses hair and her face for a moment. Rose had dark brown hair with some natural waves in it. She decided to braid the sides into a half up half down hairstyle. She weaved the hair carefully with her fingers and fluffed out the braids to make them look bigger and more romantic. She tied the ends with a small hair tie and threaded out a few strands of hair at the front to frame Rose's face.

"There you go." said Amira, as she admired her work.

Rose turned to admire herself "Oooh, I like it! What does it look like from the back?" said Rose.

Amira handed her a handheld mirror for her to view the back of her head.

"It's so cute and girly. I love it, thanks. What time is it?" said Rose.

Amira looked at the clock beside her bed and read out the time.

"It is 19:16. Let's get dressed, and then we will check the group chat." said Amira.

Amira pulled on her pretty pink dress and slid on some pink kitten-heeled sandals. Rose had a deep blue A-line dress with a deep V-neck that really showed off her two best assets.

They both looked at themselves in the mirror.

"We look gooood" Said Rose.

They laughed and turned to get their phones and pulled up the group chat conversation. They saw that a group of boys from the class were already at the pub and on their second drink. Everyone else was still getting ready. Amira typed:

'Me and Rose are setting off. See you all soon.'

Amira and Rose grabbed their small bags and stuffed their IDs, money, and phone inside them and went downstairs where Amira's mum Sharron was eagerly waiting with a bottle of wine. Sharron had her phone out and began taking lots of photos showing how grown up her little girl looked, going on her first night out, for her 18th birthday.

"You both look gorgeous. I can't believe how grown-up you look." admitted Sharron.

"Thanks mum. Do you think you could take a picture of us with our phones too? For our social media" Asked Amira

"Yes, of course!" Exclaimed Sharron, who was glad she was trusted with such an important task.

Sharron moved towards the girls who fished their phones back out of their small handbags and handed them over to her. Sharron took some care in giving the girls directions and poses to do, she went through quite a few different angles, and eventually handing Amira and Rose back their phones. Sharron gave Amira a big hug.

"Have fun; now if you need anything ring me ok?" said Sharron.

"I will mum, I love you. And thanks for the dress." She hugged her mum back.

It was time to go so Amira grabbed her house key and placed it in the zipped compartment of her little bag. Amira and Rose left and began to walk into town.

It was a nice night, very few clouds, and a warm breeze that passed through them every so often. After a 10 minute walk, they arrived at the pub that the lads were in. When Amira and Rose walked through the doors they were greeted almost immediately.

"AAAAYYYYYYY THEY'RE HERE!"

Amira and Rose couldn't help but smile and laugh as all the boys cheered and invited them over. They seemed pretty drunk already. They got Amira and Rose a drink as they sat down to join them.

"So, who else are we waiting for now?" Asked the drunken boy, who was called Steve.

"Just a few more people, three of them are coming as a group, and Tammy is coming on her own I think." replied Rose.

"I've heard that Tammy takes ages getting ready." said James.

"Yeah, are you surprised? It must take her a while from what I've seen of her on nights out. You'll understand when you see her, Amira." said Steve as he looked at Amira's confused face.

Amira looked to Rose for an explanation, and she said...

"Lots of makeup."

They had a drink and a laugh. Rose and Amira posted a few of the photos that her mum had taken of them and put them on to their social media. A group of three arrived soon after. A few people tried to message Tammy but no one could get through, so they decided to move to the next place. Rose wrote on the group chat the pub's name so Tammy would be able to find them. The boys decided a karaoke bar would be the next best place to go. Amira and Rose had hardly stopped laughing since they met up with the boys. They really were great fun. After a few more drinks and the boys singing happy birthday to Amira while giving her a sort of sexy dance, Tammy finally arrived.

"Holy shi...." said James.

Rose stood up and waved over Tammy. "Tammy, we're over here!"

Amira barely recognized her; she was a different color, covered with fake tan, lots of foundation, lots of eye makeup with a massive thick pair of eyelashes and bright red lipstick. What surprised Amira the most was the outfit. A see-through crop top with a pattern over the chest that just covered Tammy's nipples and a shiny bright blue skirt that looked like it was made of latex, finished with a pair of very high heels.

"Oh my god, Tammy, I didn't recognize you!" gasped Amira.

Tammy smiled. "I won't give you a hug guys I don't want to get my makeup on you." said Tammy.

Tammy gave Rose and Amira an air kiss each, and then pulled down her skirt a bit to cover her modesty as she sat down on a stool next to them. Tammy looked around the room and then at the rest of the party.

"They're drunk already? I'd better catch up. Back in a minute, I'm off to get a drink." said Tammy.

She got up and walked towards the bar, balancing as best as she could in her stilettos.

"Oh my gosh! I had no idea she was so… racy." said Amira, still in shock.

"Yeah, she gets a lot of attention." said Rose.

"Every time I come out she's kissing some other guy, but she's good fun, she's up for anything, bet she will be on this karaoke in no time." said Steve light-heartedly.

Tammy came back to the table with a full glass in one hand and finishing off whatever was in the other glass in her other hand. After she drank the last drop out of her second glass, she sat down and placed both empty glasses in front of her.

"What were those?" asked Rose as she gazed at the empty glasses.

"Two triple vodkas and Lemonade, they have a deal on Saturdays. That should help me catch up." said Tammy.

And it did. It wasn't long before Tammy put her name down and danced and sang along to every other song that came on the karaoke. Amira sang a Taylor Swift song, and Rose got up and sang a one direction song. When Tammy got up it was a big laugh. She sang S&M by Rhianna and gave a very questionable lap dance to some guy that didn't know what was happening. It wasn't extremely sexy. But Tammy was having a great time, and it was really, very funny. She got a huge applause and laughs from everyone at the pub. After Tammy had her turn at the karaoke, everyone in the party decided to move on to the club. Amira was the first to get inside the club, and she bought everyone a jaeger bomb with some of her winnings from the college presentation. They were a big hit, and everyone raised their glasses to Amira before they all downed their shots. Soon everyone was on the dance floor. Rose's new guy was in the club already and went straight over to Rose, lifting her up and giving each other a big kiss. It made Amira feel all warm inside. 'God, look at how they are with each other' thought Amira as she observed them together.

Rose introduced him to Amira "Amira, this is Josh, Josh; this is my business partner Amira."

They shook hands and Josh's attention went straight to Amira's ring that gave a very quick and small flash.

"Nice to meet y…. WOW, where did you get that from?" said Josh as he gazed at the ring.

"I found it on eBay." Said Amira smiling as she looked at Josh and then at Rose, as her eyes met Rose she and gave her a little nod. Rose knew what it meant after talking about Amira's special gift at sensing if people have found the one. Amira's nod and facial expression confirmed that this was indeed the case, and it made Rose smile very broadly.

Josh and Rose went away and danced together on the dance floor. Tammy was swinging around a pole she found at the side of the dance floor, and Amira was dancing with the other members of her college class and had started interlinking to dance the cancan. The night went on like this for some time, right up until it was time for the club to close. Amira was feeling very drunk now. Luckily a few of the boys had grabbed a bunch of water bottles and handed them around to the rest of the group. One of the lads looked after Tammy and was now trying to hand fed her the water as best as possible. Half of Tammy's face was smeared from kissing a guy on the dance floor. Everyone decided to grab some food at a takeout and then sat on some benches outside to eat them, to help sober them up before they all went home. Steve tried to get Tammy to eat something, but she seemed more interested in falling asleep.

"Does anyone know where Tammy lives? I think I'd better take her home." said Steve.

"She just lives up that road there at number 34. It's only 3 minutes away." said Rose, who was sat on Josh's lap, hand feeding him chips.

"Ok, I'll be back in a few minutes, hold this, and don't eat any!" said Steve as he handed his pizza box to James.

Steve walked over, and picked up Tammy, putting her over his shoulder and began walking towards her house. James was sat next to Amira, and he offered her a slice of Steve's pizza. She took the smallest piece and began eating it, it tasted good, it had mincemeat and a slice of garlic sausage on it.

"So, how's your business going with Darren Wilson?" asked Amira.

James took a bite out of his own chicken wrap "its ok, it's more different than I thought. He's sort of taken over the whole thing; he hasn't given me much to do. What about you? Will you go through with your dating agency?"

"Yes, Rose is my business partner now, we've joined forces, and we've already made a start on it." said Amira who was making the most out of the small slice of pizza.

James looked at Amira in astonishment, and then he smiled and went back to eating his wrap.

"What it is?" asked Amira.

"I thought I was the best one in that class, and then you, out of nowhere, started acing everything. It really put me down, but now, I think I'm inspired." Confessed James, he took another big bite out of his chicken wrap.

Steve came walking back and extended his arms out to the box of pizza he had asked James to look after.

"Did Tammy get home ok?" asked Rose.

"Yeah, her mum answered the door, didn't seem surprised." He took the pizza box, opened it and grabbed the biggest piece there and wolfed it down, not noticing that a slice was missing and that Amira was still eating that slice. After a while everyone had finished their food and decided it was time to leave, they all hugged each other and agreed that this should happen again in the future. They all left and went off in their separate groups. Josh gave Rose a big kiss and a cuddle and said goodbye to Amira. He left with one of the other group of boys. Amira and Rose began to walk back to her house.

"I can't wait to lie down and take these shoes off." said Rose.

"Yeah, it was a great night though, wasn't it?" Replied Amira

"Was the best night ever, I can't wait to do it again sometime." said Rose as she linked her arm to Amira's.

"So, what do you think? Is Josh the one for me?" slurred Rose.

"He's the one for you, twin flames for sure." confessed Amira.

"Don't you mean soul mates?" asked Rose, who was defiantly a bit drunk.

"No, anyone can have a soul mate, and anyone can be a soul mate. Only one person can be your twin flame." Said Amira, in a very certain and knowing way.

Rose smiled sweetly and was very content with that answer. They found their way back to Amira's house. They took off their makeup, got changed into their comfy clothes and went to sleep straight away.

Chapter 37

Birthday Brunch

Amira and Rose woke up reasonably early the next day considering that they were out the night before. Amira rolled over and saw that it had just gone 9 am. She looked slightly to the left of the clock and saw a folded up note with Amira's name on the front. She picked it up, opened it up and read the note written in her mum's handwriting.

'Me and your dad want to take you out for a birthday brunch at 11. Love mum x x x'

Amira looked at the time again just to be certain she had read it properly, 'that's good, got loads of time to get up' Amira thought to herself. She looked next to her where Rose had slept to see if she was awake yet.

"I'm just off for a quick shower. Do you want one after I've been?" Said Amira to a sleepy Rose whose once beautifully platted hair was now messy and covering her face.

"Err, yes please, I think I should." She sniffed herself, sat up immediately, and began to detangle her hair as Amira left and went into the bathroom. Amira gave her hair a quick shampoo and rinse. She quickly applied some mango shower gel to her body and rinsed off with the shower nozzle. She got out of the shower, dried herself and thought to put out a fresh towel for Rose to use so that it would be easy for her to find. Amira wrapped a towel around her body and let her wet hair hang about her shoulders as she grabbed the handle of the door to leave the bathroom. She had barely managed to leave the bathroom before Rose was already walking straight past her to get to the shower.

"Sorry, but I really need a shower." said Rose as she shamefully scuttled by.

"That towel on the rail is yours." said Amira as she laughed.

She heard a muffled reply as the door closed and then heard the shower turned on straight away. Amira went into her room, dried her hair with a towel and brushed it through to let it dry on its own for a while. She found some fresh clothes to put on ready for when she had brunch with her parents. Amira picked out some casual jeans and a red top. While Rose was in the shower Amira thought it would be a good opportunity to get out the cheat journal that Thomas and Johnny had put together for her and make a head start copying from it before Rose could see it. She reached into her bedside drawer and pulled out the journal Johnny and Tommy had given her. She admired the penmanship as she flipped through it to phase 2 and began copying the list down onto her other notepad. When she finished, she threw the journal back into the bedside drawer, closed it shut and began to read through the list properly, making sure to take it all in. Just then, Rose came back in the room looking much happier and refreshed. Rose had gotten changed into her fresh clothes while she was in the bathroom and had styled her clean wet hair into a neat bun on top her head.

"Better?" asked Amira.

"Yes, thank you." replied Rose.

Rose plonked herself down on the bed next to Amira and let out a satisfied sigh. Rose felt much better after her shower. She saw that Amira was focused on her notepad, so she leant over to read what was written on it.

"Is this phase 2?" She asked as she grabbed the notepad from Amira to read for herself.

After a minute of reading the list, Rose leant over the edge of the bed, found her bag and pulled her own notebook out of it. She borrowed a pen that was sitting on Amira's desk and began jotting and copying the list down onto it. After she had done that, she and Amira discussed sharing the jobs and what they would involve. They spent an hour talking and going over the plans and deciding who would do what from the list. When Amira looked at the clock again, it was 10:30.

"Oh, I'd better dry my hair." said Amira in sudden realization.

"Okay. Why?"

Amira pointed to the side of the bed where the note was, as she was fishing her hairdryer out of a storage basket full of her hair things.

"Aw, that's lovely. Are we meeting up next week? " Said Rose as she began to braid her hair down one side of her head.

"What are you up to today?" asked Amira, who was now untangling the wire of her hairdryer.

"Sunday roast with the family and Josh is coming too." Rose smiled as she said his name.

Amira plugged the socket into the wall and blasted her hairdryer on full to get as much wetness out of her hair as she could. When Amira's hair was dry, Rose had also finished braiding her hair. Rose collected all of her things ready to leave, -checking that she remembered her notepad with the list for Phase 2 on it, along with all of her notes that she had made talking it over with Amira. Amira walked Rose downstairs to the front door to see her out. They both said goodbye and wished each other a lovely day. Amira's mum waved goodbye and shouted after Rose, saying she was welcome anytime.

"Shall we set off then?" suggested Sharron.

"Yep!" Said Amira happily, and the thought of food, her belly made a rumbling noise.

They walked into town and went into a local café. When they got there Paul was already sat at a table and greeted Amira with a special big birthday hug.

"Happy birthday, scrunchy!" Said Paul, he was very excited and besotted to see his 18 year old daughter, all grownup.

Amira ended up having to pull away when her dad started messing up her hair in his excitement for her birthday, much like he did when she was smaller. They laughed, sat down, and looked at the menu to pick out a special brunch treat. Amira decided to go for the American special with pancakes, Streaky bacon and scrambled eggs with maple syrup. Sharron ordered eggs benedict, and Paul ordered the full English breakfast. As they waited for their food to arrive, Paul placed a medium-sized box on the table wrapped in birthday paper and slid it over to Amira.

"This is from both of us." said Sharron.

Amira tore open the wrapping paper to reveal a plain brown box. She opened it to find the latest model Apple laptop. She looked up at her mum and dad with delighted shock.

"You guys got me a laptop?! I was going to buy one with the money I won from Darren Wilson." confessed Amira.

"Well, we wanted to help you too. You save that money. You never know when you might need it when you're starting up a new business." said Paul wisely.

Amira's eyes began to fill with a few tears of happiness. She felt so lucky to have two such great parents.

"Thank you guys so much. It's perfect. I can't wait to set it up and use it." said Amira as she gave both her parents a quick hug over the table.

Paul folded the box up, carefully placing the laptop back inside and set it under his chair so that it was out of the way.

"I've also got a little news. Sophie and I have set a date for the wedding." said Paul.

Sharron's hands made little claps of excitement, and Amira gave an excited gasp.

"When?" Asked Amira

"In ten months' time." said Paul, who was smiling broadly.

Their food arrived, and Amira covered her modest stack of pancakes in maple syrup and tucked into her scrambled eggs and streaky bacon. They all ate their brunch and talked about the wedding, their jobs, and Amira's dating agency until they were all full. Then they paid the bill so they could go home. It felt so nice to have the family back together.

Chapter 38

Getting a Sign

A few weeks went by, during which time Amira and Rose were very close to almost finishing phase 2 of the business plan. Amira also finally met Sophie, her dad's fiancée. They went out to play mini-golf and had a meal together afterwards. Amira was happy to see that just like her dad had done, that Sophie had also noticed the ring almost as soon as she had met Amira. Amira noticed similarities between Paul and Sophie and Rose and Josh as couples. They were ecstatically happy and supportive of each other. Sophie and Paul bought a glamping camp together and were currently doing it up so they could open it in a month or so. Her dad was doing maintenance work and some cleaning with the glamping camp while Sophie did most of the planning and organizing.

One night during those weeks, when Amira went up to her room, she threw a bag of Doritos everywhere when she saw two handsome men appear suddenly in front of her. Only to realize it was Johnny and Thomas, who happened to find it all hilarious and couldn't stop laughing at her for at least 5 minutes. They had popped by to see her, just as they promised, in exactly one month to see what progress she and Rose had made.

"So, have you finished phase 1 of the list yet, my dear?" asked Thomas.

"Phase 1? We finished that in the first week. We're on phase 2 now." boasted Amira gleefully.

Johnny and Thomas gave each other a high-five.

"That's fantastic." said Thomas.

"You don't mess about, do you, Hun?" continued Johnny.

"It's been really fun, and Rose is so great to work with. You know Rose has met her twin flame in the club of this very town?" Admitted Amira, who knew the chances can be quite slim for that to happen on its own.

"We meant to ask you about Rose. That's great. When you're starting a business like this, it's always best to start off locally. That girl called Tammy; she could be your biggest protégée." said Johnny knowingly.

"Poor lost soul; she was good fun on that night out of yours, wasn't she?" said Thomas with a cheeky wink.

"You were there?" said Amira who began to go red.

"Well, we came to scout for potential twin flame matchups, that Tammy will take some work. But her twin flame is about her age and living, so that's something at least." said Johnny.

"Really? Where is Tammy's twin flame?" asked Amira as she leaned in to soak up the information.

"Scotland "stated Thomas.

"Flipping heck, that's a bit far from here, isn't it?" said Amira.

"Well it's actually very good. He could have been on the other side of the world. At least he's on the same Island as her." pointed out Johnny.

"Well, he has just booked a lad's holiday to Ibiza, and his soul is in great condition, much better than Tammy's is. Your friend Rose will have to work her magic on her. This time next year he will be in Ibiza. The three of you could go together, and with some luck, Tammy will meet the guy, and they will recognize they are each other's twin flame. Then ta-da!" said Thomas.

"I'll add that to the list, shall I?" said Amira with a smirk.

"Yes, please do. His name is Shaun Ewan." said Johnny.

Amira was quick to scribble down that name at the back of her notebook, and also the current date for if she was ever able to manage to convince the girls to go to Ibiza this time next year.

"Maybe wait a few months before you bring it up, though, the holiday." added Thomas quickly.

"Yeah, wait until Tammy's had enough of this town then bring it up a few days after her meltdown." said Johnny excitedly.

"A meltdown? Why?" Asked Amira

"She will defiantly want a change of scenery then. We have made a prediction that she will break down very soon, going by her behavior. And Rose will agree to the Ibiza holiday because it will be a chance to get away with Josh." said Johnny.

Amira sat and jotted a few more things down in her notebook.

"Now, how have you been finding the ring? Have you used it much?" asked Thomas.

"Well, people who have already found their twin flame notice it right away. But everyone else just doesn't see it unless I point it out to them, and its awkward asking them what color they see." admitted Amira.

"There's a loophole to that. Wasn't it in the journal we gave you?" asked Johnny.

Amira shook her head 'maybe I missed that part' she thought to herself.

"You simply make the ring have contact with the other person's skin. Like if you put your hand on theirs. The ring will then reflect what they see back to you, to show you how they see the ring." explained Thomas.

Amira sat for a while to absorb what they had just told her.

"Wait. So if I go downstairs and hold mums hand with my ring hand, I'll see the ring how she's seeing it?" summarized Amira.

"Yes, exactly" Said Johnny as he gave her a thumbs up.

"We will leave you now, my dear." Said Thomas as he stood up and pulled Amira in for a hug.

Thomas passed her straight over to Johnny for a hug immediately after.

"Remember to use your angel cards to communicate with your guardian if you ever get stuck or need help or guidance." reminded Thomas.

Johnny pulled away from hugging Amira, gave a little wave and extended his other arm to hold Thomas's hand. Amira watched as the light consumed them both, and they vanished as the light dwindled. A breeze swept through Amira's room, blowing her own hair in her face. She had forgotten about the angel cards that Johnny had just mentioned, they had arrived a week ago, but she hadn't opened them yet. She decided to open them and flick through them and learn how to use them. She opened the box and took out the cards. She took the time to look at them all individually, one by one. They were beautiful, each with a symbolic picture and a few words written below summing up the meaning of the card. She looked in the box and there was a little booklet with instructions. She opened the book and was happy to see some descriptions were more than a paragraph long about the meaning of each card and what they interpreted as. She decided to put it to the test with the question option from the booklet that required her to spread out the cards, ask a question and then select three cards to get the answer. Amira held the cards to her chest, sat upright and closed her eyes as she asked a question.

"Will Rose and I have a successful business?"

She picked out her first card that read 'Transformation'. It had a beautifully drawn picture of a woman surrounded by light, and it reminded Amira of how Thomas and Johnny come and go. The second card she selected was a simple card that said 'Yes'. She moved along and selected the last card that said 'Learning experience' with the picture of a wise older female.

Amira sat there for a moment and felt chills go down her spine at the thought that she was literally communicating with her guardian angel. She thought it was odd how people would go from life to life forgetting they had ever met their guardian angel, but that their guardian angel would never forget and would be with that soul right until the day they died after meeting their twin flame. 'I wonder if it's sad being a guardian angel', she thought to herself. She looked at her ring and admired how it shined in the light. She couldn't believe that she could have seen how others saw the ring all this time. She shook her head in disbelief. How could she have overlooked that in the book? She wanted to try it now 'wonder if mum is still awake?' she thought to herself.

She looked at the time, and it was only quarter past nine in the evening. Amira grabbed her empty water bottle from her desk and went downstairs, where her mum was sat in front of the TV with a glass of red wine in her hand.

"Not asleep yet?" asked Amira as she turned on the tap to fill up her water bottle.

"No, it's not even ten o'clock yet." replied Sharron.

Amira came over and sat next to her mum on the sofa. Sharron was watching her favorite game show. She looked at her mum and the full glass of red wine and thought something must be on her mind.

"Anything the matter, mum?" asked Amira.

Sharron looked at her little girl and held Amira's ring hand.

"I'm just thinking about grandma Lena." said Sharron sadly.

Amira looked down to see what the ring looked like, and it didn't look shiny but slightly dull. The stone wasn't completely clear but was sort of cloudy. 'That's not so bad' Amira thought to herself.

"I bet she's thinking about us too mum." said Amira as she put her head on her mum's shoulder.

"I just wish I knew that she was ok." said Sharron as she began to cry.

Just then, the lights in the room flickered and danced for a couple of seconds, enough to get both of their attention, then stopped. Sharron looked to Amira, who was shook by such a mere coincidence. Amira knew that this is what mum needed to feel better and move on with her life.

"I think she just told us that she's ok." said Amira.

Sharron and Amira shared some tears together and hugged each other close. They watched the rest of the TV game show together. Amira wondered if Runa played the lights or if it was her mum's guardian angel providing her with much-needed comfort. But either way, it didn't really mater, she could feel mum was not worried or sad anymore. Sharron was grateful to have Amira sat with her right then, and continued to hold her hand until it was time to go to sleep.

Chapter 39

Ladder of Success

(10 months later)

It was the big day of the wedding, and there was going to be a big party, after all the success that Paul and his soon to be a wife, Sophie, had from their new glamping resort. After a few months of hard work, their small resort had been classed as a luxury glamping site, thanks to the star rating team that came by to inspect and stay at the facilities. Amira and Rose were also having great success from their own business. After opening their first dating agency, they decided to call it 'To find love and love yourself' It was great for Rose, it turned out she had even more clients than Amira did. Rose was a big hit and had put together online self-assessments, quizzes and programs. Amira had now matched up 27 twin flames, it didn't seem a lot, but some of them were pretty hard work. Business was really beginning to take off, and they had over 70,000 followers on their social media platforms now. Amira couldn't wait for the holiday that she and the girls booked to Ibiza a few months back. Tammy had just about kissed every guy in the town by then and had gotten herself a bit of a reputation. Remembering what Thomas and Johnny had said months before, Amira brought up the Ibiza idea, both Tammy and Rose jumped right on board. Since then, Rose has given Tammy some special attention by taking her under her wing and giving her some free help. Tammy seemed much better in herself. The ring used to be a dark reddish-brown color when Amira last held it up against Tammy's hand, but now it was just a light cream color.

Amira and her mum arrived at the wedding reception venue and were about to get ready alongside Sophie; the bride. After Sophie and mum eventually met up again, it was as if they had never been apart. In fact, they got along so well (just like old times) that Sophie ended up asking mum to be a bridesmaid too. As Amira and Sharron were making their way to the bride's room, they decided to stop by the groom's room, where Amira's dad was getting ready, to wish him luck. They knocked on the door, and his best man answered.

"Hi Adam, just wanted to wish dad good luck before the ceremony." explained Amira.

"Course, Come in!" He said as he held the door open for them both to come in.

Amira and her mum placed their zipped up bridesmaid dresses on the arm of one of the chairs and wished Paul the best of luck and said to have a great day. Paul began to tear up, overwhelmed by how amazing this day would be for him. Amira gave her dad one last hug, then she and her mum left him to finish getting ready, picking up their dresses from the chair before they left.

They went down to the other end of the building where they found the bridal suite.

When they got there, Sophie was just having the final touches done to her hair, her face was already made up, and Sophie was still wearing her purple tracksuit with 'Bride' written in diamante on the back.

"You look gorgeous!" squealed Sharron in excitement.

"You look stunning; I can't wait to see you made up like this with the dress on as well." said Amira.

"You're just in time! I can see you both are pretty much ready yourselves. You both look perfect." said Sophie, who was glad that she had asked them both to be her bridesmaids. She lost all of her friends when she and Paul had gotten together.

Amira and her mum had gotten their hair and makeup done back at home before they set off. Amira did her mum's, and her own hair. Sharron of course took pleasure in doing both her makeup and Amira's while applying her new technique to work with the natural features of the face.

"Shall we help you into your dress? Or do you want to chill for a bit first?" asked Amira.

"I am a bit nervous. I think I'll have another glass of champagne first. You girls get ready." pleaded Sophie.

Amira and her mum both put on their dresses and stood side by side in the mirror. They looked like a couple of bad rom-com characters, but Sophie thought they looked perfect. The dresses weren't too bad at all. They were elegant, slender, navy blue satin dresses. They did look great on; it was just odd for Amira to see her mum wearing the same dress as she was. They had some girl-talk about the big day and had a few good laughs together as they got ready. By the time Sophie had polished off her third glass of champagne she was ready to get into her wedding dress. It took both Amira and her mum to help get the dress on. It was heavy and needed to be held into place while Sharron did up the corset and buttons at the back.

"You'll be going to Ibiza soon, won't you?" asked Sophie to Amira.

"Yeah, can't wait, we're all excited. I think Tammy has booked us into some places there already, for some parties and the clubs and stuff." said Amira.

"You do right. You need a holiday! You have been working so hard. How is business going?" said Sophie.

"Really well actually, we're getting more followers every day, me and Rose have started talking about maybe doing some seminars abroad. Most of our followers are from America and Australia, you know?" Informed Amira who was still holding up the front of the wedding dress

"Wow, that's amazing. Just like her mum, she travels where the work takes her." said Sophie as she nudged Sharron.

"She learnt from the best." said Sharron as she tied a bow in the ribbon on the corset.

She came to the front and put her arm around Amira's shoulders.

"Finished. Are you ready to see yourself?" asked Sharron to Sophie.

Sophie nodded and took a deep breath as she spun around to where the mirror was. She looked at herself and was speechless, almost as if she didn't recognize herself, or maybe because she had never seen herself as a bride before, until that very moment. It was a champagne colored, full-length A-line dress, with a sleeveless sweetheart neckline, an overlay of sparkly lace, with some added layers that left a slight trail behind her. Her eyes began to well up until Naomi, her makeup and hairstylist, edged in and pointed a warning finger at Sophie to not ruin her hard work. Sophie laughed, then looked at the time and began to fluster at how close it was for the wedding reception to start.

"The bride is always the last one there anyway, so there's no need to worry." laughed Amira.

The logic was flawless and made Sharron and Sophie giggle; they were both as excited as each other. It was time to leave. Amira and Sharron kept an eye on the dress as they walked towards the reception area, where Sophie's dad Walter was standing wide-eyed and proud as he looked at his daughter, Sophie, in her wedding dress.

The ceremony was beautiful, with cream and blue flowers everywhere. Sharron and Amira were the perfect bridesmaids; the whole ceremony was a big hit. The after-party was even better, food, drinks, great music, everyone had tremendous fun. Amira was asked to dance by a handsome 21-year-old boy called Niall, who was a cousin of Sophie's. They had a nice time and agreed they would meet again.

Sharron was currently dancing, with the bride Sophie and a bunch of other women, to an Abba song while screaming along to the lyrics. Amira made sure to distance herself as far from them as possible at that point, to avoid any further embarrassment. Sophie's dad Walter got so drunk he had tied to do the splits, and was still sat at his table now with an ice pack held between his legs.

After a few hours, it was time to see the bride and groom off on their honeymoon. They were both in smart but casual clothes, and they told Amira and Sharron they would ring them a few days after they get back to arrange going out for a meal. Everyone waved them goodbye until their car had disappeared over the horizon. Amira looked at her mum, who was mid-blink and struggling to stand in one place. She was very drunk.

"Let's go home." Amira said to her mum, who nodded in agreement.

Amira called a taxi, and they were home in less than half an hour. Sharron crashed on the sofa and was out for the count as far as Amira could tell. Amira pulled out the overthrow blanket from the cupboard, threw it over her mum, and took off her shoes. She decided to test her ring to see if her mum had changed since the last time she checked. So she put her ring hand on top of her mum's shoulder and the ring looked like it hadn't changed, it stayed the same. 'Can that be right?' thought Amira. She took the ring off and gave it a shake and put it back on, and tried again. Amira looked for change in the ring, but it didn't change at all, it remained a very clear stone. 'She's ready to find her twin flame' Amira thought to herself. She smiled at her mum, tucked her in properly and went up to bed to get some sleep.

***

A week had passed since the wedding and it was time to go to Ibiza. Josh picked everyone up, Rose sat in the front of the car next to him of course, and Amira, Tammy, and one of Josh's friends, who happened to be James from Amira's college class, were sitting in the back of the car. They were eager, packed and ready to go. Tammy almost had a 22kg suitcase to herself, but luckily Amira convinced her to share it with her. It was only for a week, after all. Rose and Josh shared a case and everything James wanted to bring all fitted snuggly into his carry-on luggage. Amira was glad James was there, she didn't like the idea of looking after Tammy all on her own. But with any luck from the information that Thomas and Johnny had given her about Tammy's twin flame, Shaun, she wouldn't have to do any looking after at all. That is, if they ever meet each other.

They had only been there a day when Amira recognized a guy's face inside a club and saw that it was Shaun Euan, Tammy's twin Flame. She had recognized him from his Facebook account she had found. Amira suggested going into the club that Shaun had gone into that night, and there were no objections from the group. It was full of people, everyone was dancing, and couples were kissing all over the place. After some time in there, Shaun was right next to Amira as they were queuing at the bar, so she made a decision. She slid on the other side of Tammy and pushed her right into him. Amira watched as Tammy covered her face in embarrassment and looked up to him to apologize. Amira had never seen it happen before (unless her grandma and king Toke counted). Usually, in her job, Amira just sent people off on dates with their twin flames or to places where their twin flame would be, and then see when they came back whether they had met their twin flame or not. But now it was right here in front of her. Tammy and Shaun seemed lost for words as they stared at each other. You could tell they wanted to say something to each other at the same time. Eventually, they introduced themselves and began to walk off somewhere when Tammy turned around as if she was asking permission to go. But Amira caught Tammy's hand before she left. Tammy's attention went straight to the ring. It gave a small flash; Amira knew her work was done. But they were still abroad in a club, so Amira took the necessary precautions.

"Don't worry! I'll tell Rose where you are! Just keep messaging us, or post on Snap chat, so we know you're ok!" said Amira.

Tammy looked so grateful and happy at that moment and wrapped her arms around Amira to thank her. Amira watched as Tammy left and roamed the club with Shaun 'she had come a long way in just a few months,' thought Amira as she smiled to herself.

Shaun seemed to be with them for the rest of the holiday. Josh and James were very happy that there was another man in their group. Amira and James had shared a drunken kiss one night but agreed it was only the drink and laughed about it the day after. Overall, it was a great holiday. Amira had a small holiday romance with a guy called Jessie. It just so happened that he only lived an hour or so away from Amira back at home. They hung out together a few times while still in Ibiza before it was time for everyone to go home. Tammy was heartbroken to leave Shaun, but he promised her that they would get a place together as soon as possible.

When everyone got home, Tammy expressed a desire to join the dating agency team on Roses side of the business. Rose thought it over and decided it was perfect because the workload was beginning to get too much for just one person. Rose had already given Tammy all the training and information needed to help with the client load, so it was perfect.

"And who better to hire than someone who has completed all the processes and found their twin flame?" said Amira to Rose, who was already in complete agreement.

Chapter 40

The Journey

(10 years later)

Amira heaved her suitcase onto a very fancy king-size bed and began to unpack, taking out a bunch of holiday clothes and putting them to one side. A pair of arms came around her, lifted her up, and threw her on the bed. She laughed and was hugged by a nice set of arms, which were attached to a tall and muscular body that held her close to his, and she hugged him back just as tight.

"Can we go to the beach now?" said the man as he pulled away from Amira to look at her.

Amira admired his beauty, tracing her fingers along his square jaw line, stroking his fresh fade along the side of his head and looking into his cheeky blue eyes.

"Maybe, if I get a chance to find an outfit for the beach first." She said in a teasing cheeky way.

He gave her a tender kiss and pulled away while grabbing her hands and pulling her up too. He gave her a playful slap on her bottom as he walked away.

"Ok, you find your sexy beach outfit and I'll pack the beach bag."

Amira dug into her suitcase and pulled out a pretty electric blue bikini and found a simple floaty white beach dress to slip into. She grabbed her phone from the mattress and looked at the pile of clothes and the half-empty suitcase, 'I'll do that later' she thought to herself.

"Liam, I'm ready! Let's go!" She said as she slid on a pair of flip flops.

"Then let's go."

Liam came around the corner of the room with a full beach bag; his muscular body was still on display. This time, instead of jeans, he was wearing some dark blue swimming shorts and a pair of top-gun sunglasses. They made their way down to the beach that was right in front of the hotel. Amira had never been to Cancun before. She was glad everyone had agreed to this as their next company vacation, she was very excited, and the whole place took her breath away. Liam laid down the towels on one of the many luxury beach beds, and they laid closely to each other, Amira resting her head on Liam's chest.

"So when are the others getting here?" Asked Liam, Amira would never grow tired of his German accent, which had faded a lot in the last two years from when she had first met him.

"Soon, their plane should land in about 4 hours. They're all on the same flight." replied Amira.

Liam held Amira tighter to his chest and let out a big sigh. Amira felt his whole body relax beside hers. Amira relaxed too and stroked the fuzzy feeling hair down the side of his head. They enjoyed the sun, the warm breeze and fresh sea air together until they felt recovered from travelling. After a while, they decided to swim in the sea and had some fun chasing and splashing each other in the water. When they had done, they grabbed a few drinks at the bar and took them back to their sun bed to drink while they dried off a little. When they had dried off and finished their drinks they felt like they had enough sun for the day. Liam and Amira decided to go back to their hotel room and have some time before Rose and Josh arrived with Tammy and Shaun. Amira and Liam had finished unpacking and got fully settled into their hotel room. When Liam saw that Amira had finished getting settled, he took her by the waist and pulled her into him for a sensual kiss. Amira's body tingled from the kiss, and Liam led her into the shower while holding her close.

When everyone else had finally arrived an hour or so later, they all met up at one of the hotel restaurants. Rose and Josh had been married for about 8 years now, had two kids, and never stopped being crazy about each other. This was also true with Tammy and Shaun. After they had parted ways in Ibiza, Tammy got a job with Amira and Rose at their business and turned out to be a big asset to the dating agency. Shaun had founded his own company in luxury travel. In less than six months, they were living together and happier than ever. They had been engaged for two years now. Tammy was still fun but more held together, and sure of herself. It reflected in how she carried herself and how she presented herself.

A little ping went off. Amira looked at her phone. She had received a message from her mum that said:

'Have a great holiday, love mum and Danny x'

Amira smiled. Her mum met Danny, eventually, in Newcastle. Her mum had been to Newcastle about 30 times before she managed to finally meet the guy. Sharron moved to Newcastle after she and Danny had married. Amira and Sophie were bridesmaids at their wedding, and Paul was one of the groomsmen.

There had been a few times in Amira's life where she had felt down about not being ready to meet her twin flame yet. Her soul still needed more life experience. Amira had had a few love affairs in her time, two of which she had ended up reuniting with their twin flames, which did hurt Amira a little. On one of their many visits, Amira had talked to Thomas and Johnny about it once when they had dropped by to see how she was getting along. She always felt better about things after talking with them. She learnt that just because it isn't a twin flame doesn't make it less meaningful and that it is still love that can still be passionate, beautiful, caring, amazing and inspiring. Life was supposed to be enjoyed, and people are supposed to love and to be loved. Amira looked to her handsome muscular boyfriend as everyone was laughing and joking around the table. She had met Liam 2 years ago on holiday like this one but in Thailand. At first Amira thought he might be shallow as he was there doing some modeling, a photo shoot, for some big brand. But he had a temperament similar to Amira's with a thirst similar to hers to enjoy life, she greatly admired that. Amira felt undeniably attracted to him with a lust she hadn't experienced with anyone else before. A few months after dating and getting to know each other Amira felt a deep emotional connection to Liam. She decided to surrender herself to him. She decided to be completely his when he finally confessed how he felt about her one night, when they met up near London, a few months after they had first met. She spoke to Thomas and Johnny about Liam and found out that they both had some part to play in how they met. They said Liam was not in line with his twin flame either and that Amira never had to worry about that. As long as she still loved Liam and he still loved her, then she would have nothing to worry about and could spend her life with him if she chose to do so.

Amira looked around the table and couldn't believe how lucky she was. Her two best friends, Rose and Tammy, were the best business partners in the world. Thanks to their joint efforts and hard work, they have the biggest, most successful dating agency in the whole world. Amira looked to her gorgeous boyfriend Liam, he brushed a loose strand of her hair over her shoulder and leaned over to kiss her neck, and warm flutters filled Amira's body. She loved life, she loved her friends, her family, and she loved Liam. Sometimes Amira's mind pondered about how strange it all was. How she went from that shy girl who always put herself down, self-doubted and never dared to admit what she was passionate about or wanted to do, to being a confident, successful woman who is now surrounded by people she loves. How different her life would have been if she had kept on being that shy girl. Just then, Amira zoned back into the conversation at the pretty restaurant in Cancun with her boyfriend, friends and business partners.

Rose held up her glass to make a toast and said, "To the next chapter."

Everyone else picked up their drinks and held them up as well. "To the next chapter"

Amira, Liam and their friends continued to do what made them happy. Amira overcame losses, highs and lows, just like anyone else did, but overall, Amira and Liam had a wonderful life together.

The End

Printed in Great Britain
by Amazon